monster lover

Monsters of Durnbone

emilia rose

1
the demon

TWO NAKED SUCCUBI danced against each other on the table in front of me, their hands gliding around the other's ass and breasts, groping, biting, teasing. I stared at them emptily with a couple of other demons who were at The Inferno for *royal duties*.

These demons sure as hell didn't know what the fuck that meant. They hadn't been able to take their gazes off the succubi all night. We hadn't even spoken a sentence about what would happen when the current demon queen, Queen Agool, stepped down from her throne.

I sipped from a glass of wine and sat back on the maroon velvet couch. I didn't even know why I had come. I would never inherit the throne, and I had better things to do than watch some girls touch each other. Plus, I'd had plans at the Dead Candle Tavern forty minutes ago.

"Relax," my brother, Erthrol, said to me. He sat on the couch next to me, gaze glazed over with lust and a smirk on his pretty-boy face.

"Live a little, Xorgor," some demon kid who supposedly had royal blood, Jaroth, said. Apparently, he was dating this human from a couple of towns over, but he couldn't keep his hands off these girls tonight. "We got all these beautiful women here for us."

"No," I growled.

"Bella!" Erthrol beckoned one of the succubi to come forward.

She sauntered over to us, swaying her hips back and forth, then sat with her bare ass on the table and her legs spread to give him a view.

Erthrol stared longingly at her dripping pussy, then nodded to me. "Help my brother relax."

For a brief moment, Bella tensed. Then, as if she hadn't reacted at all, she stood back up and walked around the back of the couch. She dragged her manicured fingers across my brother's chest, leaned down, and whispered something along the lines of, "But I want you," into his ear.

His eyes darkened with lust, and Erthrol grabbed the woman's chin and tugged her into a long kiss. He looked over at me and chuckled. "We can share her, Xorgor. Hmm?"

So much for a caring brother. He didn't give a damn.

I averted my gaze and glared at the wall to my left. I didn't know why the fuck I came here to these unimportant meetings. We never talked about our duties, and it wasn't like anyone expected me—the oldest son—to inherit any throne. An ugly bastard like me could never rule.

Nobody would take an incubus who didn't get *any* seriously.

Deciding that this wasn't worth my time anymore, I stood. When nobody even spared a glance at me, I walked to the exit of this club and stepped out into the darkness of Durnbone. After using magic to cloak myself, I headed toward the Dead Candle Tavern without being noticed. I didn't want to deal with the staring, the gawking, the looks of disgust on everyone's face when they saw how ugly I was, especially for an incubus.

When a group of werewolves opened the door to the Dead Candle Tavern, I slipped into the building, glanced toward the bar, and spotted a human barkeep with huge blue eyes and light-brown hair that fell just past her shoulders.

She was here.

I walked to the bar and took my usual empty seat at the far end. Dishes were stacked in front of me, piles of silverware next to them. I glided my thumb across my black, red, and gold family ring, watching her pour drinks for a group of succubi.

Unlike the other bartenders, she had tied the strings of her blouse tightly together, completely concealing her chest. Matter of fact, most of her body was clothed, to the point where I doubted she made *any* tips from the rowdy animals who came here.

She tucked some hair behind her ear and smiled at a fae couple. With my body invisible, I sat there all night, watching her pour drinks and talk innocently with the crowd. She didn't know who I was, nor would she ever find out.

No fucking way would I ever let her see me as the monster I was.

A grotesque devil lurking in the shadows.

An unwanted spawn of Satan.

An ugly, evil, disgusting man who wanted the most beautiful woman in Durnbone.

What would she think of me?

A vampire at the end of the bar leaned forward and curled his finger around a strand of her hair, tugging on it. She tensed and lightly pulled away, but kept that tight smile on her face. He beckoned her to come closer.

After nervously furrowing her brow, she shook her head. But he grabbed her wrist and pulled her closer anyway, whispering something into her ear. She gulped and smiled tensely again, as if she didn't want to piss him off.

"We'd like another!" one of the fae called to her.

As if she hadn't liked the attention from the vampire, she hurried over to the couple. The vampire stood up and walked to the restrooms in the back. I shot up from my seat and followed after him, fury rushing through me.

In the restroom, the vampire stood with his cock in his hand, pissing into a urinal. I slammed the door and locked it behind me, uncloaking my body. After shaking the last bit of piss out of his dick, he stuffed himself back into his pants.

"Listen, buddy, you don't want to fuck with me—" When he glanced over at me, his eyes widened. "Fucking hell."

I took a step toward him, hands balled into fists by my sides.

"Y-you're him," he muttered, moving backward and pressing his ass against the urinal. "You're the demon everyone talks about in D-Durnbone. Look, I don't know what I did to you, but I don't want trouble. I'll get the fuck out of here. I'll leave town. I'll do—"

Before he could finish his sentence, I snatched his wrists with a tentacle-like black appendage that extended from the muscles in my back whenever I was *aroused*—emotionally, physically, or sexually—pulled him into the air so we were face-to-face, and held his wrists against the wall. He breathed raggedly, his chest rising and falling quickly.

"Do you have fun, making women uncomfortable?" I asked, clutching his jaw in my hand.

"N-no," he stuttered. "Of course n-not."

"And the barkeep?" I asked, gripping his chin harder and harder by the second. My talons sank into his cheek, becoming drenched in his vampire blood. "You sure liked making her uncomfortable."

"I-I just wanted her to loosen up a bit," he said. "She's so uptight."

"What's it with people like you wanting others to loosen up?" I growled.

"I won't do it again." A bead of sweat dripped down his forehead. "I-I promise."

"No, you won't." I extended another black appendage from my back and aimed it at this vampire's chest.

He shook his head and begged—pleaded—with me to let him down, set him free, and promised me that he wouldn't do any shit like that. But I didn't trust a man like him not to flirt with the woman I liked again.

I thrust my appendage straight into his chest, wrapped it around his cold heart, and tore it out of his body. Blood rolled down my appendage as his heart beat weakly against it. I tightened myself around it and watched as it burst in an explosion of blood and guts.

The vampire's corpse became dead weight, so I let him drop onto the urinal. I crouched in front of him and looked into his empty eyes. "You won't get a chance to touch her again. She's mine."

2
the barkeep

maxine

"HE'S A DIABOLICAL MONSTROSITY," a succubus with luscious red hair murmured to her scantily clothed friend at the bar in front of me. "I'll tell you, I've never seen an incubus so ugly before. Half-human, half-demon. Jagged teeth. Sharp talons. Utterly disgusting."

"Not only that, but I've heard that Xorgor can't even make a succubus orgasm," a third succubus said as I poured her a glass of red wine. She grabbed it from me, her manicured fingers clicking against the glass.

"You're kidding," her friend whispered. "I'd be ashamed to have a son like that."

"I would never let someone who looked like him into my bed."

After suppressing an eye roll at how superficial they all were, I walked over to a fae couple that had been at the bar almost all night now. They kept flirting innocently with me. As I took their empty glasses and handed them their bill, I continued to listen to the drama unfolding with the succubi.

"Isn't he supposed to inherit the demon throne?" the scantily clothed demon asked.

"There are rumors, but there is no way that his family would let him. He's such an ugly bastard. His younger brother or Jaroth is set to take the throne next, I believe. Thank fucking Asmodeus."

While all the succubi degraded this man they had probably never met, I wiped some alcohol I had spilled on the counter with a rag and carried empty glasses to the sink. They must've had boring lives if all they did was gossip and demean people.

It was because of people like them that I didn't wear more provocative clothing around here, like my manager had suggested, to reel in more tips. If they saw the scars that lay on my chest from a wolf attack over a decade ago, they'd shrivel back in disgust.

The fae couple left a tip twice their bill with a note that read an address and a comment on how they wanted me to visit them tonight at their hotel. I tossed the note into the trash and found myself tightening my blouse, hyperaware of the scars hiding underneath it.

Sure, people might've flirted with me here, but … once I went home with someone, they always asked how a pretty girl like me could look so ugly underneath her clothing. I didn't have the energy for it anymore. Or maybe … I just wanted to protect myself.

Because their words were true. I was ugly.

"Of course you're still working in this lousy bar," a shrill female said behind me.

I turned around to see Valerie—the one person I'd despised the most, growing up in Durnbone—sitting at the counter. She tucked some silver hair behind her ear and drew her tongue across her sharp vampire fangs. "Never made it that far out of Durnbone, did you?"

With royal blood running through her veins, Valerie was fourth in line to inherit the vampire empire's throne. But honestly, I doubted that she'd ever make it as a queen. She was too nasty and way too annoying, even to vampires.

"I'd rather not leave," I said. "My family is here."

"Family?" She chuckled. "You still have family left after that wolf attack?"

I gritted my teeth and poured her a drink. No, I didn't have any family left, but I didn't want her to know that I hadn't left Durnbone to explore the world like I'd always wanted because I didn't have the money. I had an old home that my grandfather had left me, but I had to work for every scrap of food.

"Do you happen to still have those scars?" she teased, smirking menacingly at me. "You know, the ugly ones across your chest." She shivered, as if she was disgusted at the mere thought of them. "I remember the first time I saw them."

Despite wanting to strangle her to death, I gave her a polite smile and hoped that she would feel enough pity for me to leave a better tip than the last vampire I'd served at the bar. He had left without giving me anything.

"How's that girl you always used to hang out with in school? What was her name? Sina?"

My throat dried, and I tightened my hand around a wineglass until it nearly shattered. "She's doing fine," I said quickly, though I hadn't seen her in years.

Four years ago, she had disappeared with her father without a trace.

After that, I made myself busy with other customers until everyone left the bar, except her. Once I finally convinced her to leave way past closing time, I pulled on the string of my blouse to loosen it. It fell open a couple of inches in the front, enough to reveal the top of the diagonal scars that lay across my chest. Nobody was here, so it didn't matter anymore.

I grabbed a mop and a bucket of warm, soapy water, desperately wanting to get this over with and go home for the night. It would be the same thing tomorrow and the next day and the day after that.

A wooden board creaked. I snapped my head toward it and gripped the mop tighter.

"Is someone there?" I called, heart beating a bit faster.

Sometimes, rowdy men and women tried grabbing a drink after they were finished fucking a monster at The Dungeon—a brothel where monsters, especially incubi, paid to fuck humans—down the road, but it had never been this late or this quiet.

When no one answered, I sucked in a deep breath to calm my racing heart and continued to mop the floor. I didn't exactly know what it was, but I felt like I was being watched from the shadows, like someone was definitely here.

But all the lights were still on, and this place was empty.

I mopped, the eerie, ominous feeling staying with me the entire time. Once I finished, I poured the dirty water out into the back room sink and threw my hair up into a high ponytail. Another floorboard creaked, and I froze.

"Is someone here?" I asked again.

Sometimes, the floor at my grandfather's house creaked, but … it rarely ever happened at work.

"Hello?" I continued, stepping back into the main room.

A shiny black, red, and gold ring with the royal family's crest lay on the floor that I had just mopped. I stared at it through wide eyes and crouched down to pick it up. Maybe one of those succubi had left it, but I didn't think that they were that close to the demon royal family.

Besides, I swore that I had picked up everything off the floor before I mopped. I would've seen this. But where had it come from? There wasn't anyone in here with me, and no royal family members had been here tonight either.

The gold glistened under the dim tavern lights, illuminating the demon horns and shattered heart on the face of the ring. My stomach twisted at the thought of how much this could be worth. Thousands of coins, maybe a million.

If I left it here, someone could break in and steal it. But if I took it home with me, I'd be responsible for keeping it safe. I'd be responsible if someone robbed me while I walked home tonight, if someone broke into my house.

After checking the schedule for tomorrow morning and realizing that Arleth, a money-hungry human bitch, would be opening the tavern tomorrow, I tucked the ring away in my pocket and grabbed my belongings. She couldn't be trusted with it.

I vowed to return it to whoever it belonged to by myself. I'd do whatever it took, and maybe they'd be so generous to give me some coin for returning it.

3
the first touch

xorgor

I'D FUCKING LOST my family ring.

After Maxine closed the Dead Candle Tavern, I uncloaked myself and searched every inch of that place. It had to have fallen off when I tried to make a quick escape as she mopped. But it wasn't here. Not anywhere.

Which meant that Maxine must've had it. Maybe she had found it and taken it. Did she plan on using it to get some coin? Blackmail? Why the hell would she have taken it home? There was a lost-and-found box behind the counter.

I needed to get the ring back before returning home.

When I reached the house that she owned, just on the outskirts of Durnbone, I grasped the familiar door handle. I wasn't obsessed with her—that was what I told myself—but I had been here more than once.

I usually followed her home when she worked late to make sure she got in safe. The people who frequented The Dungeon down the street from the tavern weren't known to be nice.

Slipping through one of the back doors that she had forgotten to lock again, I cloaked myself in magic and wandered through her old home. Most of the furniture was covered with plastic, as if it hadn't been used in months. Cobwebs hung in the corners of the room.

Her purse and work pants lay on the ground in the middle of the living room. I rummaged through her purse and found a couple of old coins and a picture of some girl I had never seen in Durnbone before.

After slipping my hand into her pants pocket, I found the ring. I blew out a deep breath and slipped it around my finger, then placed her pants down where I had found them. I didn't know why the thing was so important to me.

Fuck that, I knew.

One day, I hoped that I would have a shot at the demon throne. I could only get on it with this.

The black, red, and gold glimmered in the moonlight, shining brightly around my thick finger.

Suddenly, Maxine screamed from her bedroom upstairs. Without hesitation, I sprinted up the stairs and into her bedroom, stopping completely when I spotted her on the bed with her legs spread and a vibrating dildo plunged into her bare pussy.

A grunt escaped my mouth, my cock growing hard.

Maxine froze. "I-is anyone there?" she whimpered, glancing nervously around the room.

I ground my jagged teeth together and tried to convince myself to leave, to walk out of the house and to not look back. But I found myself moving closer to the bed, crawling up onto it with her.

Even in the comfort of her own home, even while she was naked, she clutched a thin white sheet over her chest. As if she didn't want anyone in this house to see underneath it. As if *she* didn't want to see underneath it herself.

The bed creaked, but Maxine didn't notice as she went back to pleasuring herself and turned up the vibrations. I sat between her legs, my cock throbbing at the sight of her pussy. I wanted nothing more than to take her. I had been dreaming about this night for fuck knew how long.

She lay back against the mattress, spreading her legs even wider and holding the vibrating dildo in her pussy. Desperate to touch her, I slipped my fingers into her snug pussy right against the vibrator so she wouldn't suspect a thing.

I moved my fingers in a way that a vibrator never could, massaging her G-spot until her pussy was crying all over me. She pressed her head harder against the pillow, eyes rolled back and lower back arched.

"Fuck," she moaned, pulling her legs up into the air and showing me her pussy.

Really making it hard for me not to want to taste her.

For weeks, maybe months, I had sat in that tavern, watching her. Now, I was moments away from surrendering my control, to sneaking a taste of her while she made a mess of herself in the middle of her bed.

The strong scent of her juices made my blood warm. I dipped my head between her legs, my lips millimeters from her salivating cunt, and took another long breath of sweetness, imploring myself not to do it.

If I touched her with my forked tongue, I wouldn't be able to stop. I wouldn't be able to pull away or take my hands off her for the rest of the night. I would be completely helpless and bent to her will.

"Oh, please," she cried out. "It feels so good."

I froze to ensure my cloak of magic still shielded myself from her.

If she saw me, she would flip the fuck out.

"It feels too good. Too fucking good!"

Maxine was an achy, needy mess in my grasp, begging me to take her, to touch her, to taste her. Every tremble from her pushed me closer and closer to the edge of my breaking point, to completely losing control.

Another soft moan escaped her parted pink lips.

Unable to stop myself, I gently replaced the vibrator with my mouth and sucked on her clit. She slapped a hand over her mouth and screamed into it, the muffled sound making me so hard that I had to grind myself against the bed.

She drove me fucking wild.

"Oh my gosh," she cried, squeezing her eyes closed harder and squirming around on the bed.

I gently seized her hips to hold them steady and continued to flick my tongue across her sensitive bud.

"Fuck!"

With her feet posted on the bed, she lifted her hips and bucked them back and forth against what she thought was her vibrator. She drew her cunt against my mouth, letting me taste every bit of her.

I buried my fingers deeper into her and continued to curl them against her G-spot. Her legs trembled on the bed, a puddle of cum forming underneath her. She screamed out in pleasure again, body seizing.

Once she lay back against the bed, she blew out a deep breath and let her chest rise and fall quickly. I gently played with her clit, sucking on it and flicking it with my tongue. Maxine whined and lifted her legs.

"It's too much," she whispered to herself, holding the vibrator close to her clit again. Moonlight flooded into her bedroom, illuminating her pussy lips, glistening with her juices and my spit. "But I can't stop. It feels too good. Gods, it feels *so fucking* good."

4
the missing ring

maxine

AFTER YAWNING, I stepped into the Dead Candle Tavern and walked to the counter to clock in for the night. Four wolves sat at the center of the bar, talking gruffly with one another. I inhaled sharply, the scars on my chest burning from the memories of the wolf attack years ago.

Once I took a deep breath, I forced myself to smile and ask for their drink order. My eyes were heavy, the need to sleep overwhelming. I didn't know what had gotten into me last night, but I couldn't stop touching myself. I must've been up until four in the morning, teasing my aching clit, desperate for release after release.

When I placed four pints of beer in front of the four wolves, I spotted a demon who resembled someone from the royal family walking out of the bar. I believed his name was Erthrol.

"Excuse me!" I called, hurrying out of the tavern to catch him and return the ring.

When he looked over at me with his curious yellow-tinted eyes, I swallowed hard and clasped my hands together. While I had worked here for over a year now, I hadn't talked to an incubus other than asking for his drink order. And I didn't know what had possessed me to say something now. It might not even belong to him.

After he raked his gaze down my body, lingering on my covered chest, he smirked at me and stepped closer, the air around us suddenly becoming heavy. "I sure hope that I'm not in trouble with you, Miss …"

"Maxine," I said, my palms sweating. "You can call me Maxine."

My heart pounded against my rib cage, my mouth drying. Was this what it felt like to talk to not only an incubus demon, but also one from the royal family? I had heard they had powers that could make the strongest people fall to their knees in lust.

As he continued to stare at me, I pulled my gaze away and smoothed out my shirt, my nipples piercing through the thick material of my bra. "Um … no. You're not in trouble. I just …"

Oh gods, why is this so hard?

All I seemed to think about was how an incubus would be in bed. But, hell, I didn't know if anything could beat last night. My pussy still ached from how many times I had come over and over again, the never-ending bout of lust swirling through me.

"Hmm?" he asked, eyes darkening.

"I found a ring," I forced myself to say before I made an even bigger fool of myself.

He stepped even closer. "A ring," he said into my ear. "Is that so?"

With his breath on my neck, I looked down at my feet and squeezed my eyes closed. What the fuck was wrong with me? I— reluctantly—talked to people all day at work, but I could barely speak tonight. All I needed was to hand over the damn ring.

"Yes," I said, stepping backward to put space between us. "From the royal family."

"Where is it?"

"Right here." I shoved my hands into my pockets to retrieve the ring.

Nothing.

My breath hitched, and I shook my head. Nerves rushed through my body.

"I swear I had it," I said, stuffing my hands deeper into my pockets in an attempt to find it.

If I couldn't find it, I would be screwed. I had brought it home with me to stop someone from stealing it, and now … now, it looked like I was the one who had stolen it to sell it for money or something.

"I must've left it at my house."

But that wasn't the truth. I knew I hadn't left it at home, and I hadn't dropped it on the way over. I had shoved it deep into my pocket last night before I left for work, and I didn't take it out once. It hadn't fallen out either at home.

The demon hummed, and my skin warmed. Thoughts about last night rushed through my mind, and I found myself pressing my legs together.

Why was I thinking about last night? Was it because I had stayed up for so long, been so high off of coming, that I might've accidentally left it there this morning?

No. Right?

"Your cheeks are red," he said. "And you can't look at me. Are you lying?"

"No," I breathed quickly, glancing up at him and shaking my head for emphasis. "I swear I'm not. I found it last night after I closed the tavern, and I brought it home so nobody could steal it here."

"What'd it look like?"

"It was black, gold, and … red, I think."

"It belongs to Xorgor," he said. "My brother. His has a little nick in the side like this one does."

"Xorgor," I repeated, my heart suddenly racing. "Isn't he—"

"An ugly motherfucker?" he finished. "You wouldn't forget a face like his."

My stomach twisted and turned, his words not sitting well with me. After those succubi had completely criticized Xorgor last night,

I couldn't help but feel bad for this man I had never met. Now, even his brother was poking fun at him.

I touched the buttons on my shirt, ensuring that it was still pulled shut. If he was saying that about his brother ... gods only knew what he would say about me if he saw the horrid scars across my chest. It had been over a decade, and I could barely look at them.

"I haven't seen him," I whispered. "He wasn't here last night."

The demon tilted his head down at me, like he didn't believe me.

"I swear."

"Xorgor, that piece of shit." He chuckled to himself after another silent moment, the deep sound making me warm in all the wrong places. "I should've known he would skip the royal gathering to visit a sexy thing like you."

My cheeks burned with embarrassment. He wasn't speaking sense.

"He-he wasn't here last night."

"Don't worry. I'll tell my brother that you had it and let him deal with you." He moved closer to me and curled his finger around a piece of my hair, tugging gently on it and moving his lips millimeters from my jaw. "Or I can return and deal out the consequences of losing a royal family ring."

"Y-you will?" I asked, voice barely above a whisper.

While I had lived in Durnbone for all my life, I couldn't even begin to think about what kind of torture a demon would be capable of with me. I didn't want to end up like one of those girls in The Dungeon, who monsters used and abused, doing whatever the fuck they wanted with them.

I-I couldn't do that.

I'd promised myself that I would make it out of this town one day and find my best friend who had disappeared four years ago. Sina had to be out there somewhere, waiting for me to show up. She had to still be alive.

"I'm sure I'll be seeing you later, *Maxine*," he purred into my ear. And then, in a moment, he vanished into thin air.

I stared at the ground with tears in my eyes and sprawled my hand over my chest, my fingers grazing against my scars underneath my shirt. If I didn't find that ring, then I would be done for.

They'd put more scars like these all over my body. They'd destroy any last hope of me ever finding love. Because nobody liked a woman with scars mapped onto her body, with shame written into her skin. Those monsters would make me uglier than I already was. They would make me into a monster.

5
the meeting

xorgor

"WHAT'S the point of being an incubus if you're not getting any pussy?" Erthrol asked, walking backward down Durnbone's stone road with his arms outstretched.

It would sound like a lighthearted joke to anyone who didn't know him, but Erthrol never made jokes without cruel intentions behind them.

This joke was aimed at me, the monstrosity that plagued my family—a half-human, half-demon beast with one curved horn, jagged teeth that even my lips couldn't hide, and skin charcoaled from the depths of hell.

I balled my hands into fists and walked after him to wherever the fuck he wanted to go tonight. Usually, I wouldn't even think about coming into town without being cloaked, but he had coerced me into it.

Yesterday, he had told me a girl named Maxine from the Dead Candle Tavern had come up to him and told him that she lost my ring—the same ring that I wore on my finger right this very second. But she didn't know that, and neither did he.

He had been too caught up in making me jealous. He knew I had gone into the tavern, cloaked for a reason, and he had probably concluded that the reason was her. Demons loved corrupting pure girls like Maxine.

Walking, I stuffed my hands into my pants pockets and kept my head down, loathing the way everyone here stared at me. I'd rather cloak myself and become invisible to the world so I didn't have to listen to the whispers from the townsfolk.

Erthrol stopped in front of the Dead Candle Tavern, and I tensed.

"Why are we here?"

"Come on, X," Erthrol said, throwing an arm around me and waving to the succubi girls through the window, who giggled and waved back to him, not even sparing me a glance. "It's your death day. Have some fun. The girl who lost your ring is working here tonight. I thought you might want to … *punish her* for it."

My body turned even more rigid as I looked at Maxine through the window, who was tending to some rowdy customers at the bar. I turned away quickly so she wouldn't see me, not even through the foggy window.

She'd never once seen me like this, and that was the way I wanted to keep it.

"I don't want to punish Maxine," I said. "Let's go back home. I don't want to drink tonight."

"It's your death day."

"I said, I don't want to drink tonight."

"What a joke," Erthrol said, tightening his grip on me. "An incubus running away from a sexy woman he could have some fun with. That's why you don't ever get any, X. You're too afraid, scared of what they'll think of you."

Again, another jab.

The only fucking reason I looked like this was because of him—that's what our parents had told us–and all throughout our childhood, he had made sure that I knew it too—that he was the only damn person in our family the girls gushed over. It was never me, and it never would be.

"I don't want to," I said again through jagged teeth.

If I admitted that I liked her, then Erthrol would go into that bar and bring Maxine home by himself, just to fucking spite me. And I would never let him get her alone like that. Maxine didn't even know who I was, but I wouldn't let my asshole brother taint her.

"You stare at her all the time, don't you?" Erthrol asked. "One of the guys even felt your presence in the tavern the other night. He said you were using your magic to cloak yourself. Why is that, Xorgor? Are you too afraid that Maxine will think you're an ugly prick, like all the other girls do?"

If I could kill him and not be banished for it, I would've a long fucking time ago.

"Stay here for as long as you want," he said, a smug look on his face. "But I'm going to go say hi to her, maybe have a drink and bring her home for the night, or maybe …" He chuckled menacingly. "Maybe I can make her my little toy."

When he entered the bar, I glared at the door, then followed him. Anger, rage, fury rushed through me. I hated this man almost more than I hated myself. But there was no way that I'd let him make Maxine his toy, not even if she wanted to be.

Dressed in a button-up blouse that covered her entire chest again, Maxine pulled some glasses off the counter and dropped them into the sink. Erthrol slid onto the stool in front of her, and I gathered all the fucking courage I had left and sat beside him, jaw clenched and … hoping that Maxine wouldn't fall under my brother's charm, like everyone else did.

A couple of people looked over, even some of the succubi, wondering what I was doing here. They didn't have to say it out loud—I could see it in their disgusted glares and their scowls.

After setting some napkins on the counter in front of us, Maxine placed her small hands on the bar and leaned toward us. "What can I get—" She looked up at me and paused mid-sentence, her gaze traveling across every inch of my fucked up face.

I expected her to turn away, to direct all her attention to Erthrol, like all people did, even our parents.

Except she didn't.

Instead, she stared at me quizzically. "Have I met you before?"

Erthrol slung his arm over my shoulders. "You probably have, as *you* lost his family ring."

She widened her eyes, stepped back, and glanced down. "I'm so sorry. I-I brought it home to prevent someone from picking it up in the lost and found. I-I swear I don't know where it went. I checked every inch of my house. I can do anything you want. I'll—"

"It's okay," I said.

She snapped her gaze up to me, goose bumps rising on her skin. "I'm sorry."

"It's fine."

For a moment, her gaze dropped to my mouth, and she furrowed her brow, the same way she had last night when I found her lying in her bed and touching her sweet little cunt. She almost looked *aroused*.

But I didn't know why. All I had said to her were a couple of words. I'd barely kept eye contact with her for more than a couple of seconds. I didn't want her to know how much I fucking wanted her, didn't want her to see right through me and sense that I had been here every night.

"Um … what can I get you guys tonight?"

"You," Erthrol said, dragging her attention away from me. He leaned across the bar and lightly brushed his fingers against her skin, the hairs on it rising. "We want you to come home with us tonight. You know, as *punishment* for losing a royal family ring."

"Erthrol," I snapped, showing him my jagged teeth and wishing he'd shut the fuck up.

"Me?" Maxine's cheeks flushed, and she sucked in a breath. "I … I have to work tonight."

Erthrol stood up and slapped me hard on the back, staring at the tavern boss. "We'll see about that."

When he walked away, I glared at the bar with my jaw clenched and my hands balled into fists by my sides. What the fuck was he even doing? I couldn't … Maxine wouldn't want to do this anyway. She was just making excuses.

"You're Xorgor, right?" she asked once Erthrol started talking to her boss. She wiped the counter with a rag and peeked up at me. "Why don't you ever come around here? Your brother is here nearly every night, always flirting with someone."

I glanced up to see her staring at me again. "I come here."

"I've never seen you here before. Do you come in the mornings?"

"No."

What the fuck was wrong with me? I couldn't even keep up a conversation with her.

Before I could try to start up something else, Erthrol swung his arm around my shoulders again and leaned forward. "You're done for the night, Maxine. And all ours."

Maxine stared between Erthrol and me, nervously chewing on her cheek. "Are you sure? I—"

"Get out of here, Maxine," her boss called. "We got things covered tonight."

6
the night

TWENTY MINUTES LATER, we stood in my home, which I had really torn apart to look for Xorgor's ring. Erthrol stood behind me with his strong hands all over my body and his hot breath on the crook of my neck. He undid the buttons on my shirt, starting from the bottom and working his way up.

I stared at Xorgor nervously and covered my chest. "I, um … don't usually do this."

Hell, I had never done this before. If this was what they wanted in return for losing his family ring, then I would much rather do this than have them scar my body all over.

Plus, when I had first seen Xorgor sitting at the bar …

Warmth spread throughout my core. I pressed my thighs together as the last button on my shirt came undone and kept my hands over my chest to hide the werewolf scars. I'd felt like I had met Xorgor before.

I knew I had.

Somewhere.

Xorgor stared at me through one red eye and one green eye and parted his jagged teeth. "You don't have to do this," he whispered, his voice so low that I didn't think that Erthrol had heard him.

"You have nothing to worry about," Erthrol whispered in my ear, drawing his hands down my sides and touching me the way that I had wanted someone to for so fucking long.

It was all I could dream about, all that I imagined.

Nobody had ever touched me like this.

Erthrol kissed my neck and pulled my arms away from my body slowly. I stared at Xorgor as Erthrol exposed the nasty scars on my chest and hoped that Xorgor wouldn't run away, disgusted at them. I wouldn't blame him if he did.

When I caught him furrowing his brow angrily at my chest, I frowned, my gaze faltering for a moment. "I …"

"You're the sexiest woman that I've laid eyes on," Erthrol whispered into my ear, cupping my breasts from behind, then glancing over my shoulder at his brother. "Don't worry about him. He'll join in if he wants, or he'll run off, like he usually does."

Moving his hand against my chin, Erthrol tilted my head and kissed me on the lips, his tongue slipping into my mouth. I gasped sharply, eyes meeting Xorgor's for a moment. Emotions crossed his face that I couldn't seem to decipher. And then, because I wanted someone to touch me like this after thinking that I was the most disgusting woman alive, I kissed Erthrol back.

His hands were all over my body, just as Xorgor's gaze was. He stood inches from me, and the feeling of him being here with me before rushed through my head.

Suddenly, I pulled away from Erthrol and grabbed Xorgor by the shirt collar, tugging him closer to me and pressing my lips against his, wanting to feel how he felt. For the second time tonight, his entire body went rigid.

His teeth felt long and sharp against my lips, his touch familiar. When he didn't kiss me back, a wave of rejection rushed through me.

I pulled away from him and leaned back against Erthrol, who moved his lips against my neck. "I'm sorry. I should've—"

Before I could finish my sentence, Xorgor wrapped his arms around my waist and pulled me back toward him again, crashing his lips down against mine and really kissing me back this time, like I had been wanting him to do since the moment I had seen him at the bar.

I wrapped one arm around his shoulders, fingernails digging into his rough skin. When I moaned into his mouth, his dick throbbed against the front of his pants that he pressed against me. All I wanted to do was rip off all his clothes and let the monster take me, let the monster love me.

He was like me.

Different.

Scarred.

Ruined.

Erthrol wrapped his hands around both of my elbows, pulling me away from Xorgor and whispering filthy things into my ear, making me moan again. Xorgor drew his hand up the front of my soaked panties and grunted, slipping his fingers into my underwear and gently rubbing my clit, making sure his talons didn't scrape against me.

I inched my legs apart and stared up at him, nipples stiffening. Erthrol growled and ground against my backside, hands gripping my elbows even tighter when he saw how I reacted to Xorgor and not him anymore.

"More," I whispered.

Xorgor moved his fingers against me like he had touched me before, like he knew exactly what I liked—the exact spots, the exact speed, the exact pressure.

"More, please ..."

Erthrol tore off my panties from behind and pulled himself out of his jeans. He spit on his cock, forced me to arch my back, and slipped himself into my ass, forgoing my aching cunt altogether.

When Xorgor slipped a finger inside me, I moaned and glanced down at his hand. My pussy tightened around him, my eyes widening when I spotted a red-and-gold ring on his finger. He'd had it this entire time—this entire fucking time.

H-how did he get —

He curled his fingers into me, hitting my G-spot the way my vibrator had last night.

I whimpered at how familiar his fingers felt inside me and lifted my gaze to his eyes, a wave of realization hitting me hard. I'd brought that ring home last night. He had come to retrieve it. He had to have. And when he did—oh God, when he did … he had touched me.

Unless I was going crazy.

"Y-your ring," I whispered.

Xorgor lifted his harsh gaze toward me, curled his fingers inside my crying pussy, and didn't say a word. His piercing eyes seemed to glow a tinge brighter, his jagged teeth glistening under the moonlight that flooded into the room.

When he moved his fingers faster inside me, I whimpered. Erthrol pumped into me from behind, but I couldn't seem to focus on him. All I could think about was how … Xorgor had touched me like this before. My gaze dropped to his forked tongue, and I nearly came.

"Tell me to stop," he said.

I'd heard rumors that some demons had abilities to use magic to make their bodies invisible and that incubi, in particular, visited innocent women like me late at night, touching them as they pleased. Nobody had even wanted to look at me after they saw the scars on my chest.

"D-don't stop," I begged, remembering how he had felt last night. "Please, give it to me."

In one swift movement, he lifted me into the air, leaned me against Erthrol, and rested my left leg on his shoulder, cupping my right thigh and spreading my legs further apart. Pulling his cock out of his pants, Xorgor gripped it at its base and drew his thumb over the head, coating it in pre-cum.

In shock, I stared down at it with wide eyes. His cock was almost twice the size of Erthrol's, larger than anything I had ever seen before—even when things got out of hand at the tavern and some monster decided to whip out their dick to harass some succubi.

He glanced down at my pink pussy, spread and drooling for him. Instead of thrusting himself inside of me, he pushed against my entrance to get himself a bit wetter, then rubbed his swollen head against my clit, making me moan again.

"Fuck," Erthrol grunted, thrusting in and out of my backside.

I watched Xorgor rub his hardness against me, then glanced up at him, lips parted slightly. "Please," I said, the word barely audible. "Please, I need it so badly. Just—just like last night. Give it to me."

He growled, the sound ferocious, which only made me clench harder. He moved his dick between my fat pussy lips, rubbing the head of himself harder and faster against my swollen clit. Panting, I tossed my head back and screamed, my legs trembling hard in his hands. Finally, he pushed himself into my warm pussy, and my walls clenched and gripped his throbbing cock. With every inch that he thrust into me, I tightened even more and whimpered.

"It's too ... too big."

Xorgor stepped closer to me and dipped his head by my ear. "I'm not even at my full size, baby," he whispered.

I moaned again and furrowed my brow, my pussy suddenly becoming wetter somehow and easier for him to slip into. When he thrust himself as deep as he could go, he stilled inside of me and sprawled his hand over my stomach.

My stomach was swollen with the bulge of his dick. He pressed hard against my cervix, but the pain slipped away quicker than I'd expected. As he pulled himself out, he grunted. I glanced down at his dick, seeing how much of my juices coated his cock already.

"More," I pleaded, pussy pulsing on nothing. "Give me more."

He thrust himself back up into me hard, over and over and over. I dug my nails into his thick shoulder muscles and moaned again, my gaze focused on him. And while Erthrol might've been fucking me from behind, I couldn't seem to focus on him at all.

"Oh God," I breathed out, pressure rising. "I'm going to come again."

Fuck.

He pumped faster into me. Unable to stop myself, I pulled him closer to me and kissed him, and as soon as my lips touched his, he grunted. I threw my head back against Erthrol's shoulder and cried out in pleasure.

Wave after wave rushed through me, my pussy pulsing on his huge cock. Xorgor pulled out of me, holding his thick cock in his hand. Desperate for his cum, I scrambled out of their hold, pulled Erthrol out of me, and dropped to my knees, sticking my tongue out and staring up at Xorgor.

I took them both in my hands, so as not to be rude, and stroked them. Quickly, Erthrol came all over my face and stumbled back onto the bed to catch his breath. I dropped his cock from my hand and placed both my hands around Xorgor, unable to wrap around it fully.

If he really wasn't at his full size ... he would've torn me apart.

"Come for me," I begged him, my cunt aching. "Please, fill up my mouth."

As soon as I sucked only the head of his cock into my mouth, he grunted loudly and filled my tight throat with his cum. I stroked him faster, milking so much out of him that I choked on it and spilled it out of my mouth and let it rush down my chin.

"Swallow it," he ordered.

I squeezed my lips around his cock and swallowed, eyes watering slightly. When he pulled out of me, more of his cum pooled in my mouth. I swallowed again, then drew my fingers across my chin, catching the last of his cum that had run out of my mouth. After sticking my fingers between my lips, I licked off the rest of it.

Instead of standing back up, I couldn't stop myself from wrapping my hands around his cock again and sucking his head back into my mouth, stroking him back and forth to get every last fucking drop.

"More," I whispered. "I know you have more for me."

"Fuck, Maxine," he grunted, lacing his hand into my hair.

I bobbed my head back and forth on him, barely able to take more than a couple of inches into my mouth. "Please, give me mo—"

Again, he filled my mouth to the brim with his cum as I sucked on him until my cheeks flushed. I swallowed hungrily and continued to stroke his cock, one hand massaging his balls.

When I had literally sucked him dry, he grabbed me by the front of my throat and lifted me into the air. "The next time I fuck you, my cum is going to be gushing down your legs from your tight little cunt, Maxine. The next time I fuck you, you'll be *mine*."

7
the sorrow

xorgor

THE INFERNO REEKED of demonic lust tonight. I sat across from my parents and next to Erthrol on a maroon velvet couch, sipping on Rum Delight—Erthrol's favorite drink—and wishing that they hadn't invited me out to dinner.

We might've lived in the same castle, but I hadn't seen them in weeks, and I liked it.

My parents and Erthrol watched Bella, a succubus that Erthrol had tried to hook me up with last time I was here for royal duties, dance around a pole to our left. I sipped on the drink that wouldn't even get me drunk and stared at the charcuterie board on the table in front of us.

"So," Mother said, eyeing Bella's tits, "it's rumored the demon queen will step down in a few months. She has no children, and we have the best claim to the throne." She finally turned back to us but looked at Erthrol only. "I expect you to stop messing around every night and take this seriously."

Erthrol rolled his eyes. "I'm an incubus. I have needs."

"And I have needs, too, but I've done everything I can so you can take the throne."

"If you don't take it, then Jaroth will take it," Father said.

"Wouldn't want that," I said emptily. "It's all on your shoulders, Erthrol."

Never on mine.

"I expect you to help out too, Xorgor," Mother said, barely sparing me a glance.

Honestly, I was surprised that she had actually invited me out to be in public tonight with her. Usually, she hated being seen with me, almost more than she hated looking at the monster her son was. It must've been a political ploy.

The handsome incubus hanging out with his ugly older brother.

A fucking sob story.

"I have to piss," I said, placing down my glass on the table and standing.

Instead of heading toward the restrooms, I walked out of The Inferno and into Durnbone to get some fresh air. I didn't want to be part of their plans. They didn't have any need for me—until now anyway.

With my body cloaked, I walked down Durnbone's empty streets and toward the Dead Candle Tavern. A cold wind chilled my charred skin. I stopped outside and blew out a low breath, thankful that the others hadn't followed me.

Through the window, I spotted Maxine pouring drinks for a vampire couple. Shirt buttoned to the top, she dumped a couple of glasses into the sink and furrowed her brow, dark circles underneath her eyes.

I drew my forked tongue across my jagged teeth. It had been five days since the night I had spent with Maxine, and I didn't know what had come over me with her that night. I'd told her that she'd be mine the next time I fucked her.

Why had I assumed that there would be another time, that she would willingly go home with me alone and not with Erthrol? Gods, I had fucked up big time. So much so that I hadn't been able to convince myself to visit her again or even step into the tavern since Friday.

When I closed my eyes, memories flashed through my mind. Nobody had ever looked at me the way that she did on Friday night, like she was actually enjoying herself around me, like she wanted me more than she wanted Erthrol.

But what if Erthrol had put her up to it? What if he had offered her money or diamonds or power in return? Had he told her to make me fall in love with her, so then he could sweep her off her feet and take her away from me?

Sounded like something he'd do.

Maxine was the kindest and most beautiful woman in all of Durnbone. She gave her spare change to the monsters who lived on the street and brought out some leftover food to the kids in the demon sector on her way back home from work.

She wouldn't want a man who had bloodied his hands for her— a woman he'd yet to meet—a demon who killed anyone who looked at her the wrong way, an incubus who would never lead his kingdom because he was too hideous.

She'd be much better on the throne, next to my younger brother.

"Fine piece of ass, isn't she?"

I gritted my teeth and glanced over at a demon stumbling toward the tavern door. Usually, when I was cloaked, nobody could sense me around, but demons who were skilled in the same type of magic could.

He hiked his thumb back to The Dungeon and laughed. "Got kicked out of The Dungeon for not paying my way, but who the fuck cares to pay for human pussy when that cute little barkeep walks home alone at night?"

My body phased back into existence as anger flooded through me. "What the fuck did you just say?" I asked, balling my hands into tight fists, my talons sinking into the thin skin on my palms.

"Come on," he said, slapping me on the shoulder like we were old pals.

I doubted that he was sober enough to even realize who stood in front of him.

"Don't tell me that you haven't thought about it. She's gotta be hiding something under those frumpy clothes. And nobody cares if a woman like her goes missing for a few days. It's not like she's important to any—"

Before he could say another word, I grabbed his hand still attached to my shoulder, twisted it back, and broke his arm cleanly in half, his humerus and ulna bones cracking in opposite directions.

He wailed out in pain, clutching his arm. With a slight flick of my wrist, I tossed him to the ground and dragged him against the cold, dirty stone to one of the many back alleys near the Dead Candle Tavern.

I dumped him behind the dumpster and stood above him, jagged teeth aching to tear into his neck. "Stand up."

After drunkenly shaking his head, he scurried back against the brick building and clutched his arm. "You broke my arm!" he cried, the bones still protruding at grotesque angles. "You fucking broke my arm."

"Poor fucking kid," I said, crouching in front of him. "Let me heal you."

Placing my hand over his elbow, I healed his wound. He could've done it himself, but he was far too drunk, and I wanted to help out a fellow demon … because I wasn't finished with him yet.

Breathing heavily, he gently rubbed his elbow and glanced up at me. "Thank—"

I snapped it again, this time harder so the bones actually shattered inside his body. He wailed out in pain, throwing his head back and grasping his elbow. And because I wanted him to shut his fucking mouth and never let one of those thoughts rush through his head again, I wrapped both my hands around his pathetic throat and tore him into two pieces, right down the middle.

Whether or not Maxine wanted me, she was still mine to protect.

8
the ugly

maxine

"SWEETHEART, WE'LL TAKE FOUR GLASSES," a succubus said, sitting with her demon girlfriends in the corner of the bar. She glanced back at the women and smirked. "Red wine, girls?" After her friends nodded, she turned back to me. "Red wine."

I sucked in a tired breath and grabbed four wineglasses, placed them on the counter, and then plucked the finest red wine from our cabinet. Three more hours of this, and I'd get to leave for the night. But I would be back tomorrow for the same shit.

"I asked Erthrol if he wanted to party with us tonight," another succubus said to the group. "When I mentioned that we were headed here, he shuddered with disgust and told me he'd never set foot in here again."

Once I set the glasses down in front of them, I hummed to make conversation, not really caring why Erthrol didn't want to come back down here—this place wasn't the best for the royal family to drink in Durnbone.

"Why not?"

The gossiping demon leaned forward. "I'm surprised you haven't heard. I know how people in Durnbone talk nonstop.

Anyway, apparently, he slept with one of the girls who works here."

Fear ran my blood cold. "Wh-what?" I whispered. "Really?"

"What'd he say?" another demon asked, leaning closer.

"That she was a lousy fuck." She laughed. "And that she looked better with clothes on."

Laughter erupted from the group. I clutched a wet cloth in my hand and aimlessly wiped down the clean counter, desperately trying to convince myself that Erthrol could've fucked any one of the girls I worked with, that they weren't talking about me.

It had been almost a week since I'd slept with Erthrol and Xorgor anyway.

A week, and I still couldn't get Xorgor out of my head.

But the more the girls laughed, the tighter my stomach became. Neither of them had shown up at the Dead Candle Tavern or contacted me. And, sure, I understood that it was a one-time hookup but ...

Xorgor ...

I dumped the wet rag in the sink and chewed on the inside of my cheek.

"Do you know who it is?" the woman said to me, wanting gossip.

"Oh, um ..." I bit back a whimper. "No, I don't."

The demons turned back to each other to gossip, and I forced myself to walk to the other end of the bar. Pain shot through my body, my heart aching at the thought of Erthrol saying something like that about me.

If any of the other girls had slept with him, I would've heard the gossip.

Erthrol had told them about me. Me.

If he thought that I was ugly after continuing to call me the sexiest person he'd ever seen, what did Xorgor think of me? Did he think that I was a bad fuck too? Was that why he hadn't shown up here since then?

Nerves built up inside me, and I found myself aimlessly wiping down the bar again to busy my mind. But it wasn't working. I couldn't fucking stop thinking about it. About how I had thought that I was actually attractive to someone for a few moments.

How am I that stupid?

"So, did you see him?" Valerie—the vampiress with royal blood and my high school bully—asked to my left suddenly. I hadn't even realized that she was sitting so close. With a half-smile plastered on her face, she clicked her tongue and shook her head. "Isn't he an ugly bastard?"

"Who?" I asked, my mind buzzing with worry.

"You know who," she said, sipping red blood that sat in her wineglass. "Xorgor."

I stared with wide eyes at the bar in front of me and gulped, my dinner gurgling in my stomach. I hadn't been able to get him out of my head; he had been haunting my every dream. He had actually been in my room before, had touched my body.

She sucked in an excited breath and leaned forward. "Oh my gods, you did! He never shows his face in Durnbone. When I heard he came here, I needed to get the deets from you! Tell me how ugly he is. I've only seen him once in passing."

Nervously, I played with my sleeve and turned around to grab three shot glasses for a group of fairies who sat next to Valerie. I didn't want to get into this. Not here and not now. Looks weren't everything. At least, that was what I'd been trying to convince myself of for the past decade now.

Trying.

But after listening to people like those demon girls gossiping, I had never convinced myself that personality ever trumped looks. People didn't even give you a shot when you were ugly.

When I didn't answer Valerie, she took another sip and rolled her red eyes. "Come on, Maxine. Tell me what you thought of him, the one person in all of Durnbone that you're probably more attractive than."

My chest tightened, and I stared at the counter, internally pleading with myself not to give her the satisfaction of seeing me break. She had always taken jabs at me, especially when I didn't give her the reaction she wanted.

"You know, with those scars on your chest and all," she continued.

She didn't know how much her words hurt, or maybe she did and didn't care.

Once I handed the fairies their shots of a glowing liquid called Luminance, I forced myself to smile, though tears sat heavily in my eyes. "Xorgor isn't ugly," I whispered.

He might've looked like a monster to everyone else, but to people like me … he wasn't.

To humans who could never heal a wound instantly, could never perform magic, could never have a power such as his, he was remarkable. Humans were the ones in this town and in this world who could never even be as remotely as attractive as he could.

"Are you saying that to make yourself feel better?" she asked, taking another sip.

When my manager walked behind the counter, I told him that I needed to take my break now, hurried into the restroom, and locked the door behind me. Tears welled up in my eyes, and I grasped on to the sink and stared at myself in the mirror.

One of my shirt buttons had come undone during work, the tops of my chest scars visible. In a fit of sorrow and pity and shame, I undid the next three buttons to see the repulsive blemishes marked on my body forever.

If I had been born into this world as a demon or a wolf or a vampire, I would've been able to heal these scars a couple of moments after the werewolf attack. My body wouldn't be the ugly, disgusting mess that it was.

Maybe Xorgor wouldn't have frozen while staring at my chest the other night. Maybe he would've shown up at the tavern since he had slept with me, asked me out on a date, told me that I was beautiful, like his brother had. Obviously, Erthrol had been lying to make me comfortable enough so he could fuck me. Still, the thought of Xorgor calling me pretty or sexy was a nice fantasy.

I drew my fingers across the rough skin and shuddered. Valerie had always been right, ever since we had been just kids. My body was repulsive, foul, nauseating. Nobody—not even a monster like Xorgor—would ever really like me or want me.

Not for my body and not for myself.

Lifting my gaze, I stared at my teary eyes in the mirror and grasped the sink tighter. Why hadn't he called me back or shown up at the bar or even in my home, if he didn't want to be seen in public? Was I ugly to the monster that Durnbone had titled the ugliest? What did that make me, a nobody who'd be working in this tavern for the rest of her lousy life? Would anyone miss me if I disappeared, like my best friend, Sina, had?

Nobody in Durnbone cared about me.

My chest tightened. A single tear raced down my cheek.

"Ugly," I whispered, my voice trembling. "I'll always be ugly."

9
the disbelief

xorgor

"A GIRL at the Dead Candle Tavern was talking about you," Jaroth said, stepping out of The Inferno after a demon meeting with all those who had royal blood.

It was Friday night, and I had plans to walk by the tavern tonight to see Maxine. I didn't have time to chat about just anything.

"Who?" I asked.

"Someone behind the bar. A group of succubi told me."

"Maxine?"

"Sounds familiar," Jaroth said, glancing over his shoulder at Erthrol, who stepped out of The Inferno with his arms wrapped around two succubi's waists. "Is that the girl that you and Erthrol slept with last weekend?"

I drew my tongue across my jagged teeth and glared at Erthrol, still pissed at him for knowing what it felt like to be inside Maxine. I wanted her to be mine, but she would've never agreed to it any other way. No other fucking girl had.

"What'd she want?" I asked.

Jaroth chuckled. "Shit, it was her. Heard she wasn't that good, huh?"

"What the fuck does that mean?" I growled, wondering who he had heard that from.

"J, you gonna make me take both these pretty ladies home by myself tonight?" Erthrol called to Jaroth.

Instead of answering me, Jaroth gave me a measly head nod, as if to say bye, and jogged over to Erthrol.

After glaring at him, I stormed from The Inferno and hurried down the walkway toward the tavern. I wanted to cloak myself, but if Maxine really wanted to talk to me, then … I'd have to show up like this.

When I reached the door, I swallowed hard and stared into the windows, watching her pour drinks for a fairly empty bar. I stepped into the pub and briefly held the door for the wolf couple walking in behind me. Truthfully, I wanted to be here, but I didn't want to talk to her. Fuck it, I really wanted to talk to her, too, but I didn't want to be disappointed in what she had to say.

Maybe she wanted me to hook her up with Erthrol.

The wolf couple leisurely strolled into the room, and I released the door from my grasp, nervous as fuck to turn around and head toward the bar. Part of me wanted to walk back out and never come in here again, but I couldn't do that.

I needed to hear what she had to say to me.

When I turned around, Maxine was already looking at me. I sucked in a sharp breath, glanced away, and walked to the counter. I never came into town, especially alone, looking like this. Not only that, but I also didn't know what to say to her. She was everything that I'd ever wanted, and yet I couldn't believe she had been asking about me.

"What can I get you?" she asked softly, playing with her fingers. "Anything?"

"A Midnight Moon," I said, sliding onto the seat in front of her.

After a moment's pause, she turned arould to grab my drink. I finally glanced back up at her—long brown hair cascading down her back, wide hips that I couldn't stop thinking about, and a scent that had been haunting my fucking dreams for the past week.

She placed the glass onto the counter in front of me, gaze lingering on me. "Here you go."

Swallowing all the fucking anxiety about this shit, I grabbed the glass. "Thanks, Maxine."

Her eyes widened. "You-you remember me?"

She thinks I can forget her?

"What do you mean, do I remember you? Of course I do."

"Oh," she said, voice barely above a whisper. She nervously looked away. "I just thought … that, um … you've probably been around so many people this past week that our little thing on Friday was … sorta, um … unremarkable for you."

Before I could respond to her, she quickly grabbed a damp towel and returned to wiping down the other end of the bar.

Did she really think that I was like all those other demons, especially incubi, who fucked a new girl or guy every night?

Could she not see how fucking ugly I was? Why would anyone want to get with me?

As she scrubbed down the bar with a rag, she kept glancing over at me, like everyone else in this damn tavern, probably wondering why she had slept with me last weekend. She could pick to go home with anyone in Durnbone, and she had gotten stuck with me.

When she finally made her way back over to my end of the bar, I cleared my throat. "So, you wanted to see me," I said, wondering why she had been asking around. "You found me." I knocked back my drink, tired of these damn stares, and placed the glass on the counter. "Now, stop staring and talk."

Her cheeks flushed. "Who said I wanted to see you?"

"Word travels fast, especially when you tell demons who love gossip."

After sneaking a glance down the bar, she turned back to me. "I … um," she whispered, playing with the knotted ends of the rag. "I don't know how to say this, so I guess I'll just come out with it."

I clenched my jaw, the pressure in my chest building as I prepared for her to say the fucking worst. She probably wanted

Erthrol's number or was going to tell me to bring him along next time because she wanted to flirt more with him.

"What?" I growled.

She stared down at the counter, clutching the wet rag in her hands. Nervous lines appeared between her furrowed brow. She took one peek up at me, then quickly looked away. "I can't stop thinking about the other night."

My chest tightened even more, my blood running hot. *Fucking Erthrol.*

I was right.

But I didn't want her to see how this fucking affected me, how I had been waiting so fucking long for her, how long it had taken me to get up the fucking courage to walk into this bar tonight without being cloaked to talk to her alone.

So, I shook it off. "If you want me to set you up with my brother, get in line. He's got a fucking group of fangirls who love to follow him around and jump on his dick whenever they get the chance."

She shifted uncomfortably from foot to foot and gnawed on the inside of her cheek. "No." She dropped the wet rag into the sink, grabbed my empty glass to refill it, then handed it back. "That's not what I mean."

"He's busy tonight, out with some succubi. He can't swing by."

"Forget it. Forget it," she whispered, dropping her head and turning around. She lowered her voice to a tone that she must've thought she could only hear herself. "You wouldn't understand. You're an incubus demon with royal blood, and I'm just ..." She tensed and shook her head.

"If it means that much to you, then I'll give you his numb—"

Before I could finish my sentence, Maxine twirled around and finally looked up at me, tears welling in her eyes. "I don't want Erthrol's number. I don't want Erthrol at all. It's you that I can't stop thinking about. You."

My hand tightened around the glass of alcohol. I stared at her for moments, maybe even minutes, rage building inside me with every second that dragged by. She wasn't serious. Erthrol had put her up to this.

He had to have fucking put her up to this.

"No," I said between gritted, jagged teeth. The thought of her lying to me about actually wanting me hurt like hell itself. I wondered how much Erthrol had paid her to say this to me. I stood up and walked out of the tavern without looking back at her once, unable to believe this. "No."

10
the night alone

maxine

CANDLES FLICKERED AROUND MY ROOM. I stood in front of the dirty mirror and undid the strings of my top. It fell open slightly, and I frowned at the werewolf claw marks that lay across my chest.

"Ugly," I whispered.

Tears welled up in my eyes as I pulled off my top and stared at my breasts, at the scars that everyone picked on me for. I hated the scars almost as much as I hated myself. And tonight, I was really loathing everything about me.

It had taken me so long to gather the courage to confess my feelings for Xorgor today.

And all he had done was stare back at me angrily—like he would never even think about being with someone like me—then walked out of the bar without sparing me another glance.

Was I really that ugly to him? I hadn't thought so last Friday night, but apparently, I wasn't enough.

How could I have been so fucking stupid? I had never been anything special to the world around me. I was just a girl who got looked over every single day of her life. Why would someone of his power and standing even consider someone like me?

A shiver rolled down my spine, wind drifting into the room through the open window. I balled my hand into a fist and hurled it at the mirror. I was so fucking ugly that even an incubus—a man who came from a group of demons who fucked anyone from any race, no matter how different they looked—didn't want me.

Just before my fist could collide with the mirror again, someone wrapped their hand around my wrist and stopped me … except nobody was in the mirror behind me and nothing was wrapped around my palm. But there was this force; I could feel skin—rough skin—against my wrist, squeezing tightly.

I swallowed hard and tried to pull my arm away, but whoever it was wouldn't release me.

"Tell me that you were lying," Xorgor whispered deeply into my ear, his body appearing before me. "Tell me that my brother made you say what you said in the pub … that you can't stop thinking about me."

My heart raced. "I … he-he didn't."

Xorgor squeezed my wrist tighter, a charcoal-colored appendage wrapping around my ankle and sliding up my leg to my thigh. "That's not what I want to hear," he said through those clenched, jagged teeth. "Tell me my brother put you up to this."

I furrowed my brow at him. "I'm sorry that it's not what you want to hear. I shouldn't have said anything. I didn't mean to make you angry. I just … I thought by the way you were touching me and looking at me the other day … I stupidly thought that you might've been thinking about me too." I yanked my wrist away from him. "But that's what incubi do," I whispered. "They tell ugly girls pretty little lies."

He stared down at me for a long time, the veins in his neck swelling and twitching. "Ugly?" he asked with distaste.

I looked away from him, unable to keep his wicked stare, and wrapped my arms over my chest. I hated showing people my scars and tried to avoid it when possible.

He snatched my chin and forced me to look up at him. "You think you're ugly?"

I sucked in a deep breath and stared down at my feet, my scars in my peripheral vision. I hated admitting it aloud because it made it so much more real. I didn't want to be ugly. I didn't want to be made fun of over and over again. It just happened, and it made me feel like shit.

"Look at me." He seethed, voice with a demonic edge to it now. When I glanced up at him, he pressed his teeth together. "You think you're ugly?"

"Yes," I whispered, tears welling up in my eyes. "I … I have this nasty scar on my chest. No man has ever wanted to sleep with me. People just gloss me over, looking at the succubi or the vampires or the she-wolves at the tavern. It's never—"

"It's never what?" he whispered in my ear. "It's never you? It's never been me either." He flared his nostrils and stared at me with so much pain behind those eyes of his. "But last Friday, it was me and you." He paused. "I had been waiting months to be able to spend a night with you, not with anyone else from town. You."

My lips quivered, and I shook my head up at him. "You're lying."

"If I was lying, I wouldn't fucking be here," he said. "I'm going to show you how much I want you."

Two snake-like appendages emerged from Xorgor's back and wrapped around my ankles, sliding up my calves, around my knees, and up my thighs. While my feet were posted on the floor, they tugged my thighs far apart. I let out a surprised gasp and stared up at Xorgor, feeling so exposed and bare to him even though he had seen me like this last Friday.

This time … this time, it was just us though, just like I had wanted.

This almost didn't feel real.

Stepping closer to me, he rested one hand on my waist and fondled my pussy with the other, retracting his talons into normal human fingers and slipping two of them inside of me, pumping them in and out in a steady rhythm.

Inching closer to me, he placed his tongue on my collarbone and licked to my jaw, the ridges of his forked tongue making me shiver as they glided against my throat. I let out a low moan, my eyes closing in delight. All I could imagine was his tongue inside of me again, inside my mouth and my pussy, lapping around the folds before slipping into it.

I boldly rested my hand against the front of his pants and stroked him through the thin material, feeling him grow underneath my touch. He pushed my head to the side, letting his hot mouth and tongue move down my chest and capture my nipple. Sucking it into his mouth, he bit down on it with his sharp teeth.

Whether this was a dream or not, I needed this so badly. So fucking badly.

I slipped my fingers around the waistband of his pants and pushed them down.

Hanging to his mid-thigh, Xorgor's cock was bigger than even his brother's—the demon people always raved about—and already bigger than last time. I pushed him onto my bed, which could barely fit him, and crawled between his legs, lying on my stomach and wrapping two hands around the head of his cock—almost unable to get my fingertips to touch.

As I stared up at him, I opened my mouth and sucked as much as I could, just his head—anything more, and he'd tear me apart for sure. My eyes watered slightly, yet I stroked up and down his cock with two hands, hoping that I could make him feel good.

Because I liked making people feel good. I knew what it felt like to feel like shit, to feel like you were the ugliest person alive. And I didn't want him to be staring at my scars, like he had last time. I wanted him to focus on something else.

He rested back against the headboard and placed one hand on the back of my head, curling his fingers into my hair. "You do that so fucking well," he said to me. With his free hand, he grasped his horn, abdomen flexing hard.

Two of his snake-like black appendages slithered down the side of the bed, wrapping around my waist just above my belly button and around my thigh. One slipped into my pussy as the other pulled my right leg to the side to spread my legs wide for him.

As he thrust it in and out of me, I tightened around him and took more of him into my mouth. He hit the back of my throat, making me gag. Instead of pulling him out, I flicked my tongue against the ridges and the veins of his cock and stared up at him through teary eyes.

Is this a dream? Or is Xorgor really here with me?

He gently started to thrust in and out of my mouth, somehow sliding even deeper each time. When I barely even took half of him, he wiped the saliva and spit dripping down my chin onto the rest of his cock.

"You can take more than that," he said down at me, hand wrapping around the front column of my throat. He strummed his talons against the sides of my neck, thrusting harder this time.

The deeper his cock slid down my throat, the faster his appendage fondled my pussy. Pleasure surged throughout my body as he thrust himself in and out of my cunt. I closed my eyes, letting my jaw relax as I moaned out on him, giving him the chance to stuff more of himself down my throat. Something about being filled by him made me come even harder.

My legs trembled. Tears fell down my cheeks. I stared up at him with wide eyes when the base of his hips met my lips. All of him—I had taken fucking all of him inside me.

"More," I mumbled out—or at least tried.

He rolled us over so I was lying on my back with my head hanging off the edge of the bed. He didn't take his cock out of me even once as he started to throat-fuck me the way I had only dreamed of—one hand around my throat, squeezing hard, and the other rubbing my clit.

So much spit and drool ran down the sides of my face, onto my forehead, and into my hair. I gagged every time he hit the back of my throat, sloppy, wet sounds coming from my mouth. My legs trembled, and I moaned again, the pleasure already rushing through me for a second time tonight.

When he finally pulled out of me, my throat was sore. He rubbed it gently with his fingers and flipped me onto my stomach again. After picking me up off the bed—my back against his chest—he walked toward my cracked mirror and positioned his cock right at my entrance. Clenching down, I stared at my reflection, nipples bare and taut. The snake-like appendages wrapped around them, squeezing and tugging hard.

Tension rose in my core, and I knit my brows together. My nipples ached, hurt. Goodness, it felt so good … so fucking good, the way he touched me all over. Those jagged teeth glided against my throat.

"Come," he ordered into my ear, tugging on my nipples even harder and watching me with his glowing red eye in the mirror's reflection. "Get your cunt wet and ready for me. You're going to need it."

I gazed at the mirror, my eyes dropping to the head of his cock as he pushed it against my entrance. I let out a loud moan and exploded all over it. My body trembled in his arms, and he pressed against me a bit harder and let me relax.

"Hands on your stomach," Xorgor said to me when I came down from my orgasm. "I want you to stroke my cock as soon as you feel me inside of you."

Swallowing hard, I placed both my hands on my stomach. He started to push the head of his cock into me, opening me up. I bit down on my lips so I wouldn't scream out in pain. He paused briefly to let me relax before he continued to slide himself inside of me.

When I felt the bulge under my fingers, I gently stroked him as a way to distract myself from the pain. He was at least six inches deep inside of me, and my hands moved faster and rougher against the bulge, pussy tightening around him.

"Look at it, just sliding in there," he whispered into my ear as I stared into the mirror. "Your pussy is hungry for my cock, isn't it?"

He tilted the side of his face and growled low, thrusting more of himself inside of me until there was a huge bulge nearly the girth of a forearm in my stomach. "Swallowing up as much as it can."

Hands spreading my legs even further, he thrust the last of himself, disappearing inside of me completely. The pressure in my core made me clench and whimper out in a pleasurable and thrilling kind of pain. He dug his sharp teeth into my neck.

"Shh, shh, shh. It feels good, doesn't it?" he asked, voice lower than it usually was.

I furrowed my brow, looking at how much of a mess he had made of me already, and nodded, my pussy pulsing around the base of his cock. "Please, give it to me," I pleaded. "I haven't stopped thinking about you filling me like this."

He began thrusting in and out of my pussy, wasting no time in destroying it with his huge cock. "If I come inside of you," he murmured against my ear, groaning against me, "you won't be able to hold it all inside your pussy. It'll spill out before I can even take myself out of you, run down your thighs, drip onto the floor. You'll have to clean later."

He slipped his fingers from my thigh to my pussy and started to rub torturous little circles around my clit. I closed my eyes, feeling pleasure from the way he pulled his entire dick out, leaving me empty, then filled me with it again. I wiggled in his grasp, trying to hold off another orgasm, and eventually surrendered to it—the tension inside of me too much.

With trembling legs, my pussy pulsed around his cock and coated it in my juices. I rested back against him, my head in such a daze that I didn't think I could even think straight anymore. All I craved was for him to come inside of me, for him to claim me as his own.

Using his hold around my legs, he bounced me up and down on him, ramming his cock into me as I dropped onto him. I tightened even more when he tore his teeth into my skin, the pain shooting through my body as mere pleasure.

"Mine," he growled through gritted teeth.

Harder. Thrusting into me harder.

"Fucking mine."

Faster. Rougher.

"You're fucking mine." He suddenly stilled and held me down deep on his cock, forcing me to watch in the mirror.

When I felt his hot cum fill my pussy, I couldn't stop myself from coming yet again.

He was still buried deep inside of my cunt when his cum started to spill out of me, the thick fluid dripping from my creamed pussy and right onto the wooden floor, creating a puddle underneath us.

As he pumped a few more times up into my pussy, he thrust his cum deeper into me. "My cum this deep in your quivering little cunt marks you as mine." He sprawled his hand against my stomach to feel himself inside of me. "I'd destroy the fucking world now and watch it burn. All for you."

11
the confession

xorgor

AFTER I PULLED out of Maxine, she collapsed onto the bed on her back and pulled her knees to her chest. Her chest heaved up and down, her cheeks flushed pink.

"Oh my gods …" she said in a breathy whisper. "That was amazing."

I sat on the edge of the bed next to her, my talons running across her bare leg and creating goose bumps. She pulled the blankets over her nakedness and stared up at the ceiling, her breath quieting.

She was mine now. All mine.

Nobody would touch her. Nobody would look at her wrong. Nobody would even talk about her.

Once a few silent moments passed, Maxine tensed and scooted up the bed to the headboard. Hundreds of vile emotions swirled through her confused eyes until she finally pulled her leg from my hand and stared at me, brow furrowed.

"What?" I asked, wondering if she was coming to her senses and regretting it.

It wasn't like this hadn't happened before with other girls.

But as cliché as it fucking was, Maxine wasn't like other girls. I'd never liked anyone as much as I liked Maxine, and I barely knew her. Yet something so deep, so feral drew me toward her, pulling me closer and closer.

"Did you really mean what you said?" she whispered, clutching the bedsheets to her.

"What do you mean?"

"Did you mean that … you've been waiting months for me?"

"Yes." My chest tightened, as the word had been so hard to say.

The more I talked to Maxine, the stronger the pull became, and the harder the heartbreak would torture me in the end if she decided she didn't want this.

"Why?" she asked, covering her scars and staring at the space between us. "I truly don't understand."

For some fucking reason, she didn't think that she was beautiful, and that pissed me off.

"Did your brother put you up to this to make fun of me more?" she asked. Moonlight glimmered against the tears welling in her big eyes. She turned away from me and toward the window. "Did he make you do it?"

Erthrol? What does he have to do with this?

"What the fuck are you talking about? What do you mean, make fun of you *more*?"

After swallowing hard, she shook her head and stood, hurrying toward her dresser for clothes. But I shot up from the bed and blocked her path. When she tried to get around me, I stepped in front of her again, catching her wrist in my hand.

"What do you mean?" I asked again, voice raspy. "What the fuck did he say to you?"

She stared down at her toes. "Nothing. He didn't say anything to me."

But I wasn't taking that shit. Someone was making her feel like she was undeserving of love, and I needed to find out who it was. Because it wasn't everyone. And she had just mentioned Erthrol.

I clutched her jaw and forced her to gaze up at me. "What. Happened?"

While she pressed her full lips together, as if she wasn't going to tell me, she blinked once, and two tears raced down her cheeks. She quickly pushed them away and sighed softly, chin trembling.

"Really," she whispered, "it's nothing. I'm sorry I mentioned it."

"What did Erthrol do to you?"

"I don't want to get between you and him. I should've never said anything. It's my fault."

"Erthrol has tormented me for years. We're not close. Tell me."

Again, she gulped. "Are-are you sure? Will he hurt me if he finds out what I know?"

Swiping my tongue across my aching, jagged teeth, I stared down at her. Rage boiled within me. What the fuck had Maxine been through for her to think of this shit? She had only just met my brother. If Erthrol had said something to her, I'd take care of him. But it couldn't just be him hurting her.

"If he lays a hand on you, I will kill him."

She widened her eyes, pupils dilating. "K-kill him?"

My patience was slipping. "I've done it before for you."

Somehow, her eyes became even wider. "For me?"

"Tell me," I growled, my words cutting like glass. "Now."

"I just heard from some of the succubi that frequent the tavern that ..." She looked down.

"Look at me when you talk."

She snapped her eyes back up at me. "I heard them talking about how Erthrol mentioned that he'd never set foot in the tavern again because I was ... because I was a lousy fuck."

"He said what?!" I growled through my jagged teeth, aching to kill that motherfucker right here and right now.

Wherever he was, I'd find him and torture the fuck out of him for making up some shitty rumor about Maxine.

All week, he had made snide comments to me about how terrible I had been last Friday with her, about how he could've done it better if he had been alone with Maxine. He had been taunting me more than usual. He had been jealous that we had shared her.

The fuck was he spreading rumors like this for? To ease his bruised fucking ego?

"I-I'm sorry. I should've never … we should've never done what we did tonight. You're an incubus …" She pulled herself away from me and hurried to the other side of the room, clutching the sheets around her naked body. "An incubus of royal blood."

"What the hell does that matter?"

More tears raced down her cheeks. "How can you not see?!" she shouted. "I'm ugly." She rested her forehead against the window, shoulders trembling back and forth and fingers gliding against the scars on her chest. "I'm so fucking ugly. Nobody ever wants me. I probably really was a lousy fuck for him and for you too."

While succubi loved stirring up drama, I knew that this was something Erthrol would actually say. He had fucked with me for so many years, had put me down over and over and fucking over again. He would have no problem doing it to some girl.

I snatched her chin in my hand again and forced her to look up at me. "Take it back."

"But—"

"Now," I growled ferociously, teeth aching to rip apart that asshole's flesh for making her feel this way.

Erthrol could taunt me about my appearance all he wanted, but he didn't get to bring Maxine into his disrespectful and ill-mannered ways. Maxine was mine. All mine. *Really* mine now. And I would do what I had to do to protect her.

No matter what.

"Take it back now and tell me you don't fucking believe that."

She swallowed hard and pressed her lips together.

"I already told you, I would burn the fucking world down for you. If I thought you were disgusting and lousy in bed, I wouldn't have come back to you. I wouldn't have filled you with my cum. I wouldn't have claimed your body as mine."

Eyes softening, she stared up at me and parted her lips slightly. But I couldn't waste any more time trying to convince her. My monster needed to take care of my brother first before he spread even worse rumors about her.

So, I dropped my hand from her chin and walked to the bedroom door.

"Where are you going?" she whispered, hurrying after me.

She still hadn't put any clothes on, not that I was complaining, but she wasn't about to step foot outside her house, naked like this. I wouldn't allow anyone to see her the way that I had again.

"Xorgor," she cried, grasping on to my elbow. "Please, stay with me."

Knowing that I was moments from exploding in fury, I tore myself out of her grip. I didn't want her to see me like that. My looks hadn't scared her off, but the real monster inside me would. I needed to not only keep her safe, but also keep her mine.

"I'm going to handle this," I growled.

"What does that mean?"

"It means that Erthrol will pay for what he said about you." I walked toward the front door, hands clenched into tight fists by my sides, my sharp talons cutting into the skin on my palms. "He'll pay in blood."

12

the best friend

maxine

"ERTHROL WILL PAY … IN BLOOD," I whispered the words to myself, barely able to swallow them whole.

Xorgor had left my house an hour ago, hunting his brother in Durnbone and planning how he'd hurt him for calling me lousy. It wasn't like I hadn't heard worse; all I wanted to hear was Xorgor say that he didn't think so. I hadn't planned for him to *want* to hurt his brother over it.

Since he had left, I hadn't dressed myself yet. Instead, I sat naked on my bed with the blankets wrapped tightly around my body as I stared at the tips of my scars in the mirror. Somehow, someway, I didn't feel as shitty about them as I had a couple of hours ago.

They were still disgusting. Erthrol had had every right to call me that.

Like usual, just when I was feeling okay about myself, Valerie's words rang through my ears, slithering their way into my head and torturing me, like they always did. Making me feel like shit again even though Xorgor had proven and promised that I shouldn't feel the way I did.

For years, I'd wanted to get even with my bullies, like Valerie.

It wasn't fair—what she had done to me for so many years. It wasn't fair that I'd had to endure her wrath since I had been just a child. At the time, I hadn't known any better to stick up for myself, hadn't known life without the constant bullying.

But Xorgor had said he'd make Erthrol pay in blood—with violence.

The image of Valerie, knocked out and covered in blood across the tavern bar, flashed through my mind. I swallowed hard. The thought of hearing her begging me to stop, of apologizing over and over for what she had done to me, made my heart hammer against my chest.

It was wrong. Oh-so wrong.

Yet I couldn't get the image out of my head. I couldn't stop thinking about how much shit she had done to me and how much she deserved it. Everyone who had bullied me the past twenty-two years of my life … deserved it.

I closed my eyes, shaking my head and desperately trying to thrust the vision away.

No, that wasn't me. That couldn't be me. I wasn't rude to people the way they were to me. I didn't hurt people intentionally. I didn't want anyone to feel the way that I had for all those years. Except … it felt good, thinking about the pain I could cause them.

Xorgor was about to do it for me, to his own brother, to his own flesh and blood.

Butterflies fluttered in my stomach—though I knew it was so fucking wrong. I couldn't stop the small smile that was etched onto my face at the mere thought of him burning the world down for me.

An incubus of royal blood actually wanted me.

It didn't seem or feel real.

Like, at all.

"No," I whispered.

I shook my head, hair whipping around, and stared out the window. I couldn't think like this. I couldn't get attached to a guy I'd spent a couple of nights with. Nobody had shown me this much attention before though; it was hard *not* to become attached.

While I wanted to believe that more could happen between Xorgor and me, I reminded myself that it couldn't. Those of royal blood—in almost all species—didn't choose who they ended up with. Most of the time, their marriages were arranged. And even then, incubi slept with other girls on the side.

Who knew if we would even make it to the point of being *serious*? People left all the time, whether it was against their will or not. I glanced over at the nightstand, where a dusty picture of Sina sat in a rusting silver frame.

So, I lay naked on my bed and stared out at the moon, my fingers finding my scars once more. I drew the pads of my digits against the rough skin and watched the moonlight filter through the dark clouds.

Even the light could cut through the darkest of nights and the thickest of clouds.

It was almost … romantic.

I sighed softly to myself, remembering every second of tonight and finally hoping that I'd find rest. But just as I closed my eyes, my phone buzzed on my bedside table, the sound jerking me awake. I glanced over at the screen lighting up the room and retrieved it.

Unknown: Is this Maxine?

I stared at it through wide eyes and turned onto my stomach, debating on whether to answer it or not. Nobody really messaged me at all these days, but maybe it was Xorgor. Maybe something had happened.

Me: Yes. Who's this?

There was a long pause.

I nervously played with the sheets wrapped around my body and stared down at the messages on my phone. My stomach twisted at the thought of what Xorgor had done that he needed to message me over the phone instead of—

Unknown: I need your help.

Me: Where are you? Is this Xorgor?

A longer period of time dragged by this time. I worried that I had made a fool of myself, assuming that it was him. If it was

Valerie, who wanted to kill some time by fucking around with me, I'd be screwed.

She'd tell the entire town that I had a crush on the incubus demon that nobody wanted.

Unknown: No.

Another pause. It was as if the person on the other line didn't have good service or couldn't talk for long. Or maybe it really was my bullies, waiting for me to slip up and admit something else to them.

Unknown: I don't know if you remember me. I barely remember myself.

Me: Who is this?

I didn't know if my messages were going through. Whoever the hell it was wasn't making much sense. Not answering questions. Wanting to be all philosophical when I just wanted a simple—

Unknown: This is Sina.

My eyes widened, and I shot up in bed.

No way. No fucking way.

Unknown: Please, help me.

13

the brother

xorgor

STORMING INTO THE INFERNO, I headed straight to the back to the private room that Erthrol frequented. Inside, a succubus, Bella, danced naked around a silver pole, her breasts swaying near my brother's face.

"X," Erthrol hummed when he saw me. "Come sit down and enjoy the—"

Before he could mutter another word, I seized his shoulder and yanked him from the seat, shoving him toward the exit. "I'm not sitting any-fucking-where with you," I growled, tightening my grip on him until my talons sank into his shoulder muscle.

"I'll be back, Bella!" Erthrol called over his shoulder.

I pushed him out of the room and into the hallway, then slammed the door behind us. But I didn't stop there. I continued to force him toward the back door and into the alleyway because I didn't want anyone seeing this.

They'd think I really was a monster.

Because I fucking was right now.

"The fuck is your problem?" Erthrol said, trying to escape my grasp.

But I handled him all the way out the building door. When the door swung closed behind us, I released his shoulder.

He straightened himself out, brushing off his shoulder and huffing. "What the hell has—"

I hurled my fist straight into his pretty face and sent him to the ground. Blood dribbled from his bottom lip, sliding down his chin and dripping onto the asphalt below him. I ground my teeth together and growled again.

"Why did you spread that rumor about Maxine?"

Erthrol scrambled back to his feet and wiped his chin clean with his hand. "What the fuck was that for?"

"Why did you spread that rumor about Maxine?" I repeated through my jagged teeth.

"I don't know what you're talking about."

Refusing to take any more of his shit, I snatched his collar and slammed him against the brick building. He hit it with a thud, the force knocking the fuck out of him. My claws sank into his skin, piercing right through the perfect incubus exterior.

"You can bully me all you want, but you don't say shit about Maxine."

"What the fuck did I say about her?" he asked, shaking his head. "Nothing."

"She told me that you said she was a lousy, disgusting fuck."

Erthrol's innocent expression shifted into one of mischief. "So, you talked to her."

Unable to stop myself, I held him against the wall and slammed my fist into him again. He had lied straight through his fucking teeth to me while trying to play the innocent incubus, who Mom and Dad always believed. Who *everyone* always sided with.

He lifted his bloody head back up and chuckled at me. "Yeah, I fucking said that, so nobody would dare touch her again. I was doing it for you, Xorgor. Settle down. It's not like I thought you'd actually get the balls to go see her again."

"She's mine," I growled, slamming my fist into his face again. "Mine."

"She might be yours, but I've been inside her too," Erthrol hummed. "I'll always know what she feels like, and you'll always wonder if she's thinking of me while you're pumping inside her. Because why would she choose you?"

I knew what he was doing.

I fucking knew that he was playing on my insecurities—the same insecurities that *he* had created. He was being a toxic asshole, like he had always been, and it was fucking working. Even if it was just a little, just a seed …

If what Erthrol had said bothered Maxine *that* much for her to admit it to me after we had sex, did that mean she had been thinking about his words and him while I was inside her? Was she wondering why it hadn't been him who showed up at the tavern?

After squeezing my eyes closed, I shook my head, as if it would get the thoughts out of my mind. "Stop it," I said through gritted teeth. My entire body tensed as the thoughts consumed me, took hold of me, *controlled* me.

"Oh, come on. What? Did she tell you what I said about her? Was she thinking about me while your dick was inside her?" When I didn't answer, he chuckled. "She was, wasn't she? Oh, Xorgor … why'd you think she actually wanted you?"

Rage burned inside me. I snapped my eyes open and clamped my fingers down around his throat. I hated Erthrol so much for all the pain he had caused me, for everything he had done to make me feel like I was nothing.

Erthrol grabbed my wrist and lengthened his nails into talons, clawing at me to stop. "If you kill me," he said through ragged breaths, "our family will kill you too. You'll never have a chance as the leader of demons and never get to see Maxine again."

Breath hitched, I tightened my grip even more.

"Jaroth will take her as his," he said. "He's a man-whore who loves to sleep with everyone from the Dead Candle Tavern. I've seen the way he looks at her. You don't want that, do you, *brother*?"

As much as I wanted to hurt him, to kill him … the small sliver of hope that I could still be the ruler of demons held me back. If, one

day, my parents looked past my appearance and saw me for me ...
if, one day, the world saw that I could rule this demon sector ...

I wanted it so badly.

I needed it.

I had been waiting all my damn life for that.

If I killed my brother right here and right now, they wouldn't let me rule. They wouldn't even let me live. They would kill me without a second thought, just like I had killed all those men who had dared to think about touching Maxine.

I didn't know why I had been holding out hope because there wasn't a chance that I'd get my parents and the kingdom to change their minds about me. I would always be the odd one out, the ugliest demon around, who everyone thought couldn't get any.

But they didn't know that I had gotten Maxine—a woman so many other demons had wanted before me. But I had killed them. I had murdered them, slaughtered them, ripped them apart for desiring her.

Why was I letting my brother live?

He had been inside her. He had been spreading rumors about her.

After shoving him against the side of the building one last time, I released him and stormed out of the demon hangout and through Durnbone's demon sector. Why couldn't I do it? I had done it over and over to other residents of this town. And I had wanted to end Erthrol's life for so long because of his constant bullying.

If I really had killed him now, then I wouldn't get to see Maxine ever again. Some other demon, some other creature would take her, bed her, wed her, put a baby inside her. And I refused to let that happen.

She was mine.

14
the information

maxine

AFTER RUSHING OUT of my house, I headed toward the demon sector in downtown Durnbone. Sina had asked me to meet someone there to get more information about her whereabouts because she couldn't leave right now.

Wherever she is.

I swallowed my nerves and scurried into the demon sector, ignoring the hungry stares from incubi and succubi. My stomach twisted and turned, nerves nipping at the insides of it. I really hoped that it had been Sina and I wasn't walking into some kind of trap.

Stupid me. I probably was.

But she had left four long years ago without so much as a good-bye, and I really needed her. She was my everything, my fucking rock, my best friend, who I told all my troubles to. She had made me feel like I was the sexiest damn person in Durnbone when I was feeling like shit about my scars. I needed her back.

Once I made it to our designated meeting spot on a small bridge that overlooked the river, I paced back and forth and checked my phone for the hundredth time. We were supposed to meet five minutes ago, and nobody was here.

Maybe this was all Valerie's doing.

After waiting ten minutes for someone to show, I leaned against the bridge and let out a long sigh. Now, I was just standing here, looking dumb. All the demons that walked by stared at me like they had never once before seen a human being.

When a demon approached me with large curved horns and a breathtaking smile, I stood up straight. This surely couldn't be the person that Sina wanted me to meet with to talk about … whatever it was she needed to tell me about her escape.

"Are you Maxine?" he asked.

I swallowed hard and pushed my shoulders back, desperate not to seem afraid of this demon who towered over me. Objectively, Xorgor was bigger and stronger and definitely more terrifying, but I was alone with this stranger in the middle of the damn night.

"Who are you?" I asked, crossing my arms and stepping away to keep my distance.

"Jaroth," he said, the royal blood ring glimmering on his finger. "Sina's … *friend.*"

"Friend?" I furrowed my brow at the tone he had said it in. "What do you mean by that?"

Jaroth ran his tongue across his perfect pearly-white teeth. "Her ex-boyfriend."

My eyes widened. "Sina has an ex-boyfriend?"

When she had been in Durnbone, she'd had four werewolf guys from high school that she always hung out with when she wasn't with me. They were together so much that I could've sworn that they were mates. Maybe … not? Maybe she had left them too.

But Sina wasn't a gold digger. She wouldn't leave those four guys that she was madly in love with for a demon of royal blood.

"Where is she?" I asked, cutting right to the chase. "Tell me."

Jaroth leaned against the bridge, his muscles bulging underneath the moonlight. "She's with her father, about a two-day journey from here. And she's safe, so don't worry about that. She wants to—"

"What happened? Why did she leave without telling me?"

"I don't know."

I pressed my lips together and stared at him, waiting for a different response to my questions. While he was the only person who knew of Sina's whereabouts, I didn't particularly trust him. Demons should almost never be trusted, especially by humans.

Instead of answering me, he ran a hand through his luscious brown hair. "We broke up a while ago. She didn't tell me much about her life beforehand, and I haven't heard much from her since. Only that she doesn't like it at her father's estate anymore."

"So, she asked you to help her escape?"

"No, she didn't," he said. "I'm not sure why she wants to leave. I think he's being a bit too controlling of her, though I'm not positive. But she wanted me to ask you if she could crash at your place once she leaves."

"Of course she can."

"Good. I'll let her know."

When he turned back around to walk away, I took my chances and snatched his wrist. Royal blood flowed through Jaroth's veins. Touching him—*grabbing him*—was enough for him to legally banish me from the demon sector and, hell, probably cut off my own hand. But I needed more than just that. I needed to find a way to contact Sina.

He stopped and glanced down at my hand wrapped around his wrist. "I don't think you want to touch me like that, *sweetheart*. You don't know what a human's touch does to an incubus like me."

Before he could say another word, I sucked in a deep breath and dropped my hand, hoping that I hadn't overstepped to the point where he'd ... do something to me that I didn't want. "How can I contact her?"

"I can't even contact her," Jaroth said, lying straight through his teeth.

I didn't know how I could tell, but I just knew that he wasn't telling me the complete truth. There was some truth to it, but how could I know what was real and what was fake? Was Sina really safe? Why hadn't she contacted me?

"She messaged me from an unknown number this morning, just like she said she'd message you. I texted the number before I came here, but it's out of service, so the message wasn't delivered." He paused and glanced down at my pocket. "If you don't believe me, you can try it for yourself."

After yanking my phone out of my pocket, I texted the Unknown number that had messaged me earlier. I waited and waited and waited until, finally, a message popped up on the screen.

Unknown: Delivery Failed. Try Again.

Once I slipped my phone into my pocket and sighed, he turned around to leave, but I captured his wrist. "Wait."

A low growl exited his throat, rumbling through the night. "What?"

I pressed my lips together. "If you see Sina, tell her that I miss her."

Moments passed by before Jaroth finally nodded and walked down the small bridge and in the opposite direction that he had come from. I watched him depart and disappear into the night, then crossed my arms, confused about all of this.

I hoped that Sina was okay. This wasn't making a lot of sense.

When I turned around, a dark shadow disappeared into a back alley. I swallowed hard and found myself walking toward it, my heart pounding against my chest. Familiar chills ran through me as I glanced around the corner and found … nobody there.

But I could've sworn …

Suddenly, an invisible force seized my wrist, pulled me into the alleyway, and pressed me against the side of the building. As hard as I tried, I couldn't move. I couldn't break free. I couldn't even scream.

"Maxine." A deep voice drifted through my ear. "You're mine."

15
the alley

xorgor

AFTER EXTENDING black appendages from my back, I slithered them around both of Maxine's wrists, lifted her into the air until her hips were level with my face, and pinned her to the brick wall. She widened her eyes and squealed, squirming in my hold.

"Xorgor!" she shouted as my body faded into existence. "What are you—"

I stuffed an appendage into her mouth to keep her quiet.

"Mine," I growled.

I pulled off her pants, spread her legs with my hands, and rested her thighs on my shoulders, nestling myself between her legs. She stared at me through wide eyes, her mouth full. I extended my forked tongue, running it between her pussy lips.

"Mine."

"Xorgor," she whimpered on me, some drool running down her chin.

Possessiveness pumped through every one of my veins, the need to prove myself, to show her that no other man or demon could give her what I could, running through my body. I wrapped my arms around her thicker thighs and gripped the meat on them.

"Mine."

Again, my tongue ran between her glistening pussy lips. I spread her thighs further apart to give myself better access and ate her sweet, messy cunt. I moved my tongue up and down, side to side, diagonal across her clit.

Desperate to eat.

Desperate to push her to orgasm and then even further.

Within a few moments, her legs began shaking around me. She furrowed her brow in pleasure, entire body tense, and tugged on the appendages to release herself from my grasp.

"Mine," I growled, hungrily moving my tongue all over her pussy. "Mine." I raked my claws over the soft flesh on her inner thighs, making her even more tense. "Mine."

Mouth full as drool and spit ran down her chin, she screamed out on me and stared down at me. Her legs trembled uncontrollably, her entire body spazzing. I watched her ride out her orgasm, but didn't stop eating her tight cunt.

Instead, I slithered my tongue into her hole and grunted as she pulsed around it over and over, squeezing it tighter the deeper that it went. When I found her G-spot with my tongue, she squirmed even harder, shaking her head for me to stop.

"Please," she begged out on me, wads of spit dripping from her mouth. "Please."

She looked like a desperate, dirty slut for me.

I pulled the appendage out of her mouth and slipped it underneath her shirt, tugging down one of her bra cups and wrapping my body around her breasts until her nipples hardened through her shirt and she was tensing on me again.

"Please, Xorgor," she breathed, cheeks flushed. "If you don't stop, I'm going t-to c-come again."

Reaching up, I wrapped one hand around her throat and pinned it to the brick wall. "You're mine," I growled, not obeying her wishes. She would come for me again, and again, and again. "Say it."

"I ... I'm ..." Her legs shook even harder around me, her pussy clamping down on my tongue.

I gently drew my tongue around her G-spot, careful not to hit it until she told me what I needed to hear.

She tilted her head back. "Yours. I'm your—"

I flicked my tongue against her G-spot.

She squeezed her eyes shut and screamed out, her body seizing in my hold. I massaged my tongue across her sensitive bud constantly until she finally rode out her orgasm and reopened her eyes.

With the cups of her bra pulled down, I could see her taut nipples pressed against the front of her shirt, just waiting to be sucked on. My dick twitched inside my pants. I undid my zipper and pulled myself out of them, desperate to be inside her again.

After dipping my head between her breasts and taking one of her nipples between my jagged teeth, I gently bit down on it and lined the head of my cock with her entrance. Before she could react, I dropped my appendages from her wrists and let her slam all the way down onto my cock.

She grasped on to my shoulders tightly, moaning out in pleasure, and gripped my dick with her tight hole. I wrapped my large hands around her waist and bounced her up and down on me, using her like a cute little fucking doll.

My doll.

"More, Xorgor," she cried into my ear. "Please, more!"

I leaned her against the wall and stared down at her torso, watching my dick reach almost to her ribs inside her stomach.

She stared down at it, too, and tightened even more. "Oh my gods, you're so big—so *fucking* big."

"I'm going to come inside you," I growled. "And you're going to take it. Do you understand me, Maxine? You'll take all my cum, and then—"

She breathed heavily, pussy tightening the way it did whenever she was about to explode. "And then when you pull out of me, I'll push your cum deeper inside. I promise I won't let any drip out of me. I'll take it all."

An orgasm ripped through my body at her words.

I slammed my cock as deep as it would go, threw my head back, and grunted in pleasure. She didn't know what she had fucking done to me. She didn't know that those few words that she had said meant I would never fucking let another man even *look* at her.

She was mine.

All fucking mine.

Maxine tilted her head back and moaned out, milking every last drop of cum out of my dick with her tight hole. She gripped on to me tighter, slowly coming back down from her orgasm, and watched me pull my sopping cock from her body.

When my dick smacked against my thigh, she reached between her legs and plugged herself up, stuffing my cum deeper and deeper into her cunt, like she had wanted to be bred for years now.

After a few moments, she pulled her fingers from her pussy and stuck them into her mouth, sucking off the rest of my cum. I growled and grabbed her hand, tugging her fingers from her mouth and kissing her on the lips.

"Mine," I mumbled against her. "*Mine.*"

16
the truth

maxine

AFTER PULLING my clothes back onto my body, I leaned against the alley brick wall and tried to take steady breaths. Xorgor stood feet from me, more withdrawn than I had seen him—not that I had seen him much, only a couple of times.

"I'm taking you home," he said. "You shouldn't be in the demon sector."

"I had to come," I said and left it at that.

If I told him that I had come here to meet the only person who knew where my best friend had gone, he either wouldn't believe me or would think it was the stupidest idea ever.

Hell, I thought it was a bit outlandish too.

But Sina was the only person I had left. I had been alone, trying to juggle living in Durnbone for the past four years by myself. Xorgor might've gotten made fun of by succubi in the Dead Candle Tavern, but he still had family and probably friends too.

He didn't know what it was like to be completely and utterly alone.

"You should've waited for me before coming here," he said, motioning for me to follow him.

"I … I didn't think you'd want to come." I tucked some hair behind my ear and crossed my arms, hating the feeling of being vulnerable. But that was all that I was when with Xorgor, it seemed. "You ran off to your brother."

"For you," Xorgor said between gritted, jagged teeth. "If you come to the demon sector alone, a demon will lure you back to his place and take advantage of you, like Jaroth would've done if you'd kept touching him."

"Yeah"—I laughed in disbelief—"right."

Did Xorgor actually know how people talked about me—about how *his own brother*—talked about me? He must've been on drugs or something because he was out of his damn mind.

"Don't fucking laugh about it, Maxine," he growled. "It's not a joke."

"Do you hear yourself?"

Suddenly, he stopped in the middle of the street and snatched my throat in his large hand, tugging me toward him and forcing me to look up at him. "Fucking stop it. You don't know"—another low growl escaped his throat—"how many demons I've fucking killed to have you to myself."

My eyes widened. "Wh-what?"

After staring into my eyes with his fiery ones, he dropped his hand from my throat, turned around, and grunted, "Fuck." The single word came out low and feral, sending warmth straight to my core.

"You did what?" I asked again, wondering if I had misheard him.

I mean, I had to have misheard him.

"I'm bringing you home, Maxine." Xorgor continued down the road. "Come."

Warmth rushed to my stupid core again, and I cursed to myself. What the hell was wrong with me? First, he had admitted to *killing* demons for me—which had to be a lie—but my heart had sped up. Now, he was telling me to *come*, as in to follow him, and I was all flustered.

Once I pushed the thought from my mind, I fast-walked to catch up to him. Standing at least a foot or more taller than me, he had legs much longer than my shorter ones and could make more distance in one stride than I could in three.

When I finally caught up to him, I grabbed his wrist. "Please, walk slower," I whimpered, a bead of sweat rolling down the center of my back. "My short legs don't move that fast, and I'm sweating."

"We've barely walked a block."

"Yeah, well …" My cheeks burned with embarrassment at how blatantly out of shape I was. "If you couldn't tell, the most exercise that I've done in the past few years was earlier tonight and in that back alleyway."

Xorgor peeked a glance over at me, looking me up and down. When he turned back to the street, he curled his tight lips into a slight smirk. "We'll have to change that then, won't we?" he hummed, his deep voice making me warm again.

"Xorgor," I whimpered, averting my gaze. Pressure rose in my core, my pussy clenching at the thought. "You can't say things like that to me."

"Hmm? Is that right?"

"You c-can't."

"Why not?"

"Because," I whispered, heat rising inside me. "Because you can't."

"Is your desperate pussy clenching because of me again tonight?" he purred, looking over at me with those dangerous eyes.

Another wave of heat rushed to my core.

"Does she need me to tease her aching little clit?"

Before he could say another word or make a move, I gripped his forearm, hugged it to the front of my body, and stared up at him. "Please, Xorgor … this is serious," I said, but by now … I didn't remember what had been so serious.

His fingers were dangerously close to my—

With his arm still in my grasp, he tilted his hand and gently moved his fingers against my pussy through my pants. I grabbed him harder, hoping he wouldn't continue, and whimpered. He chuckled lowly and teased my clit, rubbing it back and forth.

"What was it that we were talking about again?" he hummed, playing with my clit as we walked out of the demon sector of Durnbone.

"I, um …" I swallowed hard, the pressure rising inside me. "I was …"

I needed him to stop. I had questions. Many of them. And he was trying to get out of answering them.

"Why …" I sucked in a shaky breath. "Why did you come to find me?"

While Xorgor tensed, he didn't stop fondling my pussy. "Why did I come find you?" He moved his fingers faster, his voice more tense this time. "I was on my way back to your place and found you on a bridge with that idiot. Who is he to you?"

"N-nobody," I whispered, curling my fingers into his swollen bicep.

"Nobody," he repeated, as if he didn't believe it.

"He's … my friend's ex-boyfriend."

"*Ex*-boyfriend for a reason."

I furrowed my brow and nodded. "Yes, an ex for a reason, but he's the only one who knows where she is and how to help her get out of whatever mess she's been in for the past four years."

"Maxine," Xorgor growled, his sharp, jagged teeth glistening with saliva, his fingers still moving against me, almost subconsciously.

"Xorgor," I said his name back to him. "He's the only person who knows."

"And why is that?" he asked softly.

Not accusing. Not angry. Not furious anymore.

"Hmm?" he continued, slipping his hand into the front of my pants like he owned every inch of me and lowering his voice. "Why is it that Jaroth is the only person in all of Durnbone who knows where your friend is? You said she has been gone for four years. Why didn't she tell you where she was going?"

Averting my gaze, I stared down at the cobblestone and shrugged. "I … I don't know."

Xorgor pulled his wet fingers from my cunt and stuck them into his mouth, his long and forked tongue running across them to suck off every bit of me. "You can't believe everything someone tells you, especially a demon."

Deep in my heart, I knew that something wasn't right. She would've told me where she was going on her eighteenth birthday. She would've at least called or texted before now. All this time … I had thought that she was alive and thriving somewhere without me.

Maybe that was true. Or maybe that text message had been a fake and Sina was dead.

"I don't know, but that doesn't mean that I'm going to stop looking for her," I whispered, tears welling up in my eyes. "Even if this is all a joke. Even if Jaroth has done something terrible to her. I need to find out the truth."

No way would I sit back and cry about Sina leaving me again. No way would I pretend that everything was fine without her. No way would I feel bad about myself because I had nobody left in Durnbone.

I needed to find Sina even if it was the death of me.

17

the arrangement

xorgor

"CAN I ASK YOU SOMETHING?" Maxine said, staring at the ground between us and bouncing nervously on her toes when we reached her front door. She peeked up at me, then looked away again and chewed on the inside of her cheek. "About, um … what you said earlier?"

"What'd I say?" I asked.

We had talked about so much tonight that I couldn't be sure what she wanted to talk about now—how that fucker would've touched her if she hadn't left the demon sector or how she shouldn't be off, trusting random men who resided in Durnbone.

"You said that you have"—before she continued, she glanced around, leaned forward, and lowered her voice—"killed people for … me? What do you mean by that? Surely, you're just"—her cheeks paled as her voice became almost inaudible—"just kidding, right?"

I pressed my lips together and grimaced, averting my gaze because I couldn't lie to her face. I hadn't meant to let that slip out of my mouth earlier. It was dangerous for her to know what I had done for her, the people I'd killed and threatened to keep her safe.

"I have to get back," I said, turning around to head back to The

Inferno so I could kick in Jaroth's face and warn him to stay away from her. "People are waiting for me. Make sure that you don't—"

She seized my wrist. "Wait."

Twisting around, I stared down into her wide eyes. "What?"

"Tell me the truth."

After gently wiggling my wrist out of her weak hold, I ran my forked tongue across my jagged teeth. She stood so innocently, not knowing the true horrors of this world, not understanding what demons really did, who we truly were.

"You wouldn't like the truth, Maxine," I whispered.

Somehow, her eyes became even bigger. She pulled her hand back by her side and stepped away from me, hitting her front door. She shook her head and turned away, fumbling with her keys inside her purse. "No, I don't believe it."

Once she opened the door, I caught her wrist this time and twirled her around so she faced me. I didn't want to leave her like this. I didn't want her to fear me. Left alone with thoughts like these were damaging.

"Does it change the way you see me?"

"What?" Maxine asked, voice barely above a whisper. "You killing people?"

"Me *taking care* of them *for you*?"

"You don't have to take care of anyone for me. It's not like—"

"Don't fucking finish your sentence," I growled, knowing that she was about to self-deprecate because that was exactly what I did when I didn't believe something or couldn't fucking handle life.

"Still"—she glanced down at my hand around her wrist—"you don't need to protect me."

"You didn't answer my question. Does it change the way you see me?"

Maxine focused on our hands, then gently pulled hers away. When she lifted her gaze to me, my chest tightened. I didn't know what I was expecting, but I didn't want her to see me any differently. She was the only woman to see and enjoy me for the person I was.

"No," she whispered. "But I'm not worth more than anyone else's life."

"The fuck you aren't."

She crossed her arms and stared pointedly at me. "*Xorgor.*"

"*Maxine.*"

"I mean it. Tell me that you won't kill people for me."

Suddenly, my royal ring vibrated against my left index finger, which meant that *Father* or *Mother* needed me for once in their fucking lifetimes. I wanted to ignore them, but I didn't know how much longer Maxine actually wanted me to stay. If I lingered any longer and she coerced me to admit what I had done for her, she might kick me out.

I'd rather prolong that conversation for as long as I could.

"I need to go," I said to her. "Don't go to the demon sector alone again."

"Xorgor, tell me—"

"I can't, Buttercup."

Maxine blushed, her cheeks and nose turning bright red. She grabbed the handle of her front door, opening and closing her mouth, but not saying a single word. Then, a small smile broke out on her face.

Warmth exploded through my chest, and I headed back through the woods. When I reached a distance away from her place, I stopped and tapped the emblem of my ring three times, being transported to my parents' grand estate.

I stood outside large maroon double doors guarded by men, stared up at the prison that I had grown up in, and growled through my jagged teeth. The men opened the doors and allowed me to enter.

Royal-purple drapes hung around the rounded ceilings. The shiny white floor glistened a bit too brightly. Golden statues decorated the hallways. On the outside, this was what every demon dreamed of having.

Not fucking me.

"What is it, Father?" I called through the desolate hallways, my voice traveling.

"Come," Mother called.

I followed her voice and found myself in the dining area, where my parents sat with a young vampire woman who couldn't be any older than Maxine. She wore her silver hair down her back with golden coils holding strands of it together and smiled at me through her fangs.

"Xorgor." She beamed.

Fake. Her excitement both looked and felt so fucking fake.

"What is it?" I asked my parents, turning toward them. "I have places to be tonight."

"Sit," Father said.

"No."

He blew out a sharp breath. "Don't make this harder than it is."

Instead of listening to his orders, I leaned against the doorframe and crossed my arms. "You haven't called me to dine with you here in nearly half a decade. I didn't even want to come, so tell me what you want, and I will be on my way."

After letting out another sigh, Father stood. "Not only have I heard that you threatened your brother today, but people have also been mentioning that men are going missing and getting murdered in Durnbone by a mysterious, *invisible* force."

I gritted my teeth. *Fuck.*

"Can't say I recall hearing about that," I hummed.

"Is that so? Shall I ask Maxine?"

My face dropped. "No," I growled.

Fucking Erthrol had to open his big mouth.

"She's the girl you killed those men for? The reason you threatened your brother?"

"Father, I can—"

"You can explain?" Father said, nostrils flaring. "You will *explain* nothing. We cannot risk our family looking bad or your brother to appear weak before the demon queen steps down. He's our only shot in securing the throne."

"So, what do you want me to do?" I asked, pissed the fuck off. "Not fuck with him anymore?"

He chuckled and motioned for the vampire with silver hair to come forth. She stood up, straightened out her shoulders, and walked over to him, allowing him to place his hand on the small of her back.

"No, Xorgor, you're going to back away from the human girl and marry Valerie."

18
the vampires

maxine

I POURED two cups of blood into wineglasses and set them in front of two male vampires at the Dead Candle Tavern the next day. One sipped his drink and leaned back in his seat, shoulders relaxing.

"Ahh, Maxine," he purred. "Is this your blood?"

My lips curled into a small smile, but I shook my head. "Not today, Edward."

The other nudged his arm. "Not that she'd ever let you try."

As the two began playfully bickering back and forth, my phone buzzed in my pocket. I pulled it out to check it really quickly before my manager saw, and I spotted a message from an unknown number.

Unknown: Thank you.

While the number might've been foreign, I knew it was Sina. Xorgor might've thought I was crazy to think so, but I needed to have hope and believe in something. Sina was out there, waiting to escape to Durnbone and live her life. And I'd be there to aid her.

"Maybe another time. Eh, Maxine?" Edward joked, licking the blood off the corner of his lips and placing down his empty glass.

He and his friend stood, and he stuck his hand into his back pocket to retrieve his wallet.

After the vampires tossed me a couple of coins for a tip, I stuffed the money into my pocket and found my way to a group of chatty succubi. When I reached them, they all suddenly stopped talking and collectively scowled at me. I gulped, then plastered the best fake smile onto my face, unsure of what I had done to them, but needing to be pleasant. I didn't want to be fired.

"Can I get you girls something?" I asked, pulling out four glasses.

They all glared at me, and then one tore her nasty gaze away. "Are you Maxine?"

"Um, yes …"

God, what had I done to piss off not one, but *four* succubi?

Another scrunched her nose, checked me out, then let out a strained laugh. "*Gods.*"

"Is there something that you need?" I asked, setting my hands on the bar top so they wouldn't tremble in front of them. I didn't like confrontation, especially from girls like this. I'd much rather keep to myself and collect my tips for the night in peace. "A drink maybe?"

After another moment of silence from the women, a third cleared her throat. "Are you the girl who's been messing around with Erthrol and Xorgor?" She didn't even give me time to respond. "You know they're of royal blood and they would never settle for a human like you."

My mouth dried. "I—"

"All you humans thinking that you can steal our men," the fourth growled. "I'm sick of it."

"I'm not trying to steal anyone," I said, heart pounding. "This is a misunderstanding."

"A misunderstanding?" She laughed. "How cute. Because others spotted you in the demon sector last night, talking to Jaroth and then Xorgor. And, you know, I'd bet that *rumor* with Erthrol was about you too, wasn't it?"

"Keep your filthy hands off them. You're a human, and they're royals."

"It's not what you think at all," I began, hoping to de-escalate the situation. People started to look over at us, and I loathed this kind of attention. "I wasn't trying to do anything with Jaroth or Erthrol. I was just—"

"What about Xorgor?" another asked.

"What about him?"

"You're trying to get with him."

I pressed my lips together and stared between all four succubi, gripping a towel in my hand. Why did they all suddenly care about Xorgor? They had been making fun of him for months, if not *years*. Now that someone had shown interest in him, they suddenly claimed him as demons-only?

That was bullshit.

"It doesn't matter now, girls," another chimed, looping her arms around two of the succubi's arms. "Let's not rub it in. I doubt the poor girl knows about Xorgor and Valerie yet. Don't want her to get all flustered at work."

"Valerie …" I asked, brow furrowed. *My bully from school?* "How is Valerie part of this?"

The fourth girl giggled and leaned across the bar, eyes wide in an attempt to look sorry for me. She pinched my cheek like I was some sort of toddler, squeezing it hard. "That's so cute. She has no idea."

My heart pounded inside my chest. "What is it?"

By the way they kept leading up to it and laughing in my face, I wasn't sure that I wanted to know. But I couldn't take it anymore. Just when I'd thought things were looking up in my life, these girls hit me with *this*.

"Please, tell me."

"She's pleading now, girls." She laughed.

I furrowed my brow and stared at them, my chest tight. While I wanted to scream, cry, shout at them to tell me already, I didn't want to play their stupid little games. So, I pressed my lips together and stared at them, not saying another word.

If they didn't want to tell me, then I'd ask Xorgor.

When their laughter died down and they realized that I refused to respond, the first succubus leaned against the counter. "You want to know about Valerie and Xorgor? Hmm? Their marriage has been arranged."

The rag dropped from my hand. I peered at them through wide eyes, my heart stopping for a moment. No, I must've misheard them. I *had to have* misheard them. It wasn't true. It couldn't be true.

"You're lying."

Giggles erupted between them as they walked toward the exit without even ordering a drink.

"I'm sure you'll be invited to the wedding, or maybe the bachelor party so the royal-blooded demons can pass you around like the trash you are."

They departed from the Dead Candle Tavern, and I just stood there, unmoving. My chest tightened, and I quickly hurried toward the back room and puked into the trash bin.

Xorgor was … Xorgor was to be married. To my bully.

19
the lie

"YOU CAN'T FUCKING DO THIS." I stormed after Father around his grand estate with my talons drawn and my heart pounding with wrath. For the past twelve hours, I had been arguing with him and Mother about this arranged marriage that they had sentenced me to. "It's not fucking fair."

"I don't give a shit if it's fair or not to you," Father said, walking into his office and slamming his hand down onto the desk. "You have done nothing but hurt this family with how you look. You will do this for us and then never set foot in this house again."

"Fuck that," I growled. "I'm not marrying her. She's a damn vampire."

"A vampire with royal blood," Father said. "You will have a good life, riches, and food while living among her species. It's not like I'm marrying you off to a measly human with nothing to her name."

I balled my hands into tight fists, talons slitting through the skin on my palms. This was fucking ridiculous. He couldn't expect me to really go along with this shitty plan, just so I got out of Erthrol's hair and he received a better shot at the throne.

"How?" I asked, placing my bloody hand on the desk and digging my claws into it. "How does this benefit you in any way? How does this let Erthrol take the throne and let our family control the demons? Tell me."

"Because you won't make your brother look weak!" Father shouted. "You hurt him yesterday. And if you hadn't taken him out back into the alleyway, more people might've seen your uncontrollable wrath. We can't have someone with little control like you around."

"I don't have little control."

"As soon as you hear someone mention that girl's name, you kill them."

"Because Maxine is mine," I growled. "Mine."

Father pressed his lips together. "Not anymore. Valerie is yours."

"Gods, you're fucking relentless," I snapped, turning my back toward him and storming back to the open office door. He could demand I marry this woman as much as he wanted, but I wouldn't lay a finger on her, never mind vow to spend my life with her.

When I reached the door, Father cleared his throat. "If you don't go along with this, I will denounce you as my son. You will have your royalty stripped from you as well as everything that comes with it."

"I don't give a fuck about that shit," I said through gritted teeth.

"But you care about Maxine," Father said. "If you're not royal, I will not protect you, will not pull strings to brush all these deaths away. You will be sentenced to die and will never get to protect her again."

Rage rushed through me as my heart pounded inside my chest.

I hated this family. I fucking hated every last one of them.

"If you marry Valerie, you can still mess around with other women," he said. "As all incubi and succubi do. It's in your nature and in your blood. I'm doing what I can to keep you alive and living your best life."

Bullshit.

That was fucking bullshit.

"Since you completely ruined dinner last night, I'll arrange another meeting with Valerie tonight," Father said, stepping from behind his desk and gripping my shoulder. "Don't keep her waiting, Xorgor."

Once I ripped myself away from him, I stormed through the palace to the front doors. Guards parted them for me, allowing me to hurry out of that hellhole and down the front steps toward the forest.

What the hell was I going to say to Maxine? How would I tell her? What would she think of me for it? I wanted nobody else in this world, except her, so how would I even go on living with that disgusting vampire?

I rushed through the dark forest toward Durnbone. I needed to tell Maxine before she found out through other means, like the gossip that succubi loved spreading. If she thought that this was what I wanted …

Fuck, I didn't know what I would do. I already didn't know what I wanted to say to her. How could I just come out with it? If I told my father no again, then he might really denounce me, which meant no protection for Maxine.

Which meant anyone could try to get in her pants.

Which meant anyone could try to hurt her.

She was already so fragile, especially with her insecurities.

I refused to let someone touch or hurt her again, and I didn't want to marry Valerie, but I couldn't do both without sacrificing something. I needed to choose—a miserable life without Maxine or certain death.

20

the four wolves

maxine

I STARED into the rusty bathroom mirror at the Dead Candle
Tavern through watery eyes and pushed some tears off my mascara-
stained cheeks. Since those four girls had left, I hadn't come out of
the back because I couldn't work like this.

Xorgor was the first guy that I liked who had given me any
attention. I had let him touch me when I knew nothing about him.
How long had he known about this marriage? It wasn't any
marriage either, but one to my bully. My damn bully!

Had they been planning this together? Get Xorgor to fake his
feelings toward me—like any incubus could—and make me fall for
him, then rub this in my face? My chest tightened. Why was … why
was this happening?

Balling my hands into fists, I suppressed the urge to hurl it into
the mirror and shatter it to pieces. It was bad enough I had basically
taken off the rest of my shift for tonight; if I broke something here,
they'd really fire me.

Not caring that I should still be here for fifteen more minutes,
I forced myself to walk out of the restroom and slipped out of the
tavern's back door. When I spotted the group of succubi giggling

outside at the bar across the street, my stomach twisted into knots.

Four wolves walked by the girls, who started giggling even more uncontrollably and flirting with them. Without even looking in their directions, the guys kept walking down the sidewalk and toward the forest just outside town.

After staring at them for a few moments, I widened my eyes and straightened out my shoulders. Those weren't any four wolves, but the guys who had been Sina's other best friends in school—Calder, Thayer, Gaian, and Darius.

Once I made it past the giggling succubi without being spotted by them, I hurried down the sidewalk to catch up with them. They turned a corner and disappeared down a path in the forest, most likely heading back to their pack for the night.

Xorgor had told me that I shouldn't go anywhere in Durnbone without him, but he had also told me never to trust a demon, especially one who wanted to get into my pants. Which, *ahem*, was him.

So, I picked up my pace and stepped into the eerie forest. Mist hung low among the trees, making it difficult to see more than a quarter mile ahead of me. Fallen branches lay scattered all over the ground. Howling from afar erupted through the quiet night.

My stomach twisted again, but I continued forward.

If Xorgor was about to be married to my worst enemy, then the least I could do was find my best friend. I didn't need him, nor did I want a liar and a cheat. I ground my teeth together.

How can I be so stupid? What is wrong with me?

All I wanted was for someone to love me, someone to think that I was the prettiest damn girl in the world. Was everything that Xorgor had said a lie? Did he think I was beautiful or sexy or even the slightest bit prett—

Someone snatched the front of my throat and pinned me hard against a tree, its bark rough against my skin. I yelped out in surprise and stared up into the wild eyes of four seething wolves. Haunting memories of the night I had gotten those scars on my chest shot through my mind.

I squeezed my eyes shut, pushed the memories away, then looked back up at Sina's friends that she had left too. I wondered if they knew where she had gone or why she had left Durnbone to begin with.

"Why are you following us?" Thayer growled, saliva dripping off his canines and eyes dark enough for him to be half-demon. He squeezed his claws into the sides of my neck until tiny stars danced in my vision.

"Thayer," Darius said, "back off of her. She's just a girl."

"A girl who has been marked by a demon. Can't you smell it on her? Royal blood."

I stared up at Thayer, my eyes widening even more. "M-m-marked?"

"She's been following us since Durnbone," Thayer gritted out, slamming me against the tree again and forcing the bark even deeper into my skin. More haunting thoughts rushed through my head, but I forced them away. "What the fuck do you want?"

"Come on." Gaian grabbed Thayer's bicep and pulled him back. "You're scaring her."

"Good," Thayer snapped. "She shou—"

Calder—the alpha—seized Thayer by the back of his neck and hurled him through the air. He hit a tree so hard that the tree snapped in half and collapsed, the sound echoing through the woods. "Don't touch her. She's one of Sina's friends."

"Sina," Thayer whispered, sitting up as if he hadn't been wounded at all. He scrambled to his feet and stepped toward me again, but this time without an ounce of rage rushing through his dark demon eyes. "You know Sina?"

I smoothed out my shirt and swallowed hard. "Yes ... well, sorta."

"What do you mean, sorta? Do you know where she is?" Darius asked.

After pressing my lips together, I glanced down at my feet. "No, I don't know where she is. I was hoping that you'd have some idea.

I haven't seen her in four years now. She completely disappeared the morning of her eighteenth birthday."

Silence fell upon the forest.

My gaze traveled to each of the wolves, and then I frowned. "You guys don't know where she is either, do you?" I asked.

Calder averted his gaze and clenched his sharp jaw. "We haven't seen her since the night before her eighteenth birthday. When we went over there the next morning, all her stuff in her house was gone, like she was never even there."

The other guys stayed quiet, even Thayer, who looked pissed off again.

"Was she your … mate?" I whispered, unsure if I was stepping out of bounds. Was it okay to ask something like that? I didn't want to piss them off again and have one of them rip their claws across my face.

Instead of answering me, they continued their silence, which I took as a yes.

"I received a text message from an unknown number the other day," I admitted. "I don't know what happened, and they didn't go into detail about it, but the message was supposedly from Sina. She said that she plans to return to Durnbone at some point."

Thayer snapped his head in my direction. "Really?"

"Maybe. The messages were very vague."

Gaian stepped forward and took my hand. "Can you please keep us updated?"

"Yeah, I can do that," I whispered, nodding. "But I should be getting home."

Once I departed from the forest, I found my way back through the forest and to my home on the other side of Durnbone. When I walked up the path to my front door, I spotted a figure sitting on the porch.

The moonlight glimmered against his chiseled jaw and sharp features.

"Maxine, you're finally home," Erthrol cooed. "We need to talk. Alone."

21
the bedsheets

xorgor

"MAXINE!" I shouted, banging on her front door. "Open up!"

Silence.

After I ran a hand through my unkempt hair, I paced on her porch, my stomach in tight knots. Where the hell was she? Sleeping maybe? She had worked a few hours ago and should've been back to her house by now.

I pounded on her door again. "Maxine!"

One moment passed. Then two. Then, I decided that I couldn't wait.

The deafening silence rang through my ears. I hadn't been able to stop thinking about Maxine since that asshole had told me that my marriage would be arranged. She had been my obsession for weeks, and now, she wasn't even opening the door.

So, I ripped the door open so forcefully that the lock popped off, and the end-of-summer breeze blew into her empty home. I dropped my hand from the knob and hurried through her house, shouting her name and searching every last corner of the place.

"Maxine!" I called. "Come out … please."

What if someone had snatched her after work tonight? Usually, I walked her home—or at least, I followed her home so nobody bothered her. But I had been so worked up over Father deciding to marry me off to that vampire royal that I …

Fuck.

"Fuck!" I growled, talons aching for blood.

I ran my hand through my hair again and searched the house a second time. It was no use. She wasn't here. But it was the only thing that I could think to do. I should've fucking been there tonight. I should've been protecting her.

When I had come up empty-handed yet again, I slammed my fist right through the thick wall. Drywall coated my knuckles, but I suppressed the physical pain with the haunting thoughts of where she could've gone, of who could've taken her.

"Jaroth," I said to myself through gritted teeth.

He had been talking to her in the demon sector, *flirting* with her even. If Maxine had wandered back down there—after I told her not —to talk to him about her missing friend, then that fucker would've taken her.

After deciding that aimlessly pacing in her living room wouldn't help me find her, I walked upstairs to her bedroom to find any clues to where she could've gone off too. Maybe she had left her phone or a note or fucking something.

When I reached her room, where I had been inside twice already to search for her, I glanced through the cheap jewelry on the decades-old dresser and rummaged through the papers on her desk about her friend's disappearance.

Nothing.

Yet something felt … off.

I turned toward her bed and drew my talons across the messy blankets scattered on top of the mattress. Usually, Maxine always made her bed before she left for work, but not today. Unless … she had come back here after her shift.

After tightening my hand around the blankets, I pulled them to my nose and inhaled deeply. Maxine's scent drifted through my nose along with the stench of another demon, of another—

My entire body froze for a moment, realization shooting through me, and then I hurled the blanket across the room with so much force that a frame hanging on the wall dropped and shattered everywhere.

"Erthrol!" I snarled through my jagged teeth. "What have you fucking done?!"

Where had she gone? What had he done with her? Why had she left with him or let him into her bed with her? The blankets were drenched in both of their scents. What the fuck had happened in the past twenty-four fucking hours?

I tightened my hand around the blanket harder and inhaled deeper, my chest tightening more and more with each moment that passed. She had been with him. In her bed. Where she had been with me alone the other night.

Had she been … seeing him too behind my back? Had she just wanted to get with me to inch closer to him so she could … so she could be with him? Did she want to be with my brother and not me?

I collapsed onto the bed, rested my forearms onto my knees, and dropped my head, torturing myself with their scents again. And again. And again. Convincing myself that none of this was real, that Maxine never wanted me for me, that she just wanted my brother all along.

Of fucking course she did.

Every girl did.

But those small little moments hadn't felt like that. Those small little moments we had spent together felt so fucking real. I clenched my fist and shook my head.

What had I done to make me unlovable? What could I ever do to make her want me?

22
the drink

maxine

A VACANT STRIPPER pole glimmered underneath the dim light in the private room. Demon club music thumped heavily through the walls. I sat on a maroon couch across from Erthrol, who had coerced me into coming here with him tonight.

I sipped on some water, nervously bounced my leg, and peeked over at him. While I was still furious with Xorgor, I hadn't wanted to come down here with his brother tonight. But when I'd found him on my front stoop, I'd felt … forced.

"You sure you don't want something else other than"—Erthrol peered down at my wineglass full of water and raised his brow—"that?"

"Yes," I said quickly, focusing on the glass table in front of me. "I'm fine."

"Why don't you try a—"

"No, I'm good." I sipped the rest of my drink and placed it down. "Can you take me home now? I have work tomorrow afternoon, and I really should be getting rest. I go to bed early so I can leave for work earlier, too, and I was just—"

Erthrol chuckled, his sharp jaw easing, and sipped his drink. "No wonder why he likes you so much."

My cheeks flushed. "What?" I whispered, completely caught off guard.

Erthrol placed his drink on the table next to mine and called for a waitress to fill both our glasses. She waltzed into the room, dressed in next to nothing, with her breasts hanging heavy on her chest and her big eyes focused on Erthrol. After she filled our cups and left the pitcher of whatever Erthrol was drinking on the table, she cut a glare over to me and walked out of the room.

I stared down at my less than perfect thick thighs, decorated with purple-gray stretch marks, and frowned. No wonder why Xorgor would be off to marry someone else and not tell me about it. Why wouldn't he want someone like a succubus or a vampiress when they looked like *that*? Dressed in skimpy little clothes with the perfect bodies and the biggest fuck-me eyes ever.

Compared to me?

Ha!

It was freaking obvious who anyone would choose. I would even choose them over me.

"You've heard about Xorgor?" Erthrol asked, leaning back on the maroon velvet couch and sipping his drink again. His hooded eyes were focused intently on me, and that light expression had left his face.

Pursing my lips together, I nodded curtly.

I didn't want to show him how much the thought of Xorgor with another woman affected me. It shouldn't have. I had barely even known him for a couple of weeks. Why did I care who he married? To hell with him and Valerie. I hated her too.

"Did he tell you?" Erthrol asked.

"No," I said quickly, sipping my water. "I heard it from some succubi."

Erthrol widened his eyes. "He didn't tell you himself?"

"No. He didn't."

I balled my empty hand into a tight fist and glared at my lap, my jaw so tight that I chipped my molar. He hadn't told me or even thought about telling me probably. How long had he known about this? How freaking long?

"It doesn't matter," I whispered, more for myself. "I'm done with demons."

Erthrol chuckled once more, the softness in his face coming back and making his eyes glimmer underneath the dim light. He tipped his glass in my direction. "I'm right fucking there with you."

With the tension fading, I slowly sat back, relaxed against the couch, and glanced over at him. "What do you mean?" I asked, sipping on my water. "Don't you want to, like ... be the king of demons someday?"

"I'd like to," Erthrol said, resting his glass on his thigh and leaning into our conversation. "But that doesn't matter to me as much as it matters to my parents. Succubi are"—he rolled his piercing yellow-tinted eyes—"annoying as hell though. I'm fucking over them."

A small half-hearted giggle bubbled up my throat. "Gods, me too."

They and Valerie had caused so much trouble for me, especially now more than ever. All I wanted was to stay out of the latest Durnbone drama and find Sina. I didn't care for their spiteful glares and gossip.

"I guess we can agree on something, huh?" Erthrol said, resting his arm on the back of the couch seat and strumming his fingers against the velvet material. "To hell with succubi." He threw back the rest of his drink. "When I take the throne, my queen won't be a demon."

"Good," I found myself saying and glancing at the pitcher in front of me. I sipped the rest of my water and filled my glass with whatever kind of alcohol this was because I didn't care anymore. I couldn't.

The guy that I loved was going to marry my worst enemy.

I sipped the drink—almost immediately feeling the woozy effects of it—and leaned back on the couch. My worries seemed to slip away, to disappear almost, my body numb. I didn't want to think or feel anything.

I shouldn't have taken another sip.

But I did.

I shouldn't be here with Xorgor's brother.

But I was.

I shouldn't trust a demon.

But I had.

Blindly, I had trusted and believed everything that had come out of Xorgor's pretty mouth. I believed the lies he fed me about how beautiful I was. I believed the touches he set upon my body. I'd believed that there was more to us.

Before I could stop myself, I gulped down the rest of the drink and relaxed against the couch. Erthrol took my glass from me and set it on the table in front of us, surprisingly not making a move toward me.

I expected a horny, conniving demon like him to take advantage of a drunk, helpless human like me. But he sat back on the couch beside me and stared emptily at the wall, his light expression falling again.

"It feels good, doesn't it?" he asked, closing his eyes. "To feel nothing?"

For some reason, tears filled my eyes as I stared at the wall too. "Yeah," I whispered, knowing deep down that I shouldn't be here, knowing deep down that this alcohol didn't erase the hurt inside me. Hell, it barely suppressed it. "It does."

"You should get home," he said. "It's late, and you have work tomorrow."

"I should go," I whispered, but made no move to leave.

A stray tear slid down my cheek, but I didn't push it away. I sat in the middle of a private room that Erthrol had brought me to in the demon sector of Durnbone, crying without making a single sound.

After a few moments, Erthrol grabbed the pitcher and refilled his glass. "Do you want another?" He spoke quietly, not even looking in my direction as he took my glass and refilled it on his own.

I took it from him and sipped it slowly, letting my salty tears mix with the alcohol. "Why do you drink this? Why don't you want to feel?" I asked in an attempt to make conversation because my mind felt too heavy to ask anything deeper.

Erthrol sipped on his drink and stared emptily at the wall. "Because sleeping with woman after woman and man after man means nothing when the person you love loves someone else. And you have no say in the matter. You have no choice. No power."

"Who do you love?" I whispered, resting my head on the couch and staring at the ceiling.

"Nobody." He blew air through his nose. "At least, she has to be a nobody to me now."

I didn't know if I believed him, but his words sounded so sorrowful that I could do nothing but cry for him. Or maybe I was crying for me. Honestly, I wasn't so sure anymore. All I wanted to feel was Xorgor.

23
the forked tongue

MAXINE WALTZED into her house two agonizing hours later. When I was searching for her, I had made a complete mess of her home, but as I waited, I put everything back where I had remembered it. I didn't want Maxine to know that I was here.

I wanted—*needed*—to see who she was out with and what she was doing.

Sitting on her couch in the dark and cloaked, I gritted my teeth and expected my asshole brother to walk in after her. But she closed the door behind her, placed her back against it, and frowned.

"Why?" she whispered to herself.

After a few moments of silence, she walked through the empty house to her bedroom. I followed behind her, breathing in the scent of The Inferno, mixed with Erthrol's foul scent, on the woman *I* had claimed.

Fury boiled inside me. I ached to tear my teeth into his face, make *him* the ugly one in the family, the son who nobody wanted, the man who nobody fucking cared about.

Why … why was Maxine out with him?

Why not me?

Maxine stepped into her bedroom and stood in front of the mirror attached to her dresser. I stood behind her and stared into the mirror at her reflection from over her shoulder, cloaked still, desperately wanting to touch her, to claim her, to show her that I was the brother she needed.

Slowly, she unhooked her earrings and set them on the dresser. I curled an appendage around her right ankle and slithered it up her thigh, tightening it the higher I made it up her leg. Her body tensed slightly, but I could smell her arousal.

An arousal that my brother had given her.

Not me.

I wrapped a second appendage around her left leg and stopped once I reached her hips. She glanced down at her thighs, furrowed her brow, then peered back into the mirror. Breath hitching, she reached behind her to unclasp her necklace.

"Mine," I growled into her ear, my voice wispy while cloaked.

"Huh?" she asked, eyes widening even more.

"Mine."

She went to turn around, but I tightened my grip on her so she couldn't move. Another yip escaped her throat as she gripped on to the dresser to steady herself. She stared into the mirror, trying to find me.

I stepped even closer to her. More appendages extended from my body, wrapping around her torso and pulling her to me until she pressed against my chest. And even then … even then, I wanted her closer. I wanted her to be part of me.

She was mine. All mine.

She scrambled in my grip, pushing on the cloaked appendages around her torso. I wrapped myself around her body, using one appendage to twirl around both of her breasts so tightly that I tore her shirt. Her perky nipples swelled underneath my touch. I slipped another appendage between her tits, then slithered it around her throat and between her pouty, full lips, just as the ones around her thighs traveled up her skirt and plunged deep into her.

Body jerking forward, she gripped on to the dresser with her pretty mouth stuffed full and my appendages inside all her holes. I moved even closer to her, pressing my hard cock against her backside.

"Xorgor?" she said, voice muffled around me. Spit and slobber rolled down her chin.

"Mine," I growled into her ear again.

She might've known that I was here with her, but I didn't want to uncloak. I never wanted to appear again in front of her, knowing that she preferred my brother over me, believing that I would never be good enough for anyone.

I pushed myself deeper into her throat, her pussy, and her ass. "Mine."

After digging her nails into the wooden dresser, Maxine stared into the mirror and tightened her throat around my appendage. She reached behind herself and seized my cloaked cock in her small hand, wrapping her fingers around as much of it as she could. With her other hand, she grabbed the appendage in her mouth and pulled it out.

"Why don't you show yourself?" she asked, spit rolling down her chin as she stroked me.

Dick twitching, I put space between us, tightened my grip around her legs, and flipped her upside down so she was suspended in the air with her pussy near my face and my dick at the entrance of her mouth.

While she yelped at the sudden movement, she took my cock with both of her hands almost immediately and pulled herself closer to me, taking as much of me as she could inside her mouth. And sucking. Hard.

She bobbed her back and forth, each time sliding another inch down her tight throat. My cock swelled inside her even more, growing to its full size. She tightened around my appendages and forced herself to take every last inch until her lips pressed against my pelvis.

Even then, she didn't stop.

She continued bobbing her head like she had something to

prove, sucking my cock, trying to milk all the cum out of it with just her mouth. And she fucking would too, if she kept it up, if she continued sucking those cheeks in and tightening around me like that.

I tore off her panties and gripped her ass with my hands, my talons digging into the thickness. I pulled her pussy toward me and breathed in her arousal, my forked tongue flicking out against her clit.

When it made contact, Maxine jerked in my hold. I held her thighs apart even wider and buried my face between them, licking and sucking on her swollen cunt, needing to prove myself too, to show her that Erthrol was *nothing* compared to me, that I was the only one who could make her come over and over and fucking over again.

With my dick deep down her throat, Maxine suddenly stopped bobbing her head and tensed. Her pussy clamped down on the appendage inside of it, squeezing tighter than it ever had until I thought she'd nearly rip it off.

As I drew each side of my forked tongue across her clit, she shook in my hands. Legs trembling, body quivering, mouth twitching around me, she didn't pull back, but instead sucked harder on me and cried out.

I gripped her tightly to steady her body and flicked my tongue across her swollen clit again. She trembled harder and moaned out on my cock, another orgasm ripping through her body. She bobbed her head faster, getting deeper on me and swallowing.

I grunted and forced myself not to tilt my head back in fucking pleasure, but instead, I massaged her clit even more while thrusting my hips forward and my dick in and out of her wet mouth. If she kept this up, she'd make me spill my cum down her throat.

Gods, she was fucking amazing at giving head.

"You're going to come with me," I growled, losing my sense of control and letting my body phase back into existence. "You're going to fucking come all over my face as soon as you feel me spill out inside you."

Maxine sucked me off faster, tightening her throat around me and reaching her tongue out. When she flicked it against my balls, I fucking lost it. I pulled my appendage from her pussy and thrust my tongue inside her instead, immediately finding her G-spot with my forked tongue.

Another orgasm ripped through her body. She moaned on my cock and continued to milk the cum out of my balls with her tight throat. I released into her, drawing my tongue around her sensitive G-spot.

Pleasure surged through my body, and I slowly pulled myself out of her, flipping her right side up and setting her on the bed behind us. She stared down at her flushed thighs with drops of my cum rolling down her chin.

Fully uncloaked, I stared down at the woman I so desperately wanted to keep safe. If I refused to marry that vile vampire, then I would be sentenced to death for killing handsy demons. But if I continued with my arranged marriage, I could keep Maxine safe from afar.

I didn't know what to do. I didn't know what the right choice was.

All I knew was that I needed to keep Maxine safe.

24
the talk

maxine

I SAT on my bed in complete silence, not sure what to say to Xorgor. I was so damn confused about what he wanted, *who he wanted*.

Why hadn't he told me about the arranged marriage before his brother had the chance? Why hadn't he said anything yet?

After retracting his appendages that had just done wonders to my body, Xorgor grabbed a blanket from the bed and wrapped it around his torso. He stared down at me with hurt in his red demon eye and green human eye.

Pressing my lips together, I quickly pushed past him to hurry to my closet for clothes. The more I thought about what had just happened, the angrier I became. For the past two days, I had wondered what the hell I had done.

What had I done to get him to marry Valerie? Arranged marriage or not, he hadn't told me about it before I had to hear from the succubi, who laughed at me, and Xorgor's own brother, who had drunk his weight in alcohol tonight.

"Did you come here to get off one last time before you're married?" I said between gritted teeth, ripping my closet door open and rummaging through it for something comfy to wear. All I wanted to do was kick him out and cry myself to sleep. "When's the ceremony?"

Like I actually wanted to know.

Xorgor didn't respond, which pissed me off even more.

I pulled out some sweatpants and an oversize T-shirt that I quickly realized belonged to Xorgor. He must've left it over one night and tucked it away in my drawers. I curled my fingers around the material, tears pricking the corners of my eyes.

Why?

Why had I been so stupid? Why had I fallen for him? Why had I just fucked him?

To prove myself? To show him that I would be a better wife for him than Valerie ever could? To stop myself from confessing that he was the only person I had ever wanted and that watching him marry someone else would kill me?

A tear slid down my cheek. I twirled around and hurled Xorgor's shirt at him, hitting him square in his pretty half-demon, half-human face.

"I hate you!" I cried out, tears clouding my vision.

I never resorted to violence, but I couldn't stop myself from rushing over to him and shoving him back.

"I hate you so much!" I shouted, shoving him back. "I hate you. I hate you. I hate you."

"Maxine," Xorgor said, seizing my hands.

I ripped myself away from him and continued to push him further back until he hit the wall. And when he couldn't move any further, I dug my fingers into his chest muscle and stared up at the man who I loved.

"Why would you marry someone else? What's wrong with me?"

Xorgor dropped his hardened expression, his eyes growing wide and his brow furrowed in agony. He took my face into his large hands, but I pushed them away because I didn't want him to touch me.

But I wanted him all over me.

I hated him. But I loved him.

"What's wrong with me?" I shouted through the tears. "Why don't you want to love me? Why didn't you tell me that you were going to marry someone else? Why doesn't anyone want to be with me?"

All my insecurities that I had been desperately trying to suppress suddenly settled onto my shoulders. I crumpled to the floor and landed on my knees, holding myself tightly and feeling the scars on my chest underneath my fingers.

"I hate myself," I cried, curling up into a ball on the floor and wanting to disappear from this world forever. "I hate myself so much. I don't want to be here anymore. I don't want to do this anymore."

Pain seeped through my body, down every blood vessel, to my goddamn bones.

I should've never gone home with Xorgor and Erthrol that Friday night. I should've stayed at work and never fallen in love with him, with those different-colored eyes, with the way he looked, with everything about that man.

"It's not fair," I whispered, body heaving. "It's not fair."

Xorgor pulled me off the ground and into his arms, holding me tightly to him. I attempted to push him away, to scramble out of his hold, to tell him to fuck off, but I could barely move. My entire body was too weak, too overcome with pain.

"Let me go," I cried. "Leave me alone."

"No."

Xorgor held me tighter than anyone had ever held me, like my words had struck a chord with him too. He sat with me on the bed and pulled me into his lap, resting my head on his chest and stroking my hair.

While I didn't want anything to do with him anymore, I couldn't get myself to crawl out of his arms. So, I sat and cried like a baby in his tense embrace until I didn't have any tears left to cry and my body stopped trembling.

When I gathered the strength to sit back and look up at him, expecting to see the harsh eyes of a demon who had lied to me all these weeks we spent together, I saw the tears in Xorgor's eyes threatening to spill over.

"Don't ever fucking say that again," he whispered. "Don't ever say that you don't want to be here in this world." His voice broke. "Fucking promise me, Maxine. Don't say that ever again. Please."

"I-it's true," I whispered, hurt rushing through my body again.

His lips trembled. "Take it back."

"N-no."

"Take it fucking back, Maxine," he said, voice cracking again. "Please."

"Why?" I asked, heart pounding inside my tightening chest. "Why do you care?"

"Because I fucking love you!"

My eyes widened. "W-what?" I whispered, taken aback.

He dropped his gaze and shook his head. "I love you, Maxine, and I can't bear the thought of you not wanting to be in this world anymore, of you hating yourself. I know what that fucking feels like. I live like that every single day of my life, and I don't want you to feel that indescribable pain."

But still, it didn't make sense. "Then, why? Why are you marrying Valerie? If you loved me so much, then why didn't you tell me first? Why did I have to hear it from succubi at the tavern, then your brother?"

"My father wouldn't let me leave the palace all night. I came here to tell you, but you were out with Erthrol." He stared down between us and clenched his jaw. "You were out with him all night, weren't you? All I ever wanted to do was love you, and I wanted you to lov—"

I grasped his face and kissed him.

For a couple of moments, he tensed, but then he relaxed into the kiss. I didn't know what had taken hold of me, but I couldn't stop myself from moving on top of him with my legs straddling his waist and kissing him harder, deeper.

He settled his large hands on my hips and squeezed gently. "Maxine …"

When I pulled away, I rested my forehead against his. "You don't want to marry her?"

"Never," he whispered. "I'd rather die, fighting to protect you, than ever wed her."

25
the forever

xorgor

MAXINE STARED at me in awe for a few moments, her eyes wavering. "Really?"

I took her waist in my hands and pulled her closer to me, strumming my talons on her soft skin. While I didn't want to leave Maxine without protection at all—because the demons would definitely come for me, knowing that I had killed a couple—I refused to marry that woman.

"Really," I whispered.

No way in hell would I lose Maxine.

But Father was right.

After leading her over to the bed, I sat against the headboard and pulled Maxine on top of me so she straddled my legs. I wanted to tell her what would happen since I was refusing to marry Valerie, but I couldn't get the words past my lips.

I didn't want her to fear that I'd be killed. And I sure as hell didn't want her to feel like she had to say I should marry that vampire to stay alive. Because I knew as soon as I told her, she'd either try to break up with me because she didn't want to see me dead or force me to marry the vampire.

And I wanted to do neither.

Instead, I took her face in my hands again and rested my forehead against hers. "I promise that I will never leave you. Ever. There is nobody in this entire world that I could love more than you."

Her lips trembled, and suddenly, tears slipped down her cheeks. "I love you too."

Warmth spread throughout my chest. I had wanted Maxine for so long that those words almost didn't feel real. They sounded like a lie, like something my brother had orchestrated to get me to fall deeper in fucking love with her.

She placed her small hands on my bare shoulders and smiled through the tears. "I love you so much," she whispered, sniffling. "I never thought I'd ever say those words to anyone or hear them said to me."

Tucking some hair behind her ear, I smiled. "Me neither."

"I want to be with you forever," she whispered, drawing me in for another kiss.

I tightened my grip on her, her words replaying in my head.

Forever. Forever. I want to be with you forever.

I needed to tell her that forever might only be a few weeks or maybe even a couple of days. I didn't know what the demon queen would do to me once she found out that I had killed for this woman. But I would fight to the very end to be with Maxine.

"Maxine," I whispered, "I need to tell you something."

When she pulled away, she gently stroked my shaggy hair—not caring about my scary demon face, my jagged teeth, the ugliness that I was. She still wanted me, and she was fucking happy. I didn't —I couldn't—ruin it.

"What is it?" she asked, gently stroking her fingers over my face.

Tell her. Fucking tell her.

But she looked so whole.

Like she had never once felt this way before. Like this was what she had dreamed of.

"I ..." I tore my gaze away. "I was supposed to have dinner with my family and *her* last night, so they'll be looking for me today. I need to tell them that I'm not going through with it, that I would never. But ..."

The happiness didn't disappear from her face, and I cursed myself for not telling her the consequences of telling my family no. They would either try to force me or turn the demon queen on me for what I had done.

But I would kill those demons again for Maxine. She was mine.

"But what?" Maxine asked.

"But before I head back to their home ..."

Fuck, what do I say?

My lips curled into a small smile, but my heart fucking shattered. "I want to take you on a date first." *Because every moment with you will be cherished forever by me.*

26
the date

maxine

A DATE?

I stared up at him through wide eyes, my heart racing inside my chest. A crisp fall air drifted in through the cracked window, blowing some of his shaggy, dark hair onto his forehead, the early morning sun glimmering against the demon half of his face.

Xorgor wanted to take me *on a date?*

"It's early," Xorgor said, turning his head to peer out the window. "Breakfast?"

Grin breaking out on my face, I nodded and hurried to my closet. "Just give me a second, okay?" I rummaged through my closet, searching for the strawberry-pink sundress that I had bought years ago and never had the confidence to wear in public.

But I wanted to impress him.

Once I finally found it, I slipped into the closet, shut the door, and quickly dressed myself. When I pulled the dress over my head, I stared at myself in the mirror and eyed the visible scars on my chest. Usually, I covered them up, but this neckline fell low.

After swallowing hard, I shook off my insecurities because Xorgor just admitted to *loving* me. I pulled open the door and stepped out into my bedroom, blushing slightly as Xorgor eyed me in the sundress.

He stood and sauntered over, taking my face in his hands. "You look fucking amazing."

"You think?" I whispered, butterflies fluttering inside me.

Swiftly, he wrapped his strong arms around my legs, just below my butt, and lifted me into the air. He walked with me all the way down the stairs and out the front door. "The most beautiful woman I've ever seen."

Really? The most beautiful woman?

I almost didn't believe him.

But for once, I didn't let my insecurities get the best of me.

Fifteen minutes later, we sat in a small diner in downtown Durnbone, which was mostly attended by humans, who looked over in fear and disgust when they saw us. But this morning, I refused to care.

Xorgor had told me that he loved me. *Love.*

"Can I tell you something?" I whispered, nerves bubbling up in my belly.

Xorgor rested an elbow on the table, placed his cheek in his hand, and leaned toward me, his soft lips parted and nothing but admiration in his eyes. I blushed and glanced away, that look being so unfamiliar to me.

"What is it?" he asked.

"I've, um … never been on a date before. So, I'm … sorry if I'm awkward."

A soft chuckle escaped that pretty mouth of his. "You expect me to believe that?"

Giggles bubbled up inside me. "It's true. I've never been on a date."

He tilted his head and arched a brow. "Come on. *You?*"

"I swear." My cheeks burned. I peered over at him, butterflies fluttering around in my stomach. Warmth exploded through my chest. "Stop staring at me like that."

He reached his arm forward and curled a talon around a strand of my hair, tugging on it. The way he stared at me … it was nothing like I'd ever experienced before.

"And why's that?"

"I haven't had much luck with guys until … *you*. Everyone bullied me in high school."

Suddenly, he dropped his soft expression and clenched his jaw. "What do you mean, you were bullied? By who?" He curled his long talons into his fist, hard enough to draw blood that dripped onto the table.

Valerie's name lingered on my tongue. I wanted to tell him so badly, but I didn't want him to kill anyone else because of me. She had caused too many of my problems. Having her out of my life completely would be nice, but …

Death?

"Who?" he growled, drawing the attention of some humans.

I pursed my lips to hold in a sigh and glanced down at the table, swiping my napkin where the blood had dripped. "It was just some people from high school. You don't need to worry about it."

"Yes, I do."

"No, Xorgor," I whispered, gently taking his hands and unraveling his fists. "You don't."

"You're my girl."

When the words left his lips, I sucked in a sharp breath. Warmth spread throughout my chest again, traveling to every single fiber of my being. This man, who had been hurt by so many people … was mine. And I was his.

It felt so surreal.

Weeks ago, I hadn't even seen him. Now, I sat in a diner on my first date with him, watching him admire me from afar, letting him call me *his girl*. Those words were … freaking everything to me.

"Tell me," he repeated. "Who—"

"Maxine!" someone shouted across the diner.

I glanced over through the crowd and spotted the vampire, Edward, who frequented the Dead Candle Tavern. Even before

Xorgor, he had asked me to drink my blood more than once, had stolen drunken glances at me.

"Who's that?" Xorgor growled, glaring at Edward, who made his way over here.

"A regular from the tavern."

Once Edward walked over to us, he stopped in front of our table and gave me his attention, barely even sparing Xorgor a look. I grabbed Xorgor's hands tighter, gently stroking my thumbs against his rough skin.

"Hey, Maxine," he said. "Any chance that I—"

"I'm actually out on a date right now," I said, hoping he didn't finish his sentence.

I knew he'd ask me for blood. I knew he wanted a taste of me.

But he had always been harmless, as if he didn't know what else to say to me. Humans and vampires lived completely different lives. It was difficult—especially at the tavern—to relate to them. The blood thing had been an ongoing inside joke.

If Xorgor heard that though …

Edward glanced over at Xorgor, flashed me a half-smile, then nodded and departed from our table, sending me a, "Catch you later," and receiving a death glare from Xorgor in return.

I didn't expect that he'd show up in one piece to the tavern tomorrow night.

After eating and paying, we stood and walked through the crowd toward the doors. I stepped out into the crisp fall air and let the wind gently snake around my body. Xorgor placed his large hand on my lower back and guided me toward the path back home.

My phone buzzed in my pocket, and I pulled it out.

Unknown: I'll be at your house tonight.

My eyes widened. Sina … Sina was coming. Finally!

27

the confrontation

I DIDN'T WANT to leave Maxine alone, especially not when she had been receiving messages from a random number who *said* that they were her old best friend coming to visit tonight. It didn't sound right to me, and I would be there when she arrived at dusk.

But now, I had to head back to my parents' stupid fucking home to tell my father for the last time that I would not marry that girl. No matter what. Maxine loved me. She really loved me, and if I married someone else, it would break her heart.

While I didn't want to be sent to trial with the demon queen for killing others in our species or be sentenced to death, I couldn't marry a vampire when I had a human girl I loved.

Pissed off and preparing myself for the worst, I glared at the pavement and walked to the grand double doors. My parents—especially Father—wouldn't understand my choice. He had married a woman that he didn't want and had been allowed to spend the night with other women, if he so pleased.

Why couldn't he understand that I didn't want to marry and sleep with other women?

I wanted one girl. And one girl only.

As I hopped onto the front steps that led to the building, someone stopped in front of me. I growled and moved to the side, but they mirrored my movements and blocked me from continuing up the stairs.

After raising my gaze, I gritted my teeth at my brother. "What do you want?"

All I wanted to do was hurl my fist into his pretty face for being out with Maxine last night, but I held myself together—especially because we were on our parents' property and I didn't want to be sentenced to death just yet.

Maxine was all that mattered.

"We need to talk," Erthrol said.

"How about you start by telling me why you were out with Maxine last night?"

"At least she told you," Erthrol said, upper lip curled in disgust and his teeth gritted. He was usually a carefree asshole, not furious like this. "Unlike you telling her about your marriage to Valerie."

I moved to the side again. "I'm not marrying that bitch."

Yet he continued to block me.

"Move," I growled.

"No, we need to talk."

This man really wanted to get on my nerves today. I didn't know what the fuck his problem was. He'd had every chance to win Maxine over last night while I had been trying to convince Father not to marry me off to some chick.

If he wanted her, he could've easily weaseled his way into her life.

"Then, spit it the fuck out. What do you want?" I asked, hands balled into tight fists.

After glaring at me for a few moments, he shifted his gaze to someone behind me. I peered over my shoulder to see Valerie with some of my parents' maids, chatting with a sour, snake-like smile.

"Why aren't you going to marry her?" he asked.

"Because I love Maxine," I said before I could stop myself.

I wasn't ashamed of it, but I didn't want him to know. He knew I liked her, but if he knew that I loved her … that was different. He would do anything in his power to keep her from me, to try to steal her away.

He looked back at me, eyes wide. "Love her?"

Another growl escaped my throat. "Move."

He placed a hand on my chest. "You love Maxine? For real?"

"Move, Erthrol." I seethed. "Before I move you myself."

To my surprise, Erthrol pulled his hand off my chest and straightened himself out. "Stop fucking acting like I'll do something to hurt you. I'm the one who landed you with her. If it wasn't for me, you'd still be staring at her through the Dead Candle Tavern window and following her home like some creep."

"All you've done is hurt me," I said through gritted teeth. Memories of his scent lingering on her bedsheets last night rushed through my head, the scent burned into my memory for-fucking-ever. "You were in her bed last night."

He snorted. "No, the fuck I wasn't."

"I smelled you," I growled, grabbing a fistful of his shirt. "Don't fucking lie."

He shoved me off him. "I fucking wasn't in her bedroom last night. I waited for her on her front steps and asked if she wanted to get a drink because I heard you were fucking engaged to Valerie. I didn't step foot in her house."

"You're fucking lying."

"You can think that all you want," my brother sighed. "But why would I break into her house, sleep in her bed, then not even make a move on her? I don't even like Maxine like that. Sure, she's hot. But she's yours."

I gritted my teeth and suppressed another growl. I didn't believe a word that came out of his fucking mouth. He had always done things to make my life a living fucking hell. I didn't put this past him either. He was up to something, but I couldn't tell what it was.

And I didn't want to stay to find out.

So, I sidestepped him for the fourth time tonight, and he moved in front of me *again*.

Before I could growl out a word, Erthrol clenched his jaw and glared over my shoulder at Valerie again. "You know why Father set you up with Valerie?" he asked, voice harsher than I had ever heard it. "Because he's fucking sleeping with her."

"He's what?" I asked, eyes widening.

"And he wants her around more often," Erthrol growled, finally unblocking me, pushing past me, and rushing down the stairs. "I fucking hate him for it. I fucking hate this entire family for the way we are."

28
the knock

maxine

LIPS CURLED INTO A SMILE, I hurried through my house and prepared it for my company tonight. If the person on the other end of the phone was really Sina, then it would be the first time in four years that I'd seen her.

Not many other people knew my address, so if someone knocked on my door tonight, then it could easily be her. If she asked for my address over text, then I would suggest meeting her in a more public place.

Xorgor had been right a long time ago. *Don't trust everyone.*

At least he'd mentioned that he'd be back before tonight. He didn't want me alone with anyone besides him, especially now that he was going against his father's wishes of marrying Valerie.

I glanced down at the dirty floor, teeth gritted. *Valerie.*

I should've told him.

But I didn't want him to think about her more than he already had. I didn't want him to touch her. I realized now that … I didn't really care if he killed her. But I hadn't said anything because … *I* wanted to be the one to hurt her, like she had hurt me.

After grabbing the vacuum, I plugged it into the wall. It roared to life, sucking up all the dirt and dust covering the rug. The thought scared me because I didn't like intentionally hurting anyone for my sake.

Being hurt ripped me apart on the inside, and I didn't want anyone to experience that.

My bully though?

How many times had I thought about turning the tables, asking her about all the ugly things about her, telling her that nobody in their right mind would ever love her? And she had the audacity to not even refuse the wedding like Xorgor did.

My hand tightened around the vacuum. She had talked shit about Xorgor up until she must've found out that we had a thing together. And then … then she had decided to go along with the marriage to, what, spite me?

Pushing the vacuum back and forth, I angrily cleaned my bedroom and gritted my teeth. My knuckles turned white around the handle. Every day, I hated her a bit more. I hated her for what she had done to me in high school and what she had decided to do every night since.

Xorgor wouldn't touch her.

I would. Only if it came to it.

She had done nothing to him and everything to me.

If she decided that she didn't agree with Xorgor's terms of *not* marrying her, if she decided to flirt with him in front of me at the Dead Candle Tavern, if she decided that she would lay a single finger on him, I would make her pay.

Xorgor was all mine.

Once I angrily vacuumed my entire house—because I couldn't stop thinking about that … *bitch*—I tucked the vacuum away in a side closet and walked to a spare bedroom. My grandfather, who had gifted me this house in his will, had thankfully had the place furnished.

So, at least I had a place for Sina to sleep.

After I tore the bedsheets off the mattress and gathered the blankets and pillow cases, I walked to the laundry room and stuffed them inside the washer. I hadn't touched that bedroom since I'd moved in a while ago. I didn't know what had happened in that bed.

I tossed a couple of pods of detergent into the machine, then shut it and turned it on to *power wash*. The washer rumbled through the small room, water being shot into it and filling the container. I padded back through the house and walked to the kitchen for a snack.

Since Xorgor had left a few hours ago, I wondered if he had run into Valerie. Was she staying at their home to get closer to him? Was she attempting to come up with a plan to steal him away from me? Had she touched him yet?

The questions burned inside me, and I desperately wanted to ask Xorgor.

But I wasn't sure if I *wanted* to hear the answers.

My stomach was in knots, my head pounding. What if she had touched him—without him wanting her? What if she had flirted with him, showing off the body that any species would die for? Vampires were beautiful creatures.

If she were to—

Someone knocked on my front door.

My eyes widened slightly, and I hurried to the front room. Had Xorgor come back already? I mean, it had been a while, but I didn't think he'd be back so soon. I thought that he'd at least be gone until tonight, before Sina got here.

So as not to be stupid, I pulled the curtains apart and peered out of them, eyes widening. Warmth exploded through my chest, my mind now buzzing with excitement. I hurried to the door, in shock.

No way. No fucking way.

When I pulled the door open, Sina stood on my front step with no luggage. Just a journal, the clothes on her back, and a smile. The past four years hadn't changed her at all—her body was still to die for, her brown hair blowing in the wind, her smile still strong.

"Maxine," she whispered.

Unable to stop myself, I threw my arms around her shoulders and pulled her into a tight hug. "Sina," I mumbled into her neck. "I missed you so much."

29
the slap

xorgor

"I DON'T FUCKING care what you do to me. I'm not marrying Valerie."

Father glared at me from across his large desk and gritted his pearly-white teeth. We had been *talking* for the past hour about my marriage to her, and he hadn't gotten it through his thick head that no marriage was happening.

But I wasn't going to explain myself any more than I had.

Maxine was the only woman I cared about.

"Call the demon queen. Get me sentenced to death, like you've always fucking wanted," I growled, standing up and heading toward the door. "I don't care what the fuck you try to do anymore. I'm not marrying Valerie."

Slamming his hands down on his desk, he stood. "You will not defy me, Xorgor."

Watch me, you fucking prick.

I ripped open the office door and found Valerie on the other side, staring up at me through wide, innocent eyes.

"Y-you don't want to marry me?" she whispered, her voice a

small squeak. "But … but I can give you a kingdom we'll rule together."

"Get the fuck out of my way," I said through gritted teeth.

"If you walk out of this house, you're not welcome here ever again," Father said.

"Good."

"And if you marry that Maxine—"

"Maxine?" Valerie blurted out, her angelic expression twisting into a vile one. She poked a sharp nail into the center of my chest. "Maxine from the Dead Candle Tavern? You're going to marry *her* over *me*?!"

After days of pretending, Valerie was finally showing her fucking menacing true colors. I had gathered enough from my conversation with Maxine to know that Maxine and Valerie knew each other, but I didn't know how. And I wanted to find out.

Because nobody talked about my girl like this.

"Of course I am," I said to her, stepping back so she'd get her hands off me.

"Why?!" she exclaimed, eyes glowing red. "That bitch has been ugly since grade school, has scars from a werewolf attack across her chest, barely scrapes by as a measly human. I can give you so much more than she can. She's a—"

Valerie continued shouting foul words at me about Maxine, but I couldn't listen to any more of it. The way she bashed Maxine so freely was exactly how the people who hated me for the way I looked talked to me.

Maxine was bullied by Valerie.

I balled my hands into tight fists, claws jutting into the thin skin on my palms, making them bleed. Valerie sniffed the air, smelling blood. Vampires like her didn't care what kind of monster the blood came from. When she spotted the blood dripping onto the ground from my palm, she lunged forward.

As she seized my hand and brought it to her mouth to drink the blood, as if she hadn't drunk any in days, I slammed my palm into her face and shoved her off me toward the wall. I never hit a woman, but Valerie was an ungrateful vampire who bullied my Maxine.

"Don't you fucking touch me," I growled, yanking my hand away from her and wiping the blood on my jeans. I wrapped my other hand around the front of her throat and pinned her to the wall. "And never say a word to Maxine again, or I'll kill you."

Father was still in the room, but I didn't care. He had done more to vampires than threaten them. He had lost control of himself and fucked vampires to death before. Me threatening some prissy vampire was nothing.

"Maxine deserves it," Valerie said through her fangs.

I tightened my hand around her throat and ached to kill her right here and right now. I didn't know why the hell Maxine wanted me not to touch her, not to kill her. I wanted to so she didn't have anyone to bully anymore.

But it wouldn't make anything better if I did it.

Maxine should want revenge. To break Valerie. To kill her herself.

Realizing that I couldn't be the one to kill her, I dropped my hand and stepped back. She sneered at me, as if she had won this little argument without saying a fucking word, but I just turned around and walked out of the office.

Maxine would make the choice, and I'd support any way she chose.

Father shouted to me from his office, probably going to *comfort* Valerie with his dick, like Erthrol had suggested, as soon as I left the property. Mother didn't care, was probably off with another guy of her own.

I just wanted out of this family.

So, I cloaked myself to slip out of the house easily and without any problem and headed in the direction of Maxine's house. The biting air seared my split palm, but I ground my teeth together and continued down the path.

I couldn't fucking believe Valerie had touched me *and* bashed Maxine in front of me. I needed to confront Maxine about why she hadn't told me about Valerie bullying her before. She'd had every chance to.

Did she not trust me to take care of her? Had she wanted to just forget about it? Did she not know that I would do anything to protect her? I would kill whoever she asked, eliminate any threat or any bully, die for her.

My phone buzzed in my pocket.

Maxine: Sina is here a bit early. Her wolf friends want me to bring her to a party.

Maxine: I would love if you came with us.

Maxine: Only if you want. No pressure! Don't feel like you have to!

Sina was at Maxine's home already? She wasn't supposed to come until tonight. I'd wanted to be there for when she did because I didn't know Sina in the slightest, didn't know why she had suddenly left Durnbone without a trace. It didn't sit right with me. At all.

Me: I'll be there.

Because something was off and I didn't want Maxine alone with her.

Maxine had just become *mine*. Nobody would take her away now.

30
the party

maxine

AFTER I TEXTED Xorgor the address for the party, I followed Sina into a cute boutique in Durnbone to find her clothes for the party. She had been here only for four hours. I'd expected that she'd want to rest, but Sina wanted to explore the town as much as possible.

She didn't want to stay inside and hide away from the world. She wanted to go.

While she shuffled through some clothing racks, I pulled out my buzzing phone.

Gaian (Sina's wolf friend): Are you sure you gave me Sina's correct number?

Gaian (Sina's wolf friend): We texted her as soon as you messaged us about her being back in Durnbone, and she hasn't gotten back to us yet.

Gaian (Sina's wolf friend): Recheck the fucking number. Don't be fucking playing with us.

Gaian (Sina's wolf friend): Sorry, Thayer stole my phone. Can you recheck?

I stared at the flurry of delivered messages and glanced up at

Sina, who disappeared into the dressing room to find an outfit that she liked. I hadn't told her about the guys yet. They wanted to surprise her.

Once I re-sent Gaian her phone number, I stuffed the device into my back pocket and bounced on my toes. I really hoped that they were all mates. They all seemed so excited to see her again for the first time in years. Sina hadn't changed one bit.

The dressing room door opened, and Sina walked out in a tight black shirt that hugged her curves and showed off her breasts. She spun around and looked into the mirror.

"How do you like it?" she asked with a big smile on her face. "I haven't been able to wear something like this in years."

"You look amazing in it!" I said, clapping my hands together.

She peered over my shoulder. "You think?"

"Yes!"

The four wolves will love it.

After giggling, she twirled in the mirror again and smiled. She was the most beautiful woman I had ever laid my eyes upon. She could wear anything and attract the gaze of the hardest catches in Durnbone.

"I'll get them," she said, gathering her previous clothing and walking straight to the cashier with the new clothes still on her body. She ripped off the tags, slid them across the counter to her, then pulled out bills from her pocket.

It was unusual to see someone casually rip the tags off clothing and walk out of the store in the items bought, but Sina did exactly that. And we started toward the direction of the party with her arm looped around mine.

I wondered what Sina had done all these years. Had she not bought clothes, like … ever?

Maybe where she lived, people did things differently.

Once I shook the thought away, I continued with her toward the party. I never attended parties, but thought it'd be the best for Sina to get reacquainted with everyone, especially because she had been so excited to jump right back into life here.

Plus, Xorgor was going to be here.

It was the first kinda date that I had asked him out to.

As I pulled Sina toward the house, she peered down at her phone. I looked over at the text from Gaian's number—an unknown number on her phone—and smiled to myself. They would be here tonight to see her.

"Girl!" I said, shooing her phone away. "We're about to head into your first party since you finally got the balls to leave your father's estate and come back to town. Put your phone away!"

She shoved it into her purse that she had bought today. "I thought you hated partying?"

"My best friend is back in town. You bet your cute little tush that I'm going to party, no matter how much I hate the smoke, grinding bodies, and drunk monsters trying to crawl up into every girl's bed. Gods, I see enough of that at the pub." I laughed.

After looping my arm around hers, I pulled her into the dimly lit house. Smoke and haze lay heavily around grinding bodies. People of all species danced and drank together, actually getting along. I headed right for the bar, wanting to loosen her up.

Earlier, she had told me that she hadn't ever had a drink in her life—besides some sweet white wine that I'd never heard of. Now, even though I worked at a pub, I wasn't a big drinker myself, but this was something to celebrate! Sina was back in town, hopefully for good.

She followed me to the back. I poured two glasses of Midnight Moon, this region's strongest drink for all species of monsters. Just the scent made me tipsy at the bars sometimes, but it tasted way better than any other mix here.

Sina stared off into the crowd, smiling softly to herself. When I handed her the glass, she took it from me and sipped it slowly, her nose wrinkling.

"You don't think this is a bit too strong for a human?" she asked.

"You'll get used to it," I said.

After she took another sip, she relaxed her shoulders, blew out a deep breath, and went back to scanning the room again. She looked like she was in her own little world, absorbing all the life around us in her own way.

"You're here," someone whispered into my ear, his deep voice sending shivers down my spine. He wrapped his arms around me from behind, his body phasing into existence and his strong arms holding me.

I swallowed hard and peered over my shoulder at him, butterflies fluttering in my stomach. We had only been out in public really once together, so this PDA thing was … *new* to me, but I didn't want him to let go.

"Is this Sina?" he asked, eyeing her as she sipped on her drink.

My chest tightened. While there was no denying she was prettier than I was, I didn't want Xorgor to fall for her because of it. Jealousy bubbled up inside my belly. Xorgor was mine, but Sina was … like every guy's dream—

"Why are you worrying?" he asked, mouth against the column of my neck.

"I-I'm not," I whispered, trying to be confident for once.

"You're lying," he murmured. And while I desperately tried to come up with a response that *didn't* sound like one fat lie, he pushed some hair behind my shoulder with his talon. "You're mine—you know that, right?"

I sucked in a breath. "Yes," I squeaked.

"Say it."

"I'm yours," I whispered, turning around in his hold and placing my hands on his chest. "But you're mine too."

His eyes darkened even more, jagged teeth curling into a smile. "Only yours."

31
the kill

xorgor

MAXINE STARED at me for a couple of moments, her eyes wide, as if those two words meant everything to her, and then she glanced over her shoulder toward where her friend Sina had once been. I spotted her walking through the crowd and toward the steps.

"Where'd she go?" she whispered, breath hitched. "I need to find—"

"Let her relax, Maxine," I murmured into her ear. "She'll be back."

"But—"

"Maxine," I purred into her ear, slipping around her from behind and wrapping my arms around her waist. "She'll be back. It's her first night in Durnbone. She's probably catching up with some people and relaxing, as you should too."

Slowly, I cloaked my entire body but kept my arms around her tightly. She tensed and glanced over her shoulder.

"Xorgor," she warned. "Whatever reason you just went invisible, please don't make it be—"

After pulling Maxine to a room near the rear of the house that had an empty couch, I sat down and pulled her on top of me with her ass against my bulge. I pulled myself out of my jeans and slipped my growing cock between her thighs.

"Xorgor," she said, voice unsteady.

I ground myself between her pussy lips, the head of my cock grazing against her clit.

She moaned softly. "Please …"

Extending my appendages, I fondled her breasts through her shirt, wrinkling it right around her hard nipples. All I wanted to do was rip it off her and take her here and now, in front of everyone. Show everyone that she was mine, that a human could love the monster I was.

Unable to stop myself, I slipped my other appendages around her thighs and forced her to spread them, giving me much better access to her wet little cunt. She glanced down and spotted the head of my cock imprinted against her skirt.

"Xorgor!" she whimpered, squirming in my hold.

"Beg."

She'd either beg for me to fuck her here or I would have my way with her anyway.

"No, Xorgor, I can't—"

I stuffed an appendage between her lips and into her throat. She widened her eyes.

I gently cupped her chin and pulled her closer to me. "I'll pull it out of you as long as you beg, Maxine. Can you do that for me? Or do you want everyone to see you sucking me off?"

She shook her head.

After I slowly pulled the appendage from her mouth, I slipped my hand to her throat and strummed my fingers against it, waiting for her to beg for me, to plead for me to shove myself inside her and take her.

"Please," she whimpered.

"Please what?"

"Fuck me!"

I rubbed my cock against her entrance once more, then pushed it inside of her. She threw her head back and moaned softly.

"Oh my God. It's too big for me here," she whispered, glancing down at my dick swollen in her lower stomach.

I wasn't even at my full size yet.

"Beg."

"More," she murmured. "Give me more. Please."

Hearing her beg for me was the best fucking feeling in the entire world. I had just dropped everything for her, and I didn't regret it. At all. Maxine was mine. I had claimed her not only in private, but in public now too.

Right when I was about to let myself fill up every empty crevice of her pussy, someone pushed through the crowd. That vampire guy from the café the other day stumbled up to us, drinking blood from a red Solo cup, a drop of it rolling down his chin.

"Maxine," he said, staggering to the couch beside us.

I stilled inside of Maxine and watched him, jagged teeth gritted. Maxine tensed on me, her pussy clutched on to my dick.

"Let me have a taste of your blood tonight."

"N-no, Edward," Maxine stuttered, trying to pull me out of her.

But I shoved myself even deeper and held her to me. She wasn't going anywhere.

"Come on, Maxine," Edward said, moving closer to us and gently grazing his fingers against her elbow. "One taste of you. That's all. You're here all alone."

"E-Edward," Maxine whispered, pushing him away, "I already said no."

He moved even closer to us, but I stayed cloaked inside her. She had said not to worry about him, that he was just a regular at the tavern, but I wanted to see what he'd try to do to her, how he'd try to touch her.

"I promise, sweetheart," he purred, moving his hand toward her chin. "I won—"

When he touched her, I snapped my hand around his throat and shoved him back. He widened his eyes and grasped his neck, desperately trying to breathe. Talons sinking into his throat, I cut through his flesh and felt his blood pool around my fingers.

"M-Maxine!" he sputtered out.

My body slowly phased back into existence, and he widened his eyes, spotting the ugly monster I was. He opened his mouth to shout at me, but I didn't want to hear another word come out of his mouth.

"Maxine is mine," I snarled, ripping his throat out of his body and dropping it at Maxine's feet, still pumping her full. When the throat landed on the floor, she yelped and clenched around me.

I growled again. *"You're* mine."

32
the undoing

maxine

AFTER EDWARD'S throat landed at my feet, his body smacked against the ground in front of me. My breath caught in my throat. This was the first time that I had seen Xorgor kill someone like this —*for me*.

I clenched around him, both scared shitless and turned on at his pure possessiveness.

"Xorgor," I whispered.

Never before had anyone been this possessive and protective over me. Xorgor had killed for me because another guy had hit on me in front of him not once, *but twice*. And Edward had done it many, many times prior, when Xorgor hadn't been with me.

"You enjoyed that," he growled into my ear, cloaking himself and pushing inside me.

"Wh-what? No," I whispered.

"Your cunt is squeezing my dick tighter than it ever has. You enjoyed that."

"No," I said, shaking my head but clenching harder. "I can't."

"I'll do that to anyone you want me to," he murmured against the column of my throat.

Because I couldn't help myself, I tightened even more around him. I was so close to losing control, to screaming out to everyone at the party, to coming all over his cock. This wasn't right, but I couldn't help myself.

All I could think about was Xorgor doing that to Valerie. I had told him not to touch her, but I wanted him to be inside me while he ripped her throat out, growled at her, and told her that he would only love me.

Never her.

He slipped his appendage underneath my shirt and around my breasts, using them like rope in shibari. One of them attached onto my swollen nipple and sucked harder and harder, driving me higher.

"Tell me who you want me to kill, and I will for you," he murmured. "Anyone."

"Xorgor," I whispered, knowing that this was so wrong. "N-Nobody."

As much as I craved it, I … I couldn't. I would be stooping far below Valerie's level. I would be a monster and a killer, not the good girl that Xorgor had fallen for. It was wrong—so freaking wrong.

He sank himself deeper inside me with every agonizingly slow thrust. "Tell me."

Valerie. Valerie. Valerie.

Her name danced on the tip of my tongue.

By the way he kept pumping in and out of me, begging me to tell him the names of all my bullies, I was starting to *want* to tell him. The thought of watching Valerie take her last breath, watching the life leave her eyes …

Pressure built higher and higher inside me.

I clamped down on his huge cock and whimpered. "Xorgor, we … we can't. Not here. I will tell you later when we get home. If I tell you now, I think I'll—"

"Come?" he asked. "Does thinking about *her* life ending get you that excited?"

I didn't know how he knew it was a woman who had given me

such a headache and such heartache all these years, but he was right about everything he had said. And the thought didn't sit well inside me.

"Yes," I whispered, building up to a higher orgasm. "It d-does …"

The words were gentle, but I sounded so vile.

I nervously scanned the room to make sure nobody else had heard me.

Gaian, one of Sina's four wolves, pushed through the crowd toward us. I inhaled sharply, not ready for another guy to come over to talk to me while Xorgor was still inside me. Plus, how would I explain Edward, who lay dead a few feet from me?

After taking one long look at Edward, Gaian lifted his gaze to me.

I opened my mouth, heart pounding. "I-it wasn't me!"

Like Edward meant nothing, Gaian stepped over his body and shook his head. "You couldn't hurt anyone," he said, glancing back through the crowd. "I'm just here to tell you that we're bringing Sina back to our place. Don't tell her, but she's our mate."

Their mate! I knew it.

Xorgor pumped into me faster, his appendages sucking on my nipples. I tightened and balled my hands into fists, nails cutting through the skin on my palms in order to displace all the pleasure and pressure inside my body.

"Make him leave," Xorgor growled into my ear. "Or I'm going to fuck you harder."

"S-sure," I stuttered. "Tell her to call me l-later."

"Sounds good," Gaian said, eyeing me for a moment. "Are you ok—"

"Yes!" I said a bit too loudly. "I'm fine!"

As promised, Xorgor seized my hips harder and began pounding into my tight pussy from behind me. I gripped on to the couch to hold myself steady and not jerk back and forth from his harsh movements inside me.

"Please, leave!" I whisper-yelled.

After a couple of moments, Gaian took one last long look at me and then headed back through the crowd. When he disappeared from my view, I blew out a deep breath and gripped the couch even harder.

"Xorgor, if you don't stop …"

"Don't try to get out of my question," he growled into my ear. "Tell me who has hurt you in the past, Maxine. Tell me who you want to be removed from your life, to pay for what they've done to you."

Pressure rose higher and higher. After he reached around me with one of his appendages and trailed it against my pussy lips from underneath my skirt, he hovered it over my pounding clit.

I curled my toes, desperate for this appendage to suck on it too.

"Please," I breathed. "Xorgor."

He moved the appendage closer until it grazed against my clit. "Tell me, Maxine."

Unable to stop myself, I lifted my hips to meet his cloaked body. "Fuck."

While I thought he'd pull his appendage away, he left it against my clit, but didn't suck on it, like I wanted him to.

Instead, he chuckled darkly against my neck. "I'll allow you to come over and over all over me, if you tell me."

"Valerie," I finally whispered, exploding all over his cock. "I want Valerie to die."

33
the bath

xorgor

I LAY BACK in the warm water with my arms resting on either side of the tub, Maxine straddling my waist.

With a soapy rag in her grasp, she dragged it down my neck and sighed softly. "You have blood all over you."

"Do you want me to apologize for killing a vampire who wanted to suck your blood?" I asked as she washed the blood off me, soap and water running down the center of my chest. "They get off on that kind of thing, Maxine. He could've killed you."

"I know," she whispered. "I'm sorry for not letting you get in the middle of it sooner."

My eyes widened slightly. I had expected Maxine to shout at me for killing Edward, to demand that I never do something like that again, especially to Valerie. But … she had apologized for not letting me do it sooner.

"But," she continued, "I'm not worth your life."

Bullshit.

After taking her chin, I raised it so she looked directly at me. "You're worth more than it."

"Stop it," she scolded, body stiffening. "Please don't ever say that again. I don't … I can't lose you, Xorgor. I don't want you to get hurt, fighting anyone for me, and I don't want you to be sentenced to death by the government."

Not wanting to fight with her—but definitely not agreeing that she wasn't worth it—I took the rag from her and set it down beside us. Then, I pulled her closer by her waist. Soft fingers resting on my shoulders, Maxine let out a long sigh and relaxed in my arms.

As an incubus, I had been taught to crave one thing and one thing only—the sexual touch of another. But Maxine resting her hands on my shoulders, relaxed in my arms, breathing shallowly against me … was everything I hadn't known I needed.

Maxine didn't have the touch of a succubus, the thirst of a vampire, or the power of the mythical Paragons. She was nothing more than a human woman, lying peacefully in my arms while the world outside tried to burn her down.

And I would do everything in my power to protect her because she was the kindest woman I'd had the pleasure of knowing, the softest being I had ever laid my fingers upon, and an innocent human, who had stolen my cold demon heart.

I wrapped my arms around her waist and locked my hands behind her back, tugging her closer to me so her lips grazed against mine. I loved her more and more every single day, had claimed her the first night I spent with her.

"I love you," I murmured against her lips.

"Xorgor," she whispered, fingers curling into my muscle. "I love you too."

"Your bullies will never get away with what they did to you," I said, tilting my head against hers and wanting her to really, truly understand that I would never let anyone talk to her that way again. "Promise me that you'll tell me all the names of the people who have hurt you."

"The names?" she whispered, shaking her head. "There are too many."

Almost unconsciously, she brushed her fingers across the were-wolf scars on her chest. From what I'd gathered, she'd had those for a long time, and she had been insecure about them since the moment they had formed.

But I found no ugliness in them.

Even if she had been born, looking the way I did, she wouldn't be ugly to me.

Never.

Suddenly, Maxine pulled back to stare into my eyes. Tears threatened to spill over in her lashes and slide down her flushed cheeks. She gently took my face into her hands and brushed some hair off my forehead.

"Promise me that your bullies won't get away with what they did to you either," she said.

Little did she know that my bullies were my family. My mother. My father. My brother.

They had hated me from the moment I was born, and Erthrol had only made it worse over the years. But we were a royal family, some of the next demons to be in line for the royal throne. If what I had done for Maxine didn't sentence me to death, killing my family would.

"Xorgor," she whispered, "promise me."

She begged me to vow to do something more than just risky.

I grabbed the soapy cloth from her and gently rubbed it against her upper arm, where Edward's blood had splattered against her. If I killed my family, she'd be in so much more danger than either of us could imagine.

But I had promised to keep her safe.

From her bullies and from my family.

"I promise that they won't get away with it either," I whispered, the blood disappearing from her milky skin and soaking through the rag. I dipped it into the tub with us, the water turning a light pink around the cloth. "Never again will anyone hurt us."

"Never again," she repeated.

After I hung the rag over the side of the tub, I seized her hips in my hands and gently let my talons sink into her ass. The water sloshed around us as I pulled her even closer to me once more, her breathing quickening.

Tonight, I would bring Valerie to Maxine. Tonight, that vile vampire would die. Our hands would be stained with blood from her bullies, from the woman who had thrown her scars in Maxine's face, from the vampire who had tried to marry me to hurt Maxine even more.

Tonight, I would teach Maxine how to kill.

34
the incubus

maxine

AFTER OUR BATH, Xorgor had left to go deal with his family. I had wanted to beg for him to stay, but I had to work today, and I needed to ensure that Sina had gotten along well with the four wolves. If she needed to stay at my place tonight, she one thousand percent could.

But I wanted her to be happy too.

Walking to the Dead Candle Tavern, I hummed lightly to myself and smiled. Xorgor had affected me in ways that I hadn't thought were even possible. I wanted him to spend every waking moment protecting me from the people who hurt me, but I didn't want him to get hurt.

Or worse, wind up dead.

My phone buzzed in my pocket as I turned onto the stone road toward work.

"Hello?" I said.

"Maxine! You will guess what happened last night!" Sina said on the other end, her voice so light and bubbly, like she'd had the best night of her life. "I'm at Calder's pack house, by the way."

"I know." I giggled. "And you sound like you had a great night."

"It was great until they stole my diary!" she whisper-yelled at me.

Another giggle bubbled up my throat. "It's just a diary."

"It is not just any diary, Maxine!"

"Well, what kind of *weird* stuff do you have in there, Sina? All your fave sex positions?" I asked, my neck engulfed in heat. "Because if I had a diary like that, you bet your cute ass that I'd have a thousand locks on it."

"I didn't think the lock thing all the way through," she said with a small laugh. Suddenly, the line went quiet for a couple of moments, Sina's breathing quickening. "I have to go, Maxine. I'll talk to you later."

"Are you okay?" I asked before she could hang up.

"Yeah, it's just Gaian sneaking into my room."

Once we hung up, I stuffed my phone into my purse and walked into the Dead Candle Tavern. I hoped that nobody would start shit with me today, but I highly doubted I'd get one easy day of working.

After I slid behind the bar, I dumped my purse into the back room and prepared myself mentally for the shift ahead. Edward's buddy might come in and ask if I had seen him, or those succubi that had poked fun at me the other day might show up.

I expected it all, except …

Jaroth, the demon I'd met up with because of Sina, sat at the far end of the bar. He shooed away a bartender who flirted with him and locked eyes with me as soon as I emerged from the back room.

"Maxine!" he called, catching everyone's attention in the entire bar.

My face burned, and I hurried over to him and hoped that people would stop staring. I grabbed a glass from underneath the counter and set it in front of me.

"What would you like today?" I asked.

Even though Xorgor warned me to stay away from him, Jaroth had told me that Sina would come to Durnbone and to be ready for when she did so she could have a place to crash. Plus, it wasn't like I'd meet him somewhere alone again.

Xorgor would kill him if I did that.

"Nothing," Jaroth said. "Where's Sina?"

"Sina made it to Durnbone," I said, smiling widely. "She didn't have much with her, but you were right. She made it to my house earlier than expected yesterday. We went shopping and then to a party and—"

"Where is she now?"

"Um, I don't know the exact location, but with a couple of friends."

"Those wolves?" he growled, lips turned into an ugly scowl.

Eyes widening slightly, I stared across the bar at him. What the hell? Why was he suddenly so cold, so disgusted by those wolves? What had they done to him? I was so confused by what—

"She's in danger with them," he said, running a hand through his hair. "That's why I wanted her to stay with you. She can't be alone with them, especially all four of those disgusting animals. You know how they are." His gaze dropped to my chest. "You remember that night those beasts marred you."

"Not her friends," I said. "They didn't give me my scars."

"They're of the same breed, Maxine. They'll do that to her … or worse."

I swallowed hard and gripped the empty glass in front of me, my stomach tightening into knots. On the phone, she had sounded so happy and excited to have gone home with them last night, minus them stealing her diary.

And I couldn't even imagine Gaian letting any of the guys hurt her. Hell, I couldn't imagine any of the guys *hurting* her either, intentionally. Calder and Thayer were a little bit rough around the edges, but Darius?

They wouldn't lay a finger on her … I hoped.

"She needs to stay with you," Jaroth urged.

"I can't force Sina to stay with me," I said, putting the empty glass away. "Especially if she doesn't want to."

"Do you want her to end up dead?" he asked, standing and leaning forward. "Because that's what she'll be if she stays with them tonight. She'll be nothing but a corpse that you'd wish you'd saved."

"Jaroth," I whispered, "you're causing a scene here. Can we talk outside?"

Jaroth slammed his hand down on the counter. "You'll wish you'd listened to me."

I gritted my teeth as more people glanced over at us again. What didn't he get about not making a goddamn scene at my work? What was it with people at the Dead Candle Tavern that just riled them all up?

"If you really believe she's in danger, why don't *you* go save her?" I asked.

Jaroth stormed out of the tavern.

Without saying another word.

He was either going to save her or he was lying to me.

35
the apology

xorgor

"I'M HERE to apologize to Valerie," I said, standing at Father's office with my lips pressed together to hide my gritted, jagged teeth. Behind my back, I balled my hands into tight fists. "What I said and what I did were wrong."

Lie.

But I needed Valerie to come with me. I needed my parents to trust me.

Tonight, I would give Maxine the chance to kill Valerie. And if Maxine didn't want to bloody her hands, if she wanted to stay pure, for me to kill Valerie myself, then I would present Maxine with Valerie's vampiric fangs on a silver platter and her head on a wooden staff.

"You upset her," Father said, allowing me into his office.

I bet I did. I chose the girl she bullied over her.

"Can I see her?" I asked, lingering by the door.

I didn't want to chitchat with him. I had shit to get done, an abandoned house to lock Valerie inside of for hours, an ugly vampire to torture until Maxine finished her shift at the Dead Candle Tavern.

Father walked behind his desk—where he did devils knew what —and studied me for a few long moments, his gaze narrowing, as if he didn't believe me. But I had grown used to that suspicious, disgusted look.

While I should've pleaded, I wouldn't beg him for anything. Especially not for her.

"I want to take her out on a date," I said, stifling a ball of vomit from spewing out of my throat. "You were right about me not being able to be with Maxine. She's too beautiful for a monster like me. She'd always be in danger with me around."

After clearing his throat, Father tore his gaze away from me. "I'm glad you came to your senses. That girl wouldn't be good for you. She's a human, and you have royal blood. You'll never have a chance at the demon throne, but if you marry Valerie, you could be king of vampires someday."

I fucking hated him.

"I know," I said, pausing for a moment to make it believable. "Where is she?"

Placing a hand on my shoulder, he guided me out of the room and toward a living room with a fireplace. I stood, dwarfing him, while we walked down the hallway. This would be the last time I ever let any person in my family touch me.

Soon, I'd be out of here with Valerie.

There would be punishment for killing a member of the vampire royal family, but I didn't care. I would take the punishment, no matter how harsh, so Maxine wouldn't feel so hurt and insecure anymore, so she could finally stand up to her bully the same way Valerie had hurt her.

With violence.

Violent words called for violent actions.

People healed faster from physical wounds, but the emotional scars lasted forever.

Valerie sat on the couch with Mother, chatting quietly about something. She cut her gaze to me and flashed me her fangs, eyes glinting red. I did my best not to scowl in her direction because I hated the fucking bitch.

Father released my shoulder. "Valerie, Xorgor would like to chat with you."

A growl crept up my throat, but I pushed it back and thought about Maxine. This was all for her. Everything I had done these past few months was for the girl of my fucking dreams, for the woman who'd one day give me children.

"I'd like to apologize," I said, intertwining my hands. "And take you out to dinner."

Valerie stood from the couch, walked over to me, and smacked me right across the face. "You hurt me, you ugly bastard," she snarled. "Why would I ever go to dinner with you?" Fake tears wavered in her eyes. "I hate you."

"I'm sorry," I whispered, taking her hands in mine. "Please …"

"If my son wasn't truly sorry, he wouldn't be here," Father said, like he even knew me.

"He's right," Mother said, standing from the couch and placing her hand on Valerie's shoulder, squeezing lightly. "Xorgor has never been one to apologize. When he does, he means it. One date, and if you don't like him … we won't have any hard feelings."

God, they were good liars.

Just like their son.

Valerie wiped a fake tear from her cheek and glanced up at me. "One night."

"One night," I repeated. "I already reserved a table at Faerie's Tavern."

She pressed her lips together and stormed past me to the door. I nodded to my parents, as if thanking them for helping me to convince her. Only thing was that they didn't know that I hadn't made any plans to take her to dinner and that I wouldn't try to win her over tonight.

I'd kill her.

Slaughter her.

Give her body to Maxine.

"I promise to make this night something special, Valerie," I said, walking out the front door behind her and following her down the steps. "The most unforgettable night that you'll ever have because you deserve it."

"After what you did to me?" she snarled, stomping off through the woods and down a path toward Durnbone. Her silver hair blew in a slight breeze, the moonlight glimmering off her pale body. "Yes, I do deserve it."

"You do."

I followed her down the path and toward Durnbone, making sure to stay a few feet away so I didn't just snap and kill her now. I needed to control myself, to hold myself back, to think about Maxine.

Before I took Valerie to the abandoned house, I needed to get as far off my parents' property as possible. I didn't know who they had lurking in these woods, watching my every move. I didn't put it past them not to trust me either.

Five minutes before downtown Durnbone, I caught up to her, snapped my hand over her mouth, and seized her waist. We wouldn't make it down to Durnbone tonight, and Valerie wouldn't see another day.

36
the surprise

maxine

AFTER I CASHED out the last customer of the night, I grabbed my purse from the back room and slumped my shoulders forward. Thankfully, nobody had asked about Edward, and Valerie hadn't walked into the tavern, gloating to me about Xorgor.

Once I slung my bag over my shoulder, I turned off the lights and walked out of the tavern, locking the door behind me. Someone wrapped his arms around me from behind, invisibility snaking around my waist.

I shivered in delight and glanced over my shoulder as Xorgor uncloaked himself. Twisting in his arms, I laid my hands upon his shoulders and stared up at him, tugging on the ends of his hair.

"Why do you still do that?" I asked.

"Do what?" he said, tucking some hair behind my ear.

"Cloak yourself?"

His smile dropped slightly, and he glanced away, his body tensing. "I'm used to it."

Was he really used to it, or … was he still insecure? Did he still hate the way people looked at him? Did he loathe the side stares, the looks? My chest tightened. I hoped … he didn't feel that way.

Gently, I took his face in my hands and forced him to look at me. "Are you lying?"

He swallowed and stared down at me, eyes wavering. "Maxine."

"Xorgor," I whispered, heart breaking. "How can I … what can I do to make you not feel that way about yourself? I know how much that hurts, and I want you to … never feel like that again. I hope you don't feel that way because of me."

"I don't," he said quickly, as if he desperately wanted to reassure me. "I mean, not because of you. It'd never be because of you, Maxine." He took my hand and turned around. "Come on. I have a surprise for you."

While I followed him, I gently pulled on his hand. "How can I help you?"

He had done so freaking much to help me feel secure with myself again. I wanted to help him feel better about the way he looked because there was nothing wrong with him. Sure, he might not look like the other demons. Sure, he might have half a human face, decorated with jagged teeth.

But that didn't make me love him any less. That didn't make him ugly.

At least, not to me.

I squeezed his hand harder. "Tell me what I can do, please."

Xorgor had been the most loving, kindest person to me, even while all the girls bullied me at the tavern, even when I was the harshest on myself, even when I was standing next to Sina—the prettiest girl in all of Durnbone. He still put me first. He still … loved me.

He'd *chosen* me.

"You can't do anything for me, Maxine," he said quietly. "This is how I've lived all my life."

"But that has to be …" *Terrible.* "Don't you want to not feel that way anymore?"

Continuing down the path toward my home, Xorgor glanced down at me. I craned my head up to stare at his figure looming over me. He squeezed my hand tighter and cracked a small smile.

"I don't feel that way when I'm with you," he whispered.

"I don't *ever* want you to feel that way."

"It's not always that simple, Maxine," he said, stopping suddenly when we reached a side path I had never once been down.

Rumors were that the mansion at the end of the dirt road was haunted.

Xorgor turned toward down the road. "Come, I have a surprise for you."

I dug my heels into the dirt, eyeing the thick fog that hung underneath the darkness. The moon shimmered through the grotesque trees above us, creating shadows that resembled nightmares through the fog.

"Why don't we go back to my house?" I asked, not moving.

"Trust me, Maxine," he said. Instead of pulling me along with him, he waited for me to make my own decision. He gently squeezed my hand once more. "I have a surprise for you, Maxi, but if you don't want to see it tonight, then we can wait."

Maxi?

Butterflies fluttered in my stomach, and I grinned like a little girl. I glanced down the dark path, then back up at him. If anyone else had asked me to follow them down a dark path that led to a haunted house, I'd run the other way.

But I stepped forward and looked up at him, trusting him with my life. "A surprise?"

"I promise," he said, walking with me. "You'll love it."

Since my family had departed from this world, nobody had given me a surprise. Nerves zipped up and down my body, but I bounced down the path next to him, glancing up at the demon half of his face every so often.

"What is the surprise?" I asked, spotting the house at the end of the road. "Ghosts?"

"Not ghosts," he hummed. "I wouldn't let the ghosts who reside here even touch you."

The ghosts who reside here? Did that mean this place really was haunted and that ghosts were real? I had only heard rumors in

Durnbone about ghosts, but I hadn't seen one in real life yet. I almost didn't believe they were real.

"Then, what is it?" I asked.

"A surprise."

After I playfully rolled my eyes, Xorgor tugged me to the front door. Overgrown grass covered the cracked concrete sidewalk. Broken windows were boarded up and then spray-painted over with black markings.

When we reached the door, he jiggled the wobbly knob a few times and opened it. I stepped into the dingy-smelling, cobweb-infested room and glanced around it. Xorgor walked in behind me and grabbed a candle and lighter from a side table that I hadn't spotted.

Once he lit it, the flame flickered between us, illuminating his monstrous face. If there was a lighter and candle here, Xorgor must've been here prior to tonight. A low whistle echoed through the empty house.

I grabbed Xorgor's free hand. "What's the surprise? This place is giving me the creeps."

"No ghosts are going to haunt you," he said, chuckling slightly. "I locked them upstairs before I came to the tavern to walk you home." He walked toward door decorated with three locks, as if it was holding something bad from escaping.

"You can see ghosts?" I asked to keep my mind occupied, but my stomach was in knots.

What did Xorgor keep down here?

"Whenever I'm cloaked, I can," he said.

My eyes widened slightly as he undid the first lock. "Really?"

"Yes, really," he said, undoing the next two locks quickly. "Now, come."

The door opened with a creek, the light from Xorgor's candle illuminating stairs that descended into darkness. My heart pounded inside my chest, my throat drying. From the depths of the dungeon, chains rattled.

"Xorgor," I whispered, clutching on to his bicep now, "what is this?"

"A surprise," he repeated for the umpteenth time tonight.

"I don't like this surprise," I said. "Please, can we go home?"

He stepped onto a squeaky stair and glanced up at me. "Please, trust me."

"I do trust you," I whispered. "I don't trust whatever you have locked up down there."

"I told you that I'd protect you from anything," he said, holding out his hand. "Please."

Though nervous, I grabbed his hand and stepped onto the first stair. Xorgor lit a trail of other candles on shelves as we walked down the stairs, but when we hit the last step, the room was pitch-black.

The chains rattled harder, clattering against metal. My stomach twisted. Xorgor brought me to a far wall and lit a torch that illuminated the small prison. Whips and torture devices hung from the walls. And when I turned around, I leaped back in horror.

A six-foot wooden stake pierced through Valerie's body from her stomach to her shoulder, fastening her into the air. Black and red blood seeped down her body, a thick puddle forming underneath her. Chains were clasped around each of her wrists and ankles.

And she was alive, staring at me.

Xorgor let go of my hand and walked to her cell, unlocking it and pulling it open.

"For you, Maxine," he said. "All for you."

37

the refusal

xorgor

MAXINE STOOD in front of Valerie with wide eyes. "Xorgor, I … you …"

"I promised you that I would take care of her for you," I said, grasping her hand tighter.

While Maxine's body stiffened beside me, she gazed up in fear.

"I promised I'd take care of *you* in a way I only knew how."

By giving her, her enemy's head.

"She's on a stake," Maxine said, her mouth opening and closing once more.

Valerie jerked her body and tugged on the chains, making them clatter. Maxine sucked in a sharp breath and backed up into me, plastering her back to my front and clutching my hands.

"Maxine," Valerie said dryly, her voice hoarse. "Maxine, let me out."

Again, Maxine inched even closer to me, as if she still feared Valerie, like Valerie would break out of the chains and pull herself off the stake just to kill her. I intertwined my fingers with hers.

"Maxine!" Valerie shouted with all her might, vein bulging against her neck. "Let me out!"

"N-no," Maxine whispered.

Valerie screamed, the shrill sound cutting through the quiet room. "Maxine!"

"No," Maxine said again, this time stronger. "I … can't let you out."

"Why are you doing this?" Valerie hollered. "I've done nothing wrong to you! I've helped you out whenever you needed it at the Dead Candle Tavern, kept you company when nobody wanted to talk to you. Let me out!"

"You're lying," Maxine said, body quivering. "You're a liar."

"Xorgor!" Valerie turned to me. "Whatever she told you about me, she's lying! I didn't do anything to her. All I wanted was to be her friend, but she … she fucking terrorized me when we were younger. She—"

I growled through my jagged teeth, loathing the way Valerie lied so freely. Playing with Maxine was all just a game to her, all just a way to pass the time. She wouldn't lie and berate her anymore. Never fucking again.

Once I released Maxine, I walked toward a desk that the previous owner of this haunted mansion had down here. I opened up the first drawer and pulled out a sharp wooden stake that would fit in Maxine's hand. I had carved it out and placed it here specifically for her.

Maxine gazed down at the sharp wood in my hand and gulped. "Is that …"

"For you," I said, handing it to her.

After hesitating for a moment, Maxine placed her small hand in mine and took the stake. She glanced at Valerie and gripped until her knuckles turned white. I guided her toward the cell until we stood feet from Valerie.

"Please!" Valerie cried. "Please! Erthrol …"

"She's hurt you for years, Maxine," I murmured. "It's time for her to pay for it."

"B-but …" Maxine glanced at Valerie, then at me. "Your brother … I think they …"

Erthrol? Why did they both bring him up now? Shit always has to do with him.

"Forget my brother," I growled to Valerie. "This isn't about him."

Maxine snapped her mouth closed, clutched the stake stiffly with both hands, and stared at the girl who had bullied her for years, if not over a decade now. Tears welled up in her huge, terrified eyes.

Suddenly, the stake hit the ground.

"I don't think I can do it," Maxine whispered, turning toward me and sinking her nails into my chest. She stared up at me with tears in her eyes. "She's hurt me too much, but I … I don't want to end someone's life."

"Maxine …"

"Killing someone would make me"—she gulped and shook her head—"a monster."

"Is that what you think I am?" I whispered. "A monster?"

"No, Xorgor," she said, her fingers trembling. "I-I'm sorry," Maxine murmured, resting her forehead against the center of my chest. "I want to be strong for you. I really, really do. But I … I can't kill her. I don't want to stoop to her level. I … I can't. I'm sorry. I'm so sorry."

After taking her face into my hands, I lifted it so she looked up at me. A single tear slid down her cheek, and she clutched me. So fucking tightly. As if she didn't want me to let go of her.

"I'm sorry," she cried again. "I-I can't. Please, don't be mad."

"Angry with you?" I asked, eyes widening. "I could never, Maxine."

She slowly stopped trembling and blinked her tears away, holding me. After gulping, she took my hands into hers. "I don't want to kill her myself, but I … I don't want her to bother me anymore."

"You don't have to get your hands bloody," I murmured to her, pushing some hair behind Maxine's ear and dragging my nose down the column of her neck to her shoulder. "I'll do it for you. I'll do anything for you."

38
the head

maxine

ONCE XORGOR RELEASED MY HANDS, he tilted his head in Valerie's direction.

"She's done so much to you," he growled, stalking toward her with his muscles clenched. "So fucking much."

Appendages extended from his back, like they did just before he slipped inside me. Except … now, those tentacles were growing larger, thicker, and sharper with jagged thorns that looked like they'd pierce right through any type of skin.

"She wanted to marry me to hurt you," Xorgor said.

And while I couldn't gather the courage to kill Valerie myself, I didn't mind if she died. She had bullied me since grade school, had purposefully poked fun at my scars for her own enjoyment, and then … then she had wanted to marry my boyfriend to antagonize me.

After I kicked the stake across the room, Xorgor moved closer to her with his sharp, long talons drawn. My heart pounded against my chest, my mouth drying. She had really wanted to marry him to hurt me. She had wanted to marry *my Xorgor* so I couldn't have him.

I wanted her to know that she had lost.

I had Xorgor's heart, and he had mine. Nobody—not even a petty, pretty vampire with royal blood—could ever come between us. I was more than just a human girl now. I was Xorgor's lover, Xorgor's … *mate*.

A vicious growl escaped Xorgor's throat as he moved closer to her.

"Wait," I said, capturing Xorgor's wrist.

Inches from her throat, he paused and clenched his jaw. "Don't tell me not to kill her," he growled. "She's hurt you more than anyone in this entire town, Maxi. She deserves everything that I have and will do to her. If—"

Before he could continue his sentence, I kissed him. Right on his mouth. Right in front of Valerie. I wanted this to be the last thing that Valerie saw, her last memory in this world. Little ol' Maxine, who she used to bully until I ran home and cried … had won.

"Maxine," Xorgor murmured against my lips.

I sank my hand into his pants and gripped as much of him as I could. He let out a low, feral growl, his dick stiffening in my hand. A wave of heat swarmed around my pussy, and I curled my toes.

Craving the power I had for the first time while standing in the same room as Valerie, I slipped my tongue into Xorgor's mouth and kissed him harder. I stroked him slowly, feeling him harden more and more.

"Please," I murmured. "I need you."

Instead of wrapping his hand around Valerie's throat, he wrapped it around mine and pinned me to the wall nearest to Valerie. After he undid the button on his pants, Xorgor slipped himself between my legs.

Hands on each of my thighs, he lifted me into the air and lined himself up to my entrance. I wrapped my legs around the backs of his knees and my arms around his shoulders, clutching him tightly.

When Xorgor slid inside me, Valerie stared in horror, probably wondering how someone like Xorgor could like me, the girl she had bullied every single day of her life because I had scars and I was an easy target for her.

But no more.

No more of her *jokes*. No more of her vile comments.

Xorgor was mine.

"Kill her," I whispered into his mouth. "For me."

The monster buried deep inside me viciously swiped his claws across Valerie's throat once. Then twice. Then a third time. Blood spurted everywhere, squirting from her dark throat veins and rolling down her body, drenching her in it.

"Yes," I moaned, clenching on Xorgor and *loving* the monster he had become. "More."

Xorgor wrapped his large hand around the pieces of neck still attached to her body and ripped right through it, completely detaching Valerie's head from her body. It dropped to the ground and splattered in the pool of her own blood, spraying against Xorgor's legs.

A rush of heat surged through me, and I clenched on him even tighter. He wrapped his bloody arms around my torso and pulled me closer to him so our bodies were flush together. I tugged on his shaggy, dark hair and pulled it back, burying my face into the crook of his neck.

"I love you," I whispered, dragging my dull human teeth up the column of his throat. Gently, I bit down just below his ear, eyes rolling back in my head and pleasure rushing through my body. "So fucking much."

Xorgor shuddered and pulled me in tighter to him, his cock twitching inside me. "I love you too."

39
the marking

AFTER I PROMISED Maxine that I'd burn Valerie's body, I walked her home.

"Was that a little love bite back there?" I asked her halfway to her house.

"Maybe …" Maxine blushed and glanced shyly at the ground. "Wolves bite their mates to claim them, and I—I didn't mean that we're mates—I, um … I mean, like …" Flustered, Maxine began stuttering. "And not that I wanted to cla—"

A grin broke out onto my face. "You don't want to be my mate?"

Maxine stopped walking and stared up at me, placing her hands on my chest. "N-no, that's not what I mean. I do, but I … incubi don't have mates. They usually …" Her voice dropped to a whisper. "Don't they usually have a bunch of partners?"

"Usually."

Eyes becoming glossy, she frowned. "I-I …"

I scooped her face up in my hands. "But I don't need or want anyone else."

"But surely, you're … you're going to want someone else at some point. I-it's only natural for you, isn't it?" she asked, voice even

168

smaller. She wrapped her arms around my torso and shook her head. "I don't want you with anyone else. You're mine."

"That's why you nibbled on my neck?" I asked, amused. "To claim me?"

Again, she looked down shyly, so I dropped to my knees in front of her and bared the demon side of my neck to her. "Bite me again, Maxi," I ordered, taking her chin in my hand and gliding my thumb across her dull human teeth. "And sink these teeth into my neck. Mark me."

Maxine widened her eyes. "But I … I don't want to hurt you."

"Bite me."

After shuffling toward me, Maxine dropped to her knees, too, and stared at me through wide eyes. "Are you—" She stopped when I moved my head to the side once more and showed her the place she had bitten a few hours earlier. Crawling closer, she placed her mouth centimeters from my neck and stiffened.

"Come on, Maxi," I murmured. "Show me how much you love me."

Maxine gently placed one hand on the opposite side of my throat and pulled me toward her, setting the tips of her teeth on my skin. She shuddered and moved even closer to me, biting down softly.

"Harder."

She bit harder.

"Harder."

She sank her teeth even deeper.

"Make it hurt, Maxine," I ordered.

"B-but I don't want to hurt you."

"Make it hurt," I repeated.

"Are you sure?"

"Do it."

Maxine sank her teeth deep down into my neck as hard as she could and broke the flesh. She stayed still for a couple of moments and then quickly pulled away—probably tasting blood. Eyes wide and brow furrowed, she brushed her thumb across the wound.

"I'm sorry," she whispered. "I didn't mean to make you bleed. Can you ... heal it?"

I brushed my fingers across the skin she had bitten and growled in pleasure. Maxine didn't know that the demon side of my body didn't heal. It couldn't. Her mark would last forever on my body. The only scar I loved.

"I love it," I said, knowing that if I told her the truth, she'd hurt.

Cheeks turning red, she smiled softly. "Will you ... mark me?" she asked, her voice soft and vulnerable, like her asking was the most embarrassing thing in the world.

Did she want the same little scar on her body too?

"I marked you the first night we spent together," I said. "Incubi claim their partners differently than other species."

"How?" she asked, *so innocent.*

"With our cum."

Her face turned a darker shade, and she buried her head into my chest so I couldn't see her. "Are you being serious, Xorgor?" she asked, giggling softly to herself. "You mark your partners with your ... cum? Does that mean every girl you've slept with before me, you've marked?"

I took her face in my hands once more. "You're the only woman I've slept with, Maxine, and you're the only woman I will ever be inside of." I leaned down and kissed her on the lips. "You're all mine."

40
the tavern

maxine

HALFWAY THROUGH MY shift the next night, my phone buzzed in my pocket. I leaped up and held my hand to my heart. Ever since Xorgor had killed Valerie, I had been terrified that someone already knew and would try to hurt either one of us, especially him.

When my manager wasn't looking, I slipped into the back room and pulled out my phone.

Sina.

"Sina? Are you okay?" I asked, brow furrowed.

"Are you at the tavern?" she asked in a hurry.

"Yes, wh—"

"I'm coming down now."

When the phone suddenly turned off, I gazed down at the blank screen and frowned. She sounded rushed, but not … afraid, right? What Jaroth had told me—warned me—about the four wolves she hung out with wasn't true, right?

I swallowed hard and shoved the phone into my purse before my manager found me sneaking a call during work. After scurrying back to the bar, I found a fae couple that hadn't been served yet and set out two glasses for them.

My stomach twisted. Maybe I should've listened to Jaroth. Were those guys bad news? Should I message Gaian and ask him if anything had happened to Sina? Heck, I barely knew the guy … would he tell me the truth? If she didn't show up after fifteen minutes, I'd call him.

After filling the glasses with pink alcohol, I spotted a couple of succubi across the bar who the other bartenders looked to *purposefully* be avoiding. And I swore, if it was because they wanted me to serve them, I would actually quit.

Ever since I had been with Xorgor, I hadn't gotten along with any succubi.

Biting my tongue, I walked over to them and gave them my best customer-service smile.

"We'd like two Midnight Moons and make it quick," one said, without sparing me a glance.

Thank gods.

She continued gossiping to her friend about Erthrol, who had *apparently* slept with her last night at another club in front of a bunch of people.

I filled two tall glasses to the top with Midnight Moon and handed them to the two female succubi, who then wandered off to a table of vampires.

Royal vampires.

My stomach turned, and I quickly looked away.

If one of them saw me staring, then … they might ask if I knew about Valerie.

Once I forced myself to look away, I glanced over my shoulder and spotted Sina sitting and staring me down near the fae couple. I refilled a couple of more glasses for customers and walked over to Sina with a full glass in my hand, giving it to her. She looked like she needed it.

"Oh gods, you look like you haven't slept a wink in the past twenty-four hours," I said, scrunching my nose and stifling a giggle.

Her hair was all over the place, her eye makeup smeared slightly. "What the hell happened to you after the party?"

"They want me pregnant!" she said. "That's absurd, right?"

"What?!" I asked. "Who wants you pregnant?"

She glanced around the bar, then leaned forward. "You know … the four wolves—Calder, Thayer, Darius, and Gaian. But especially Calder. Thayer said that he wants me filled with his pups the most, and I mean, I—"

"Girl," I said, resting my hands on her shoulders, "sounds like you're their mate."

"Yeah, but, Maxine, *pregnant*?!" she asked, shaking her head. "They've all changed so much—except Gaian really—but I have barely seen them for two days. How could they want to … to …" She swallowed hard. "How could they want to …" She trailed off, her words getting lost in the loud wolves and monsters hollering in the tavern.

"To what?" I asked.

"To …" she started, but instead of finishing her sentence, she downed the entire glass of Midnight Moon. She slammed the empty glass onto the bar and sank down on the barstool, dragging a hand across her pretty face. "I don't know what to do."

Behind her, the tavern door opened, and the four wolves waltzed in. Or … more like stormed into the bar, looking angrier than I had ever seen them, especially Alpha Calder and Thayer, the psycho.

"Well, you'd better think quickly," I said to Sina.

"Why?"

"Because the four big, bad wolves just walked in behind you."

Sina froze, her eyes growing wide. "You're lying. They're not here."

I bit back a smile and hummed to myself. Oh, they would *definitely* not like the two guys sitting beside Sina and gazing over at her once they spotted her at the bar either. Sina was in trouble, and by the way she didn't sprint out of here the moment I'd said they had arrived, I could tell that she didn't fear them, nor were they hurting her.

"Save me." She leaned across the counter and grabbed my forearms. "Please, hide me."

"Why?" I asked, a smile on my face as I poured a drink for the customer beside Sina.

"Because they will not stop fucking me!!"

"That is not a problem to have." I giggled. "Besides, it's kinda sexy to see them all riled up because of you. You should've known that they'd hunt you down and find you in town."

"They were sleeping when I left!" she whisper-yelled, making herself small.

"Who're you girls waiting for?" the guy next to Sina asked.

When he leaned closer to Sina and grazed his fingers against her knee, she swallowed hard and turned away, and then Darius grabbed the guy by his shirt collar and flung him across the room. Sina's four wolves were here, ready to protect their mate at all costs.

Just like Xorgor had done with me last night.

41
the villain

AFTER I HAD WALKED Maxine to the Dead Candle Tavern for her shift, I lurked in Durnbone for a while by myself—cloaked. I had shit to do but wanted to make sure that someone like Erthrol wouldn't bother her.

When my parents began trying to contact me to come over—probably to see how it had gone with Valerie last night—I ignored them and decided to get on with my day. They wouldn't rule me. What I had done was to protect Maxine.

And I'd do it again.

Besides, it was only a matter of time before everyone found out that I had killed a royal vampire, and I needed to prepare for when that time came. I had to be strong enough. The vampire queen would come for me, and then so would my family.

Both of us were in danger. But we were together. That was all that mattered.

I walked down Durnbone's dirt roads toward the haunted house where I had murdered Valerie. After I cleaned up the rest of the mess and released the ghosts from the bedroom I had trapped them in, I needed to find Carve.

Twenty minutes later, I steered myself off the dirt path and took a branch-and-insect-infested footpath to the dirty, rotting two-story home. A For Sale sign with a red Sold sticker hung on the front door.

That hadn't been here yesterday. I drew my tongue across my jagged teeth and grumbled to myself, pissed that I wouldn't have a place to do business anymore. I guessed I would have to find somewhere else.

Taking the back entrance into the house, I walked down the cobwebbed stairs to the cellar. It reeked of blood and death—the way it always had—but now, the tinge of vampire lingered. I have taken care of Valerie's body, burned it in the dawn light earlier, but still, that bitch had to haunt me.

After lighting up a torch so I could improve my limited vision down here, the fire brightened the room. I dropped a couple of used towels onto the concrete floor to soak up her blood and any chunks of her flesh that I had missed earlier.

And once I finished, I prayed to Satan that I would never have to hear her name spoken again. Though deep down, I knew that I would never be able to relieve myself of that cursed sorry excuse for a royal.

I walked back upstairs to where I had locked all the ghosts away in a tiny bathroom. They banged on the door, nearly pushing the door right off its hinges. I undid the five locks and shoved it open for them to leave.

Wind whipped around me as they exited, chills rushing down my spine. I cloaked myself so I could speak with them, though I knew they wanted nothing to do with me. I had taken their house and used it to murder someone.

"Seems like you're going to be having company soon," I said as my body phased down the stairs. "The house just sold. You have a new owner." I walked to the front door and smirked at the vague visible male figures. "Don't give them too much trouble."

With that, I was off.

Out of the house, down the footpath, and back on the dirt road out of Durnbone territory. I walked for what seemed like miles through thicker and thicker forest brush until a heavy haze settled upon the land.

A castle peeked out through the graying darkness, surrounded by mountainous trees. I stepped onto Carve's property and gazed at the jagged pathway up to the house on the hill. I hadn't been here in decades.

After blowing out an annoyed breath, I walked half a mile up to the front door and knocked. There was a long pause, and I knew that Carve was watching me from the inside. He didn't open his door to anyone these days.

Suddenly, the door swung open, and a man almost as ugly as me answered. "What?"

"Never thought I'd see you again," I said, uncloaking myself.

When he realized it was me, he crossed his arms and leaned against the doorway. "Never wanted to see you again, Xorgor. Why the fuck are you here and not running around Durnbone, looking for your mommy and daddy's validation?"

I clenched my jaw. "I'm here because you owe me a favor."

"What is it?"

"I killed a royal vampire. Valerie."

Carve whistled lowly. "About damn time someone ended her lousy life, but what does this have to do with me?"

Honestly, I hated the thought of leaving Maxine with the craziest asshole who had been banished from Durnbone, but he was my only hope if things went terribly wrong with my parents and with the vampire queen.

"I need you to protect somebody for me. The entire town will find out sooner or later what I have done, and I need her to be safe. I killed Valerie for her. You know what that's like—to do that for the woman you lov—"

He growled. "You know nothing about my personal life."

I raised my hands. "Fine. Fine. But I helped you once decades ago. Now, it's your turn to help me."

Carve hardened his glare at me. "Who is she?"

"Her name is Maxine. She's a human who works at the Dead Candle Tavern."

"I don't involve myself with humans. You know how much I fucking hate them."

"You owe me," I said. "And the ten-year-old debt has now incurred interest."

He sharpened his glare at me. "This is the only thing I'll do for you, but you do understand that once they find out, they will kill you too. And when you're dead, I'm not responsible for what happens to this Maxine girl."

"They'll try to kill me, but I'm not going to let them win this time. Maxine will be mine for eternity."

42
the walk

maxine

WHEN MY WORK SHIFT ENDED, I expected Xorgor to be outside the tavern, cloaked. But instead of the man I loved, I found his brother with his arms crossed over his chest, his brows drawn together in anguish, and a pointed expression at me.

"Maxine," Erthrol said, stopping me.

Shit. Shit. Shit. Shit. Shit.

"Y-yes?" I asked, clutching my purse.

I needed … I needed to get out of here. I wasn't prepared for questions about Xorgor or Valerie or anyone today. Less than twenty-four hours ago, I had watched my enemy die in my lover's hands.

"We need to talk," Erthrol said, stepping toward me.

I moved back. It wasn't that I didn't trust him—who the hell was I kidding? I didn't trust him at all. He had taken me to that demon bar the other night after I told him I didn't want to go. Demons like Jaroth had been coming up to me too often lately too. It didn't feel right.

"I need to get home," I said. "It's late."

"I'll walk you."

"No. No." I stepped back. "It's fine."

"Maxine, I insist. Besides, we need to talk."

"About what?" I asked, gulping.

"Valerie. Have you seen her?"

"No."

"Are you sure? She usually—"

"No, I haven't seen her." I scanned the streets, a nervous fucking wreck. "Why don't you go find her yourself? I'm sure she's at a vampire blood bar or, um … maybe back at your place? She can't be too far."

Stop, Maxine! You're talking too much.

I snapped my mouth closed. I felt like utter shit, telling him to go find Valerie when I knew that she was dead. I had watched Xorgor kill her, slaughter her, torture her just for me. I loathed lying, but I didn't want either of us to get in trouble.

"Did she tell you where she was going? She must have come down to the tavern recently."

"N-no," I stuttered, turning away from him and gazing down a nearby alleyway that led toward a tall concrete wall that I couldn't scale if Erthrol decided I was lying. "I don't know where she is. She hasn't shown up at the tavern for days now."

He ran a hand through his hair and gazed into the tavern's foggy windows. "Last time I heard, she was going out with my brother to dinner. My parents said that they never returned. Not yet. Where would he have brought her?"

"I don't know," I said. "I hardly believe he'd go out with her."

God, I hated lying. If he kept asking questions, I didn't know what the fuck I was going to say. I was slowly weaving a web of lies, and I knew I wouldn't be able to keep them straight for much longer.

"Of course he would go out with her," he said. "To protect you."

"To protect me?" I asked, cheeks flushing. "What do you mean, to protect me?"

"Our parents gave him an ultimatum," Erthrol said, moving in my path as I started toward the direction of my home.

I needed to get out of here fast.

"He could either marry her to protect you or be with you and risk death. And you know what I think he did?" He stalked closer to me, and I couldn't really read him. "You know what I think that fucker did? I think he risked death for you."

My eyes widened. "What-what do you mean? He wouldn't do that."

"Of course he would. He loves you."

I opened and closed my mouth once, twice, three times. I didn't know what to say. I knew that he loved me. I had seen what he would do for me. But nobody could find out, not even his brother. Because his brother … I believed he was in love with Valerie.

With Valerie!

I didn't know how anyone could be in love with such a vile creature. But that didn't concern me. All that I needed to do was get away from him as soon as possible. Stop this conversation before it led down a path of more lies.

"I don't know what you're trying to get at," I said. "But if Xorgor really loved me, do you really think he would risk both of our lives like that? Because if you do, you're crazy. And I don't know where Valerie is, so please …" I pulled my purse closer to my chest and hurried past him. "I have to go home. I have an early shift tomorrow morning."

He caught my wrist and yanked me back. "You shouldn't go alone."

"I'll be fine," I said.

"Not with Xorgor lurking around," he said. "I'm coming with you."

Did he not just hear a damn thing I had said to him?!

Erthrol pulled me along the path down to my home. I scurried after him, trying to make my body as heavy as possible so he would let go. I had been nothing but friendly to Erthrol so far in our interactions together. If I started to get defensive, if I started to show guilt, he would know. He would know that I had taken part in killing the love of his life.

He would know that I'd enjoyed it.

She'd deserved everything that she got. She had bullied me my entire life.

I wasn't ashamed of what Xorgor had done or feeling guilty. But I needed it to be kept a secret.

As we walked down the street, I crossed my arms while he still held on and stiffened. I really didn't want to be here. I so wished that Xorgor had been here to walk me home tonight. I couldn't feel that cold chill I got every night when he was with me, cloaked.

But maybe he was lingering behind. Maybe he wanted to see what his brother would do to me. Or maybe, just maybe, he was waiting for us to get away from everyone else so he could take care of his brother himself.

"You shouldn't trust Xorgor," Erthrol said. "He's not the man you think he is. He's a monster. He's always been a monster."

But I didn't believe that for a second. He had been nothing but loving to me, caring. The monsters in this town were the people who never gave us a chance. The people who would bully us relentlessly because we looked a little different.

"Really," I said, "it's fine. I can walk myself home alone. I don't fear your brother."

"You should. He's dangerous."

Royally pissed off because this conversation was going in circles, I ripped my hand out of his, turned toward him, and glared. "How? How is he dangerous? Please, tell me, Erthrol, because only a few weeks ago, you were in bed with the both of us."

The way people spoke about Xorgor—even his damn brother— angered me to no end. His own goddamn brother had made him feel like shit after trying to get us together. His own freaking brother had caused all his pain.

"Come on. I thought you needed to get home," Erthrol said, ignoring my question—because he didn't have a damn answer for it

—and seizing my wrist again. He squeezed so hard that I wouldn't escape, no matter what. "Don't ask questions, Maxine. You're a human. Nothing but a human in this world full of monsters. You don't know *who* is dangerous."

But Xorgor wasn't the one who was dangerous. Erthrol was.

43
the brother's betrayal

xorgor

SHIT, *I'm late.*

Cloaked, I hurried down Durnbone's roads toward the Dead Candle Tavern to pick Maxine up from work. Talking to Carve had taken longer than expected, but I had needed to convince him to watch her, and I needed to get my shit in order.

The streets were dead, empty, completely desolate. When I turned onto the road that the Dead Candle Tavern resided on, all the lights were out on the inside.

Fuck.

I jogged toward it and phased inside the building to see if Maxine was in the back.

When I couldn't find her or anyone else, I stormed out of the tavern to trace her scent to her home. She had to be there, right? She wouldn't have gone too far, especially not after what happened with Valerie.

In a rush, I bumped into a couple of guys who were heading toward The Dungeon. Most people who attended The Dungeon were ruthless animals, looking for some women to use, to rape …

"Hey, watch it," he slurred, stumbling away with a beer bottle in his hand.

I didn't have time for this shit.

Pissed, I shoved past them and hurried down the road toward Maxine's.

"Did you hear?" one of them said from afar. "There's a new girl from the tavern here tonight."

I froze and twirled around, watching them walk into The Dungeon. *The fuck did he say?*

Because I didn't put it past one of these fuckers to kidnap my girl and drag her into their shitty little club, I stormed into the front entrance and right into The Dungeon without paying my fee. One of their measly human guards followed me, shouting that I couldn't come in.

Yet I continued through The Dungeon to make sure she wasn't here.

Girls and women were locked in cages, being auctioned. Others were walking in and out of the rooms in the back in skimpy clothes, some completely naked with monsters hanging off their tits.

The human guard seized my upper arm, but I shook him off.

"Get the fuck off me," I said through jagged teeth. "I'm looking for someone."

"Who?" he asked, following me. "We don't allow our girls to be seen without—"

With fury rushing through me, I twirled around and slammed him up against the wall. My appendages wrapped tightly around his wrists and lifted him into the air until we stood face-to-face. He wriggled in my hold, sweating nervously.

"Did you take a human girl from the Dead Candle Tavern tonight?"

"I, uh … I don't think so. We are—"

"Don't lie to me," I growled. "People are fucking advertising it outside. Bring me to her."

"We-we don't have any—" He screamed out in pain as I tightened my grip on his wrists until his left one snapped. "Fine! Fine! I'll bring you to her!"

When I dropped him, he gripped his broken wrist and hurried down the hallway to a hidden back room. He pulled a key from his pocket with his right hand and shakily pulled the door open.

Inside, a woman I didn't recognize lay on some hay, like she was an animal, trembling. I glanced at her once, then twice, wondering if I had seen her at the Dead Candle Tavern before but knowing that I hadn't.

Maybe she did work there, but the only woman I paid any attention to was Maxine.

"H-here," the human guard said. "Y-you can have her."

I turned around and rushed through The Dungeon. *Screw whoever that is.* I needed to find Maxine.

After sweeping through the place twice, I growled to myself and stormed out of the building. I didn't want to head all the way to Maxine's house without checking Durnbone first, but if she had left work fifteen minutes ago, then she would be at least halfway to her house by now.

So, I followed the path to her home deep in Durnbone's woods until I faintly smelled her scent lingering in the trees, on the wood, down the path. Each step closer to her house, the smell strengthened.

I upped my pace because something didn't feel right. Maxine was free to do as she pleased, but I didn't think that she'd leave the tavern without me, especially after what I had done.

"Let up," Maxine whimpered from afar. "Please, your grip is too tight."

A growl ripped from my mouth, and I ran faster through the woods to Maxine's house. Rage rattled through my body as another whimper drifted through the forest. I followed Maxine's strengthening scent to the front door of her home and ripped it open to see my brother inside with her, his hand around her throat as he pinned her to the wall.

I uncloaked and lunged forward, wrapping my hand around the

back of Erthrol's throat and ripping him off my girl. I didn't know why the hell Erthrol had such a damn interest in her, talking to her whatever chance he got, bringing her home.

But I feared that he already knew about Valerie.

And if he did, then I would have to take care of him before he opened his big mouth and blabbed to anyone else, especially our parents, about what I had done to protect my mate. Maxine was the only person who mattered to me anymore.

I would do anything for her, even kill my own brother.

44

the bat

maxine

"WHAT DID YOU DO TO HER?" Erthrol growled, shoving Xorgor off him and stepping forward, as if he wanted to intimidate Xorgor. "What did you do to Valerie? She hasn't shown up anywhere, and people are talking."

"He didn't do anything to her!" I shouted, adrenaline rushing through me.

On the entire walk back to my place, he had asked me nonstop what Xorgor had done to his precious Valerie. Then, he had tried to … to *hurt* me.

"Get out of my house!"

Erthrol paid me no attention.

And I hated him for it. I hated him for loving Valerie. I hated him for caring about Valerie. I hated him for hurting Xorgor, for forcing himself on my walk home, for bringing me to that bar the other night because he needed someone. I hated him for everything.

Hot tears welled up in my eyes, and I didn't even know why my stupid eyes wanted to cry. I was angry as hell that Erthrol thought he was superior to me, to Xorgor, just because he was next in line for the royal throne.

I was furious and felt so disgusted that he had forced himself into my home and thought he could intimidate me by … by touching me.

"Get out of my house!" I screamed at him, knowing that he wouldn't listen.

But I needed to do something. I couldn't just stand here while Erthrol had forced me to bring him home, and now, he was forcing Xorgor to admit something that could get him killed.

"Now, Erthrol!" I yelled.

The two brothers glared at each other, Xorgor's red eye and Erthrol's yellow-tinted ones glowing in the dark house.

"If I find out that you did something to Valerie," Erthrol growled, "I will kill you."

When Xorgor didn't say anything—stood there with a smug smirk on his face without any remorse—Erthrol growled loudly, transforming into a blood-hungry demon. Talons extending from his manicured fingers, jagged teeth growing from his pearly-whites, eyes glowing red, his demon was more like a smaller rip-off of Xorgor.

"No," I murmured.

Erthrol turned on me, his nostrils flared and his teeth bared. And while I would've been terrified, seeing a royal demon a couple of weeks ago, I had been sleeping with one almost every night, who was *way* scarier in looks and actions.

"What did you say?" he asked, stepping toward me threateningly.

"No, you're not going to kill him."

Before I realized what was happening, Erthrol captured my throat in his large hand and slammed me against the wall, holding me two feet—at least—off the ground. "Listen, you measly human gi—"

Xorgor ripped Erthrol off me again, forcing him to let go.

I fell from the air, bracing myself to collide with the ground. Inches from the hard floor, one of Xorgor's tentacles wrapped around my waist and caught me before impact. While he and his brother were going at it—furniture, tentacles, and talons flying everywhere—he gently set me down.

"You don't touch Maxine," Xorgor growled. "She's mine."

"Like Valerie was mine," Erthrol said, lunging at him.

Xorgor cut him across his pretty face, blood gushing from its wound and onto my rug. Erthrol stupidly lunged back at his brother, catching the human side of his body and right across his forearm. Immense pain shot through my body, centering from *my* forearm.

The brothers continued to fight in the middle of my living room, Erthrol intentionally aiming his attacks on Xorgor's human side. I didn't know how it was possible, but every single cut, scrape, and punch, I could feel it inside me.

It was almost as if Erthrol knew it would hurt me or … or Erthrol targeted Xorgor's human body because he hated his brother, because he was *jealous* of his brother, because he enjoyed the pain his brother felt.

And while Xorgor had the upper hand, was throwing the hardest punches and cutting Erthrol's body the deepest, the years of abuse from Erthrol seemed to get to him, the constant jabs at his human body, the snide comments about how Erthrol wanted to make every part of Xorgor ugly so not even I would love him.

"It's only fair that I do to Maxine what you did to Valerie," Erthrol growled. "But first, I'm going to fuck her and force you to watch. You piece of shit."

I stared at Erthrol in horror and shook my head, fury building up inside me. How could Xorgor let his own brother bully him for years when Xorgor was stronger, wiser, more built than any other demon around?

Maybe the same way I had let Valerie bully me—through years and years of torture.

But no more.

Xorgor had taken care of Valerie for me. And I would do the same for him.

When Erthrol lunged at my boyfriend, I grabbed the bat by the front door that I kept there because, a couple nights a year or two ago, I had been followed home from the tavern and *not* by Xorgor. I swung the bat at Erthrol and slammed it into the side of his neck, so hard that he hit the ground and didn't move.

For a couple of moments, he didn't move *at all*. But then his body twitched, and my fight instinct kicked in. I swung the bat at his head another time as hard as I could so he couldn't hurt either of us anymore. And then he was still for good.

My eyes widened as the bat slipped from my hands, bouncing off the ground in the quiet room, the sound echoing. I stepped back, my throat drying and my hands shaking.

I-I didn't mean to … to do that. I just wanted to protect Xorgor.

"I-is he dead?" I asked, my voice small. "Did I just kill Erthrol?"

45
the body

xorgor

"I'M SORRY, XORGOR," Maxine whispered, stepping back as her fingers began to tremble. "I didn't mean to hurt him. I was trying to protect you. I didn't think that I would … I would be able to do this to him. I'm so sorry."

Crouching down in front of Erthrol, I placed my fingers against his neck to check his pulse. I waited for a moment, not feeling even the slightest movement, but then … a faint beat. I gritted my teeth, pissed.

Since he had spent the night with Maxine and me a couple of weeks back, I hadn't been able to stop loathing every piece of him. He couldn't be a wingman for his brother, couldn't fucking stop himself from touching the woman I loved.

I wished she had killed him.

"He's not dead," I said.

"H-he's not dead?" she whispered, eyes widening in terror. "What will happen when he wakes up? Will he … will he hurt me?" She paced around the room, shaking her head as tears welled in her pretty eyes. "K-kill me?"

"He's not going to lay a finger on you," I said.

She hurried over to me and wrapped her arms around my waist, burying her face into my shirt. "I'm sorry. I didn't mean to do it. I don't want him to hurt me," she cried. "I-I just wanted to protect us from him."

"I know," I whispered, gently stroking her hair.

She was so close to me, shaking uncontrollably with her arms around my waist and her chest against mine. So close that I could feel her heart beating against my body. I had been inside this damn woman, but I had never felt closer to her than right now.

While I didn't want my good girl turning into a monster like me, she had protected me from *my* bully, like I had protected her from hers. She had done what she could to make sure that he didn't lay another finger on me.

And, fuck, nobody had done that for me.

I loved her more and more every damn day. I almost couldn't believe how amazing she was, how much she … she loved me too. The thought seemed so out there, so foreign. Never had anyone loved me the way she did. How could I believe it?

"We need to do something with him," she said, chin on the center of my chest while she looked up at me. She swallowed hard, pushing away her tears before looping her arms tightly around me again. "If he wakes up, he'll hurt both of us."

We needed to lock him up, but I had no place to—

"Ah, screw it," I murmured, taking her hand. "Come."

After I threw him over my shoulder, we walked out of the house and back through the woods. I shouldn't feel guilty for killing this motherfucker right here and right now, but he was my brother. An asshole and a bully, but my brother. Still, it was fucking hard, especially when he was so helpless. I had no problem with a fair fight, but killing him right now while he was unconscious felt wrong.

So, I needed to restrain him somewhere. Plus, a deep, sinister part of me wanted to torture that man for days and days to come. He fucking deserved it for everything he had done to me and to her.

At the moment, I didn't have anywhere else to bring him. I had been using that haunted house for almost a decade, doing what I wanted with it and torturing the men—and women—who had hurt the people I cared about, like Maxine.

"There is a Sold sign in the window," Maxine whispered when we approached the front. "Are you sure this is okay?"

"It's fine." *Hopefully.*

It had to be fine because I didn't have anywhere else to bring him right now. Whenever he woke up, he would hurt Maxine without a second thought. She had knocked him out cold, slamming that baseball bat hard into his head—*twice.*

He wouldn't take that lightly, especially because she was a human. He had run home and cried to our parents after I put him into his place, and I was a demon, just like him. If word got around that a human had knocked him out, he'd do everything in his power to show Durnbone he wasn't a weak piece of shit.

When I opened the door, I stepped into the house first. I had let those ghosts out of their room the other day, but I needed to set some ground rules. They had been here alone for years, but they couldn't touch my girl.

"Stay close to me, Maxine," I said to her, then cloaked my body for just a moment so I could see the ghosts lingering inside the room, hungrily gazing at the woman behind me like they hadn't seen a female in decades. "Don't touch her."

Once I brought Erthrol down to the cellar, I locked the chains around his wrists and ankles. This was to protect Maxine. Everything I did was to protect her. Once Erthrol died—because there wasn't a way that he'd leave here alive—I'd have a target on my back. *We* would have targets on our backs.

"What if the owner finds him down here?" she asked, glancing over her shoulder and back up the stairs. "Do you think they've moved in already? Seen what you did to Valerie down here? I can still smell her blood."

"They haven't moved in yet," I said to calm her down. "I'll lock the door."

"A lock won't stop someone," she said, moving closer to me and staring up at me through wide eyes. "I'm sorry for being annoying, but I just … I don't want either of us to get caught. This is the second person with royal blood down here!"

I took her face in my hands. "Don't think you're annoying and don't apologize for being yourself, Maxine. I fucking love you just the way you are. Let me handle all of this shit going on down here. Don't you worry about it."

"You shouldn't have to," she whispered. "*This* is my fault."

"It was self-defense."

"It was self-defense until we brought him here and tied him up."

After I brushed my thumbs across her cheeks, she relaxed under my touch, her shoulders slumping forward slightly as she exhaled.

"Don't worry about it," I whispered to her. "You're mine to protect now."

I needed to get Maxine to Carve's castle to stay for a few nights while everything cooled off. She'd try to get out of it to go to work, to see Sina, but she needed to stay. For her own good.

So, I scooped up her hand and led her out of the haunted house. "Come with me."

46
the knife

maxine

"WHERE ARE WE GOING?" I whispered, staring up at Xorgor while he led me through the forest just outside of Durnbone. "It's really late. Don't you think we should get home? I want to lie down with you after the night I've had."

He squeezed my hand. "I want to lie with you, but you can't stay at your home anymore."

My eyes widened. "Wh-what do you mean? All my clothes are there and everything."

"You're not safe there," he said. "Carve has clothes for you."

"Who the heck is Carve?!" I exclaimed, wrapping my fingers tighter around his.

Just by his damn name, this *Carve* sounded terrifying. Was he really going to trust a random stranger with me for who knew how long?

"Carve is a friend," Xorgor said. "Sorta."

"Sorta?"

"I've known him for decades. He doesn't like the royals. They have a long history. He'll do whatever he can do to piss them off

196

even if that means hiding you from them." Xorgor ducked underneath a low branch. "Plus, he owes me a favor."

"But what do you ..." I started, my voice trailing off once I stepped into view of a large castle that stood hundreds of feet in the air.

The full moon loomed over its highest apex, the fog sitting heavily near the top.

"How many people live here?" I whispered, walking up a cobblestone path.

"One."

"One?!" I whisper-yelled, crows cawing above me. "Just one?"

This place looked like it could house hundreds, if not thousands, of people. No castle, no mansion, no royals home in Durnbone matched the grandiosity of it all. I slowed to a stop and craned my head up to really take in all its beauty.

"You're here earlier than agreed upon," someone said from the shadows.

I snapped my head in the direction of the voice, spotting a tall figure approaching us from behind. While the man was built, he wasn't as muscular as Xorgor, but damn did he look way more sinister.

Too terrifying to even look in the eye.

When I spotted the knife he held in his hand, skillfully moving it around between his fingers, I stepped closer to Xorgor until I pressed my entire body against his back and peeked around his arm at Carve.

Why did Xorgor want me to live with him?! How long was I even supposed to be here for? Would Xorgor come back for me every night, once a week, at least one time every month? I didn't want to be away from him for too long.

"Change of plans," Xorgor said. "My brother is locked up."

"Erthrol is locked up. By who? Your parents?"

"By us," Xorgor said, taking my hand and stepping around me so I was in front of him. He placed his large hands on my shoulders, standing over me and making me feel so small, like a child he was protecting. "Maxine … knocked him out."

Carve dropped his gaze to me. "*You* knocked him out?"

"Y-yes," I squeaked, heart pounding. I inched closer to Xorgor and looked up at him, lowering my voice. "Please, don't make me stay with him. I can protect myself back home with my bat and—"

Carve hummed, lips set in a tight line. "You used a bat on Erthrol?"

"Yes."

He raised his gaze back up to Xorgor. "A bat? You taught her to fight with a bat?"

"I haven't taught her to fight at all."

Carve stepped closer and flipped the knife in his hand. "We'll have to change that. There are clothes in the guest bedroom. Go change. We start in fifteen minutes."

"B-but it's, like, two in the morning," I said.

"This isn't going to be a vacation," he said, pointing the knife at the door. "Go change."

Xorgor twirled me around and gently took my face in his hands. "He's not going to hurt you, Maxine. I'll be back tomorrow night. Please, stay here with him and don't leave. Durnbone is too dangerous for you right now."

"But …" I curled my fingers into his chest. "Xorgor …"

"I have to go," he said, resting his forehead against mine. "I love you."

"I love you too."

47

the ghost harem

xorgor

AFTER I DROPPED Maxine off at Carve's castle, I walked back to the haunted house because I needed to figure some shit out. I had really wanted to get Erthrol out of there before the new owner moved in, but the door was wide open when I reached the house.

Cloaked, I stepped into the house. There was a suitcase at the bottom of the stairs and a single light flickering in the second-floor hallway. I walked up the creaky steps and toward the main bedroom.

The door was closed, so I jiggled the doorknob to open it and stepped into the room.

What the f—

A woman was on all fours in the master bedroom with four ghosts surrounding her, their cocks stuffed into her holes and her moans getting lost in the soft whooshes as more moved around the room.

"Goddamn," I murmured to myself.

What a housewarming party.

These ghosts were even hornier than that old creep at the trinket toy shop in downtown Durnbone and his assistant, Mindy. I slowly backed out of the room before they all spotted me and tiptoed down the stairs to the locked cellar.

Once I unlocked the door, I phased through the doorway and walked to my brother, who hadn't woken up yet. I needed to figure out what the hell I planned on doing with him because those ghosts wouldn't keep the new owner distracted for long.

Or maybe they would.

Moans drifted from upstairs to the cellar, and Erthrol's nose twitched, as if he was inhaling her scent, even while unconscious. I sat across from him and stared at the dickhead that I called my brother, then dropped my gaze and shook my head. I needed to get rid of him.

"You're an asshole," he murmured.

I glanced up to see his head lolling back and forth, eyes half-opened.

I walked over to him, grabbed him by the back of his hair, and forced him to look up at me. "Who did you tell about Valerie?"

Erthrol knew what I had done to Valerie. There wasn't a reason to hide it.

He yanked his arms against the chains, trying to escape but failing. "Let me out, and I won't think about killing that human you're obsessed with, that little bitch who hit me with a fucking bat."

"You won't kill her," I said calmly. "Because I'm not letting you out of here."

"She's a human!" he shouted.

"And Valerie was a vampire who slept with our father, and you still wanted her."

"That's different," Erthrol growled. "Our father is an incubus too. He has needs."

"He had the need to sleep with the woman you loved just as you had a need to sleep with the woman I desired," I said, still unable to forgive and forget that first night.

Erthrol had used my insecurities against me to fuck Maxine when I wanted her.

"Exactly." He seethed. "And I didn't kill him."

"Because you want the demon throne," I said. "Killing another demon while trying to reach that place would get you kicked out of the royal family for good." I stepped closer to him. "And that is where we differ, Erthrol. I've never truly been part of the royal family, never had a place in line for the throne."

"Let me out!" he roared again, his eyes glowing yellow, like a true demon.

"If you loved Valerie that much, you should've killed our father."

"Or what?" he taunted. "You're going to kill me? You're not going to fucking touch me, Xorgor. You're too weak. You've always been, and that's the reason why you were never given a chance at the throne. Not because you're an ugly bastard."

I slammed my fist into his face, his insults still cutting deep.

"If you wanted to kill me, you would've done it already."

And while part of that might've been true, while he and his words still affected me in ways that they shouldn't, I wasn't going to let him go, like he was trying to persuade me. And I wasn't going to chain him here forever without laying another hand on him.

Tonight, he had threatened Maxine.

Tonight, he'd pay for it.

After rummaging through the closet drawers for supplies, I pulled out a gag—to keep him from screaming and alerting the new owner—and a knife. I walked back over to him and stuffed the gag into his mouth until he could barely make a sound.

"You've always hated me for no reason," I said. "And I put up with your shit for years because I started to believe the lies you fed me about no woman ever falling in love with me. Maybe I am an ugly bastard, but the woman I love is still alive."

He pulled on the restraints again, pitifully attempting to escape.

"Valerie died right here," I taunted him. "While I was fucking Maxine." I moved closer to him so my lips were centimeters from his ear. "And Maxine loved every single second of watching her scream in agony."

As he muffled on the gag, I smirked. He deserved this and more. They all did.

I moved the knife down the center of his chest to his abdomen and then to his pants, ripping apart the clothing and letting his pants fall to the ground. My brother had always been more attractive than me, but his dick was pitiful.

"I would stake her again and again if I could," I said. "Just to see Maxine smile."

He screamed on the gag, his yellow-tinted eyes glowing. He should've *never* touched Maxine.

He had known exactly what he was doing when he took advantage of both of us that first night. He had known exactly what he was doing when he spread those rumors around Durnbone—about Maxine being bad in bed, about Valerie being forced to marry me.

The more I thought about him, the angrier and angrier I became. How could I have let this bastard rule and ruin my entire life? He didn't deserve the praise he got from anyone. He didn't deserve the throne.

So, I would make sure he would never have it.

"What's an incubus without a cock?" I whispered, sliding the knife across the base of his dick and cutting it clean off his body. "He becomes a nobody, just like his brother."

48
the training

maxine

"YOU'RE PSYCHO!" I shouted, dodging a knife that whizzed past me.

My heart pounded against my chest, my throat dry from yelling for the past five hours straight. Carve had not given up or even let me rest. I had been training and training and training as his crazy ass threw blades at me.

Sharp blades!

"I don't think Xorgor will appreciate this!" I said, ducking.

A knife cut through the air inches from my head and lodged right into a tree trunk behind me. His throw had been so hard and precise that the entire blade was stuck in the tree, not just the tip, like I had seen at the Dead Candle Tavern when guys threw knives at a target in the back.

"Stop whining," Carve growled. "You won't learn."

"How am I learning now?!" I exclaimed, eyeing him suspiciously when he stopped.

"Take the knife," he said, gesturing to the tree.

I didn't trust him at all not to throw another knife at my wrist and pin me to the tree with it while I desperately tried to pull his first knife from it. He hadn't stopped for more than a few moments since Xorgor had left.

After I narrowed my eyes at him, he rolled his and crossed his arms. "Now."

Terrified of his tone, I scrambled to the tree and yanked on the knife as hard as I could. But the damn thing was so deep in the bark that I could barely move it a millimeter. Gripping it with both hands, I placed one foot against the trunk and used my entire strength.

The knife slipped out, and I hit the ground with a thud.

"Oh my gods, you're useless," Carve muttered, walking toward me.

"I'm not useless," I mumbled, sitting up with the blade in my hand. I shuffled to my feet and brushed the dirt off my ass, cutting my gaze to him. "I just don't usually have someone chucking knives at me."

He stood in front of me with his arms crossed over his chest again, his looming figure making me feel small—and not in the same way that Xorgor did. Carve terrified me to no end. I wouldn't be surprised if he killed me before Xorgor returned.

"I want to sleep," I said.

When he took the knife from my hand, I thought he was going to finally let me rest after a long day of work and of knocking out Erthrol. But this man twirled the blade around his hand and gave it back to me, showing me how to hold it differently than I had before.

"This is how you hold a knife if you're going to throw it."

"I don't want to throw it."

"Well, it's a little too fucking late for that, sweetheart. You almost killed a member of the royal family tonight. You don't get any take-backs. You need to learn how to defend yourself, or they will kill you."

"What if I strangle them?" *Like I want to do with you right now.*

Ignoring me, he readjusted the way I held the knife again. "Hold it like this to stab."

I gripped the knife in my hand and glared at him, gaze focusing on his chest, where I ached to stab him. Because I was cranky. And tired. And didn't want to be here right now. I wanted Xorgor.

"Stab me."

I snapped my gaze up to him. "What?"

"Stab"—he moved my hand so the tip touched the center of his chest—"me."

"You're insane," I whispered again. "I'm not stabbing you."

Before I could say another word, he slammed my hand to his chest and let the knife slide into his flesh. I attempted to yank back my hand, but he tightened his grip around it and held me in place so it looked and felt like *I* had stabbed him.

"What are you doing?!" I shrieked.

After a moment, his grip on me loosened, as if his fingers were becoming weaker. With wide eyes, he stumbled back and tripped onto his ass. And when he landed on his back and stared up at the night sky, I collapsed next to him to pull the knife out.

"Carve!" I shouted, not knowing what to do. "What did you do that for?"

Now, he was dying on the fucking ground in front of me. I didn't know what the hell to do. My heart was racing a million miles a minute. And I—

As I scrambled to hold his wound closed, Carve whipped out another knife from his belt and pressed it against my neck. "When we started, I told you to make sure that your prey was dead before you approached them."

My eyes widened slightly as the wound closed underneath my fingers. He grazed the blade across my throat, then pulled it back and leaped up, as if he hadn't just been stabbed in the chest, as if he was completely fine.

"You're fucking insane," I whispered.

"Get up."

I stood up and stepped back from him. "What the hell did you do that for?"

"To give you experience."

"With nearly killing someone?!"

"With stabbing them," he said, flipping the knife in his hand and humming. "If you don't get it over with now, you might freeze up during an actual fight." He stepped closer to me and placed the edge of the blade against my chin, lifting it. "And if you freeze, you die."

"But I don't want to kill anyone."

"Too bad," he said, turning away and walking toward his castle. "Come on."

"Come on?" I asked. "We're done?"

"Did you want to train more tonight?"

Before he could turn around and throw another knife in my direction, I sprinted toward him and headed for the castle. I hadn't even been inside yet, but I needed a ton of rest. I didn't want to wake back up until Xorgor made it back to me.

"Do you know Olenna?" he asked suddenly, walking into the castle and into a staircase before I could even explore. "From Durnbone. She frequents the Dead Candle Tavern. Short. Strawberry-blonde curls. And one of those good-girl facades, like you have."

Walking up the stairs with him, I arched a brow at the last part of his sentence and wondered where the hell he was going with this. Did he know her? I vaguely remembered a girl matching that description coming into the Dead Candle Tavern a couple of times with a guy named Ran.

"Yes," I said, still unsure.

He slammed open a door to a bedroom right off the staircase and shoved me inside it. "Next time you see her, tell her Carve told her to go fuck herself," he said, then shut and locked me inside the room for the rest of the night.

49

the dick

A MENACING ROAR exited Erthrol's throat as blood spurted from where his cock had once hung. Not very low, but it had been there. He yanked his wrists and ankles against the chains a final time, trying to escape.

"I'm going to kill you," he shrieked. "I'm going to fucking kill you and that bitch!"

Ignoring his empty threats, I grabbed his ugly dick from the puddle of blood between his feet and stepped toward him. So he wouldn't alert the woman who had just moved in—she was probably spooked from all those ghosts fucking her—I stuffed the cock back into his mouth to shut him the hell up.

He could choke on his own manhood for all I cared.

Before he could spit it back out, I grabbed the duct tape from the closet and wrapped it around his mouth and head, holding it in place. What a sad, sad man he was, and now, he was finally getting what he deserved.

More and more blood seeped out of his wound, his movements becoming weaker. He thrashed against the chains once more, and then his body went limp again—from loss of blood this time.

After thanking Satan that I didn't have to deal with his ass for another moment, I washed the blood off my hands underneath a small faucet and walked back upstairs. I locked the door behind me so the new owner wouldn't go down there and cloaked myself.

With her hair sticking up in every direction, she descended the stairs and walked into the living room to grab a moving box. She looked to be Maxine's age, maybe a year older. I should introduce them. It'd give us a reason to come over so I could still use the cellar freely.

Once she walked back upstairs, I opened the front door and slipped out of it. I'd promised Maxine that I would be back tonight, but there was a royal demon meeting today that I needed to attend and survive first.

So, I walked to The Inferno in downtown Durnbone.

Naked succubi danced against each other around silver poles scattered throughout the room. Incubi fucked demons and humans alike in large glass boxes. I growled underneath my breath and rubbed my forehead, not wanting to be here.

If I could make the rules, I would spend every moment with Maxine.

Demons with royal blood sat on maroon velvet couches in the exclusive VIP area in the back. I stepped over the velvet ropes that sectioned off the area and sat down in an empty seat in front of a succubus twirling around the pole, her fake hair extensions clinging to her body.

She stepped off the platform toward me. "Do you want a—"

"No."

"Come on," she purred. "Take off some—"

"If you touch me, I'll break your fingers," I growled. "I said no."

After she rolled her eyes, she stepped back onto the platform and continued dancing. I anxiously tapped my foot and waited for the demon queen to arrive with my father. Jaroth sat down on the couch across from me. The succubus leaped off the platform again and sat in his lap.

When the demon queen arrived with my father, I arched a brow at them. "Didn't bring Erthrol to the meeting today?" I asked, pissed the fuck off and clenching my jaw to keep up the act. "I'm surprised."

"Erthrol isn't with you?" Father said.

"Why the fuck would he be with me?" I responded, not slipping up for even a second.

I knew that he was just waiting to put the blame on me for something, to hurt me more than he already had. Why would his ugly son, who would never have a chance to lead the demons, show up to the royal meeting and not his pride and fucking joy?

"Well, we don't have time to wait," the demon queen said. "I will be stepping down soo—"

Before she could finish her sentence, someone growled from the entrance of The Inferno Club. A royal vampire stepped into the club, his beady red eyes glowing in the darkness. "Where is my daughter?"

The demon queen straightened her back. "Your daughter?"

Shit, this is Valerie's father, isn't it?

"Valerie," he snapped, storming toward us as everyone in the club quieted down. Even the dancers stopped. "What have you done with my daughter? She was promised to one of your kind. The ugly one."

Everyone turned toward me.

Fuck.

"Where is Valerie?" Father said. "I haven't seen her."

"Have you checked your bed?" I asked, arching my brow.

"Xorgor," Father growled.

I stood up to meet his gaze. I couldn't say too much, or they might suspect something, but I needed this tension between the vampires and demons, and I needed the attention off me because I had killed Valerie and might eliminate my brother soon too.

"The last person she left with was *you*," Father snapped.

"Blame the ugly son, like you always do," I growled, shaking my head. "Why wouldn't I want an arranged marriage to a beautiful woman like Valerie? Sure, we come from different walks of life, but nobody as beautiful as her would ever even consider marrying me."

"An ugly bastard like him would be thrilled to marry my Valerie," the vampire royal said, stepping toward my father. "That's what you told me when you came to my home to arrange the marriage. He would have no reason to hurt her."

Ah, this is falling together perfectly.

"He has every reason to hurt her," Father growled. "He hates her!"

"So, you lied to me." The vampire seethed, his fangs growing sharp and skin paling the way all vampires did right before they were about to attack, the power growing and gathering inside him. "You either lied to me then or you're lying to me now."

"I'm not lying to you," Father said, straightening his back to look more intimidating.

"Where is my daughter?" the vampire asked again, his voice deathly quiet.

"I don't kn—"

Before Father could finish his sentence, the vampire leaped forward at the speed of light, sank his fangs into Father's neck, and sucked the literal life out of him in a single moment. My eyes widened to keep up with the act.

But inside, I held back a grin.

This was it. This was finally the fall of the demons. The fall of bullies. The fall of a fucking empire.

50
the castle

maxine

"MAXINE!" Carve shouted, his voice traveling through his castle.

I scurried down the large hallway and ignored his shouts. I had barely gotten five hours of sleep because of that man, and I didn't want to start training again so early. The least he could do was let me explore.

"Get your ass to the quad!" he shouted. "You have training."

Man, didn't he do anything for fun other than hurl knives at innocent girls who didn't want to learn how to fight in the first place? I totally knew that I needed to, but—come on—I was only asking for a couple more hours of sleep this morning.

When his shouts became quieter, I slowed to a leisurely stroll and widened my eyes at all the paintings and murals, all the golden frames, finally able to take them in and admire the art collection that must've taken centuries to build.

How long has he been alive? He was way too grumpy to be a young kid.

And who was that girl that he had asked about? Olenna? I mean, I think I'd seen her a couple of times in the Dead Candle Tavern, and from what I could remember, she had always been so sweet. Not someone that I would ever tell to go fuck herself.

What was Carve's problem?

Maybe telling people to go fuck themselves was how he showed love.

My lips twitched into a small smile. I would have to ask him how much he loved her later.

So, I continued sneaking throughout the castle. Xorgor had said he would be back tonight, but it had been hours since he had left, and my stomach had been twisting into tight knots since he had disappeared back into the woods.

When I turned the corner and slammed into Carve, he gripped the back of my neck and dragged me back through the hallways the way I had come.

"Why were you ignoring me?" he asked. "You need to train."

I pressed my lips together—not wanting to give him the satisfaction of hearing me beg him not to throw blades at me again because he'd probably get off on it—and followed him out the door to the quad. I had known I wouldn't be able to hide out much longer.

"How old are you?" I asked, grabbing a knife from him and walking to the other side of the lawn.

"Old enough."

"Centuries?"

"None of your business."

"You're very grumpy."

A knife whizzed through the air, nicking me in the ear.

"And you talk too much."

After drawing my tongue across my teeth, I turned around to retrieve the knife that he had just cut my ear with, lodged straight into the tree behind me. Gods, Xorgor really needed to get back soon.

"So," I hummed, "were you lovers turned enemies?"

"The fuck are you talking about?" he growled.

"Were you and Olenna lovers in the past?" I asked, yanking the knife from the tree.

Before I could turn around, he had me pinned up against the bark, the wet wood digging into the soft skin of my cheek. He pressed a knife to my carotid artery, the blade against my skin almost hard enough to break it and draw blood.

He seethed. "Don't you ever say that again."

"So, you were," I said, the words tumbling out of my mouth.

"What did I just fucking say?" he growled.

Tilting my head slightly to the side, I glanced back at him and grinned. "Oh my gods, so … is it like a *friends to lovers to enemies* kind of thing?" I squealed. "That's so cute! I don't read that much anymore, but when I was growing up, that was my favorite kind of books!"

After growling again—but this time in annoyance—he released me. "This is why you're going to die. You don't have a filter, do you?" He muttered something in an ancient demon tongue and turned around. "Helpless."

What he didn't know was that I absolutely had a filter. I just wanted to piss him off because I had barely gotten any sleep last night before his booming voice woke me up this morning, yelling at someone through his phone.

I hurled the knife at his back. "I'm not helple—"

As if he had killer instincts, he reached behind his back without looking and caught the knife milliseconds before it could slice into his skin. "You have to be quicker than that if you want to kill a demon."

Throat drying, I swallowed and eased my glare. My thoughts traveled back to Erthrol, who had walked me home last night and laid his hands on *both* Xorgor and me.

"What if the demon is restrained?" I whispered, wanting an answer but also hoping that he didn't hear me.

"Erthrol?" he asked nonchalantly. "You want to know how to kill him?"

After peering around the yard to make sure nobody was watching us, I moved closer to him and nodded. I hated the thought of killing anyone, but … Erthrol was a danger to us all. He had the knowledge to sentence *both* of us—especially Xorgor—to death.

When I had hit him with a bat and thought I'd killed him, I'd freaked out a little bit, but I … I had sorta felt relieved that he wouldn't bother us any longer. And I feared that Xorgor wouldn't be able to kill him himself.

Sure, Xorgor had killed many people, but this was his brother, who had constantly teased and taunted him since they had been children. I feared that Xorgor felt lesser than Erthrol still, like he didn't have the strength or courage to kill him.

"Yes," I whispered. "Teach me how to kill Erthrol."

51
the return

xorgor

AFTER THE VAMPIRE royal sucked the life force out of my father, I had only a few seconds to enjoy the moment before he lunged at the queen of demons. Because it couldn't hurt to get on the queen's good side now that my father was dead, I grabbed the royal by the throat and crushed it in my palm. He snapped his head back into place, then thrashed in my arms, screaming at me to let him free, that we all deserved this.

The queen yanked a wooden leg off the coffee table and staked him right in the heart with so much force that the wooden plank sliced through his body. He fell limp in my hands, and I dropped him onto the ground. He landed at our feet with a thud.

She dusted off her tight dress and stared down in disgust at the dead vampire, spitting on him. "He has killed a royal demon," she announced to the entire club of demons. "This calls for war with the vampires!"

Demons roared to life in excitement, and I walked toward the exit.

They had wanted nothing to do with me for the last decade, so I didn't give a shit about what happened next. Jaroth could grab the demon throne for all I cared because my father wasn't having it. Erthrol wasn't having it. And I sure as hell would never get the chance at it.

"Where are you going?" the queen called to me.

I stopped and turned toward her. "Home."

"You will fight by my side," she said.

"You have turned away from me for decades," I said. "Everyone has."

She stepped toward me. "I have never turned away from you," she growled, snatching my jaw and forcing me to look down at her small figure. "The only reason you've been asked to come to these meetings is because I have requested your attendance. Your parents and your brother have turned you against us. I've seen your power from the start."

Gritting my teeth, I glared down at her. She never even looked twice in my direction.

"You think I'm lying," she said, releasing my jaw and holding out her hands. Her body shifted from a sexy succubus who could feed on a hundred thousand souls to an ugly, scared monster who would be banished from this world without a second thought. "I'm the same as you."

Disbelief drifted through me. *How could ... how is ...*

After a moment, she returned to her original form. "Fight by my side."

"I have a woman to attend to," I said. "I can't stay."

"Then, we will meet tomorrow for battle plans."

I gritted my jagged teeth. All I wanted was to spend time with Maxine. *Why is tha—*

"I know you did it," she said, lowering your voice. "I know you're holding your brother hostage, too, and I don't blame you after all the years of torture he has put you through. And your father—that disgusting man—wanted you to marry Maxine's bully."

"You know Maxine?" I asked, stiffening.

"Of course I do," she said. "She's a lovely girl for you."

She was being kind. Too kind.

I didn't know how to handle it. Worst of all, I didn't know why.

"You will see me tomorrow," she said, "to flesh out battle plans. Then, you will bring Maxine to my home for dinner in secrecy. Do not tell anyone else that I've invited you over. Don't release your brother. Meet me at the southern entrance."

"If you knew I killed Valerie, why didn't you say anything to the vampire?" I asked. Was this something she wanted? Had she predicted war? Wanted war? Ached for war? "And what do you want with Maxine?"

"All your questions will be answered tomorrow evening at dinner," she said. "And for Maxine …" She paused for a moment, then drew her tongue across her sharp teeth. "All I want is to meet her."

"And if I don't bring her?"

"Then, you won't like the consequences, Xorgor."

After staring at her for a couple more minutes, I finally nodded and walked out of The Inferno. Thoughts raced through my mind.

What the hell was all that? How long has she known about me? About Valerie? How did she find out?

Should I really bring Maxine to meet the queen? What does she want with her? Maxine is too sweet to be corrupted by a demon of the queen's strength. And how the hell is the queen an ugly monster like me?

Once I made it onto Carve's property, I pushed the thoughts away and followed shouting until I came to the quad. Maxine threw knives at a moving target—the moving target being Carve, who whizzed back and forth across the lawn, skillfully dodging all blades and attacks.

Deciding to hop in on the fun—because this day had been going better and weirder than I could have imagined—I caught one of the knives that he had dodged and tossed it at his back while Maxine continued to whiz blades at him. The knife lodged into his shoulder, and he stopped.

"Damn," he said, yanking it from his muscle. "You got me."

"Really?!" Maxine cheered, eyes wide and a huge grin crossing her face.

They hadn't spotted me yet, but her damn smile …

I stepped out from behind a tree and clapped. "Great job, Maxi."

Her grin widened even more. "Xorgor!" she shouted, dropping all the knives in her hand and rushing over to me. She wrapped her arms around my shoulders and jumped into my embrace, burying her face into the crook of my neck. "I'm so glad you're safe!"

"I told you I'd be back."

"After what I did to Erthrol, I thought for sure that they'd find out."

I didn't want to lie to her, but I didn't want to worry her either. So, I spun her around a couple more times and then set her on the ground in front of me. "I'm safe for now, Maxine," I murmured, placing a kiss on her lips.

"Can we get all this romance shit over with already?" Carve called, gathering the knives.

He put on a big show in front of Maxine to keep up his image, to show her that he didn't give a shit about anything or anyone anymore. But I knew that his cold, lonely heart still longed for the woman of his dreams.

Olenna.

52

the past

maxine

"COME." Xorgor took my hand. "I'll show you the castle."

"Hey!" Carve shouted, his wound closing. "We're not finished."

"Unless you want to watch me fuck Maxine," Xorgor said, "we're finished."

Heat rushed through my core, and Carve scrunched his nose. "I fucking hate romance."

Hated romance?!

But what about his *friends to lovers to enemies* thing he had going on with Olenna?

I bit back a giggle and wiggled my eyebrows at him, letting him know that I knew he really didn't hate romance. When he growled at me, I scurried along with Xorgor into the house before he threw another knife at me again.

"How was he today?" Xorgor asked.

"Annoying," I said, letting out my giggle. "He's extremely grumpy all the time, and he's tried to kill me about a hundred times since you left last night. I didn't think I would make it out alive, never mind see you again."

I decided to keep the bit about Carve teaching me how to kill Erthrol to myself for now.

"He won't hurt you," Xorgor said.

After intertwining my fingers around Xorgor's, I let him lead me through the large castle. While I wanted to go home tonight, I doubted that Xorgor would let me. So, I at least wanted to learn how to navigate this huge place by myself.

"How long has he collected art?" I asked, walking through the long corridor, filled with paintings in gold frames and statues made of the finest marble. I had been in this place earlier this morning, but I hadn't really had the chance to admire it.

I wasn't a huge art fan, but I could appreciate a five-hundred-year-old painting. I was honestly surprised with how well it had been preserved, minus the dust. It hadn't rotted, and there were minimal tears.

"Hundreds of years," he said.

"They're covered in dust."

"As most things are around here."

"Why doesn't he have a maid? A groundskeeper?" I asked, collecting the dust on my fingers. "With a home this big, he must have the money for one." I furrowed my brow and looked up at him. "Right?"

"Carve has more than enough money to hire a thousand people to work for him."

"Then, why?"

A low sigh escaped his lips. "Because he doesn't care anymore. He doesn't care about the paintings, the artwork, his image in Durn-bone. He hasn't for almost half a century now. It's quite ... sad."

After showing me a bit more of the castle, he followed me down the large hallways to the guest bedroom and walked into my room. The wind blew the curtains. And he seized my waist, bringing me down onto the bed with him.

"He was different before?" I asked. "How?"

"He sought power and possessions, threw parties so grand that everyone in his town would attend. Women he had grown up with grew old and died. The people he loved vanished. He relished in immortality for a bit, but then he became a lonely soul. The art, the gold, the status didn't matter to him anymore. The only person who did was the woman who hated him the most."

"Olenna," I whispered, heart pounding.

"How do you know about Olenna?" he asked.

"He mentioned her." *Kinda.*

"I'm surprised," he said. "He never speaks of Olenna anymore."

"He told me to tell her to go fuck herself."

Xorgor's chest rumbled as he laughed. "Of course he did."

"Did they get into a fight?" I asked.

He paused. "It's better if he tells you. I don't know the details."

After nodding, I rolled over onto my stomach and pushed some shaggy brown hair off his forehead. My lips curled into a smile, and I was so damn grateful that he had come back to me in one piece.

"What happened today?" I asked.

"I met the woman who had bought that haunted house," he said.

I sat up and stared down at him, heart pounding at the thought of him getting caught. "You-you did? Did she ask why you were there? Were you able to get Erthrol out of there before she saw him, before she said anything?"

"Relax," he said. "She didn't see me."

"How'd you see her then?"

"She was being fucked by the ghosts in the house when I—"

"You saw her naked?" I asked, possessiveness grabbing me by the throat.

He paused for a moment. "Yes, but—"

Jealousy crawled through my body, but I stayed as calm as I could, staring down at him. My stomach was in tight knots, and my nostrils flared. I didn't know why my body was reacting this way. Xorgor was a damn incubus and probably saw women naked all the time.

But I couldn't seem to stop the possessiveness.

"She's about your age," he hummed. "You should be friends with her."

"Be friends with someone who you saw naked?!"

His lips curled into a smirk.

"Why are you smirking at me like that?" I whispered. "Did you like—"

He pushed a hand into my hair, gently took the back of my head, and pulled me down toward him, crashing his lips onto mine. "I'm smirking because this little possessiveness you have going on is sorta … cute."

"You're mine," I mumbled against his lips, grabbing his collar and pulling *him* closer to me. "Only mine, Xorgor."

"Only yours, Maxi. Only fucking yours."

53
the bed

xorgor

TWO APPENDAGES SLITHERED out from my back, wrapped around Maxine's wrists, and pinned her to the headboard. A soft moan escaped her lips as I crawled between her legs and spread her thighs.

Balls heavy, I brushed the head of my cock against her entrance and rubbed her clit with my fingers. She arched her back and squirmed, but I tightened my grip on her wrists. Her clit swelled underneath my touch, and when she started moaning, I slipped my fingers into her, pumping them in and out in a steady rhythm.

Unable to stop myself from wanting to completely devour her, I placed my forked tongue on Maxine's collarbone and licked to her jaw. She closed her eyes and moaned in delight. I groaned into her ear as her cunt tightened around my fingers.

My dick grew harder, longer, thicker for her. She lifted her hips and ground her wetness against my throbbing head. Hungrily, I moved my mouth and tongue down her chest and captured her nipple between my lips, sucking it into my mouth and biting down gently.

I released her hands. "Jerk me off."

While I finger-fucked her pussy, she reached between us and took my dick in both of her small hands. After a few failed attempts at trying to wrap her hands around it completely, she whined and began stroking my cock up and down, back and forth.

Another groan escaped my throat. Gods, I wished she were sucking on it again, trying to stuff it all in her mouth but failing, only able to suck on my head because it was too big. I moved my hips back and forth in her smaller hands, getting myself off.

My appendages wrapped around her thighs to spread them even further for me, giving me better access. I plunged a third finger into her cunt and pounded them inside her. Pleasure surged through my body as I continued to thrust my hips, getting closer and closer to her entrance every time.

And when I couldn't handle it anymore, I pulled my fingers out of her, used the tips of my appendages to hold her entrance apart, and stuffed my cock deep into her pussy until my balls smacked against her ass.

She screamed out in pleasure, grasping the bedsheets and arching her back. I sucked my fingers into my mouth and growled at how good she tasted, pounding faster into her cunt. Then, I grasped her tits, my fingers finding her nipples and tugging hard.

"Come," I demanded.

Her pussy exploded all over me, her cries getting lost in Carve's empty, large castle. She trembled in my arms, which only made me pound into her harder. Shakily, she placed her hands on her stomach and felt my bulge inside her belly.

"Look at you," I cooed. "Taking it so well."

"P-p-please, I wanna come a-g-g-g—" she started, but couldn't finish because I slammed my dick so forcefully into her that she moved up to the headboard.

I refastened my appendages around her wrists and pinned them to the headboard again, crawling up to it and never letting my dick slide all the way out of her tight, drooling pussy.

"Beg me," I ordered.

"Please, Xorgor!" she cried. "Please!"

I slipped my fingers from her tits to her pussy and rubbed torturous little circles around her swollen clit. She closed her eyes, pleading with me more desperately with every thrust. With trembling legs, her pussy pulsed around my throbbing cock and coated it in her juices. Her head lolled back in a daze, her pussy milking my cock.

Using my hold on her arms, I bounced her up and down on my cock, ramming myself into her as I dropped her onto me. My balls smacked against her pussy. Pressure gripped hold of my cock, starting from the base and quickly working up to the head. I grunted and threw my head back, spraying my cum into her.

54

the royal queen

maxine

"ARE you really sure Queen Agool wants to meet me?" I whispered, grabbing tightly on to Xorgor's hand as we walked down the hallway to my guest bedroom the next day.

I had spent the entire day training with Carve *and* Xorgor today, and now … I had to prepare to meet the queen!

It sounded absurd. Why would she want to meet me? I didn't have much to offer her, didn't have any hidden special abilities, magical powers, or honestly anything that could be beneficial to her. If I had, I surely hoped that they would've helped me while knives were hurled in my direction.

"I don't know why," he said, staying relatively quiet, as if there were more on his mind.

"You're nervous."

We walked into the bedroom, and he grimaced. "I don't know what her plans are. She knows that I killed Valerie. She started a war with the vampires because of it. And she wants me to help her with it. Her intentions with me bringing *you* to dinner tonight are unclear."

I swallowed hard and glanced into the closet in hopes of finding something suitable for meeting royalty. When Xorgor had brought me here, I hadn't packed any clothes. I had been wearing these frumpy clothes, which looked to be centuries old, from Carve's guest closet.

"You're afraid she will hurt me," I said because it was the only thing that made sense.

Xorgor was stronger than most demons. I had no doubts about that. But against the demon queen? Would he be able to fight her and win if she tried hurting me? Or would we both get caught in the middle of a brawl and die because of her wrath?

Again, Xorgor stayed quiet, which made me uneasy.

I turned around in front of the closet. "We don't have to go."

"If we don't go, she'll come and find us. We must go."

Nerves rushed through me, but I turned back to the clothes and rummaged through them. Xorgor must've been more nervous than he was letting on because I had *never* seen him like this. Usually, he was calm and collected, even while kicking his brother's ass or killing Valerie.

"Don't worry about it," he murmured, placing his hands on my shoulders and dipping his head against the crook of my neck. "Whatever happens tonight, I'll protect you. You do know that, right, Maxine?"

"Yes, I know."

He had promised to protect me from Valerie, and he had. He had promised to protect me from Erthrol, and he had. Every time he had made me a promise, he'd kept it. And I knew that tonight would be no different. Still, I worried.

Because, one day, protecting me might get him killed.

"Go shower," he ordered me. "I'll find you a dress fit for meeting the queen."

After kissing him on the nose, I chewed on my inner cheek and walked to the bathroom to shower. My stomach twisted into tight knots as thoughts raced through my mind.

What am I going to do? What conversation can a peasant make with a queen? We have no similarities.

Once I turned on the hot water and stepped into the steamy shower, I blew out a deep breath to calm myself. Worrying wasn't going to do me any good. I didn't even know what she wanted from me or Xorgor yet.

"I found something," Xorgor called, his voice lighter than it had been a couple of moments ago.

I quickly finished washing my hair and body, then stepped out of the shower and wrapped a towel around myself. When I walked out into the bedroom, Xorgor held the skimpiest dress, which was basically lacy black lingerie, in his hands.

My eyes widened. "Are you crazy?! I can't wear that!"

"Why not?"

"Because I am meeting the queen!"

"I think it's sexy."

"Xorgor!" I exclaimed, glancing between him and the lingerie. "All my bits will be exposed."

"Good."

"Not good!" I said, hurrying to the closet to find myself something. "Not good at all!"

He stalked behind me and gently took a fistful of my hair, pulling it back so I stared up at him. "You're going to put on what I picked out for you, okay, Maxi?" he hummed against my mouth. "She's a succubus. She'll expect you to look presentable to her."

"I'm not fucking her," I blurted out.

He chuckled. "Good, because I'm not sharing you. But you don't want to show up to a succubus's front door with clothes that cover every single inch of your body and your skin." He kissed my mouth. "Understand, sweetheart?"

"Are you sure?" I whispered, not wanting to stand out tonight.

If I could get through tonight *without* being talked to, that would be great, honestly. Plus, I was nervous about what she would say about the scars on my chest. Lately, I hadn't cared that much about them, but I still wasn't showing them off.

I hated them. And if I wore this tiny little lingerie piece, someone would say something. My body wasn't exactly the succubus type.

My chest wasn't huge. My ass wasn't round. I had a bit of a belly. Some days, I still was in shock that I had pulled Xorgor.

"Put it on," he said. "Let me see you in it."

After gulping, I dropped my towel and grabbed the lingerie dress and put it on. The lace clung to my body, so much of my skin on full display. Xorgor stared at me hungrily from the bed, his forked tongue gliding across his lower lip.

"Maxi," he growled, "you look so fucking sexy."

My cheeks warmed, and I tore my gaze away from the mirror because if I looked into it, I would only focus on my insecurities. On those horrid scars. They were the only things on my mind right now even though they shouldn't be.

"You don't think that my scars look too—"

He took my chin in his hand and lifted it. "We all have scars that don't heal, Maxine. Even the demon queen. You look beautiful, and I hope, one day, you fucking believe it and feel like it too."

55

the castle

xorgor

AFTER CONVINCING Maxine that her lacy lingerie dress wasn't too much for dinner with the queen, we found our way from Carve's castle to the queen's palace in northeastern Durnbone. Nestled between the wooded forest and rocky cliffs, the marble palace stretched for nearly a half-mile and was guarded by the strongest demon military in the world.

Maxine craned her head up and stared through wide eyes at the grandiosity of it all. She had only ever seen the inside of human homes in Durnbone before she met me, never straying into werewolf, demon, or monster territory. So, all these castles had to be amazing to her.

"One day, you can live here," Maxine whispered, squeezing my hand. "Commander of the demons." She grinned. "You could be the king, one of the most powerful beings in all of Durnbone, Xorgor."

But I had no shot at being a king.

There were other royal demons in line who far surpassed anything that I could do. Who could be far more powerful leaders than I could be. All because they had grown up without being pissed on by everyone who was supposed to care about them.

"Yeah," I said, leaving it at that.

While I appreciated the thought, I didn't want to give Maxine these ideas that I could become a leader one day. Truthfully, with my father gone and Erthrol sitting in the cellar with chains around his wrists and ankles, I had a bit of a better chance. But ... could I truly lead?

All I wanted was to be Maxine's husband.

I swallowed hard at the thought that had never quite fully come to my mind until now. A true marriage wasn't for demons, werewolves, or even vampires. We married for power and prestige, not for love. Usually.

But, gods, I wanted to be her husband so badly.

She was more than I could have ever dreamed for. More than I had ever wanted. She made me feel a certain type of way that no other woman, no demon, no title could ever make me feel. And what really was power if one didn't have the love of their life by their side to enjoy it?

That was what Carve's sorry excuse for a life had taught me.

"Are you ready?" I asked, holding out my arm for her as we approached the steps.

She smoothed out her lacy little dress, then wrapped her hands around my bicep and nodded. I could see the hesitation on her face, could see her teetering back and forth. She really didn't want to be here, and neither did I. But we had been summoned by the queen herself.

"Follow me," I said, leading her up the black marble staircase to the double doors.

Maxine stumbled slightly in her heels, clutching on to me for greater support. I grabbed her waist, my fingers curling around her curves, and helped her onto the top step. She blew out a tight breath and smiled at me, nervousness in her eyes.

The queen greeted us at the door. "You made it." Her gaze drifted from me to Maxine, who stiffened. "I almost thought you were about to make me eat dinner alone tonight." She stalked closer to us, holding out her hand to Maxine. "It's nice to finally meet you."

While it was customary for a commoner to kiss the hand of a queen when presented with it, the queen took Maxine's hand. She brought it to her lips and kissed it softly, staining Maxine's skin with her red lipstick.

"Silly me." She giggled, still holding Maxine's hand. "I seem to have gotten lipstick all over you. And you've dressed up for the occasion and everything. Let me help you clean this up." She glanced at one of her guards. "Get me a wet napkin!"

"Yes, madam," three guards said in unison, bowing their heads.

Once they disappeared, the queen glanced down at Maxine's hand again and gently glided her thumb across Maxine's skin, the lipstick smudging. I glanced between Maxine and the queen, wondering what the fuck was going on.

Why did she call us here? And why is she acting like this?

She swiped her thumb across Maxine's skin again, the lipstick disappearing. The queen widened her eyes, then lifted them and smiled softly at the woman I loved. "Your skin is so smooth." She tucked some hair behind Maxine's ear, the way I usually did. "So beautiful."

Maxine blushed—and I didn't think it was in the flirtatious kind of way, but the *I don't know what the fuck is going on* kind of way. She teetered back and forth, smiling softly, but not accepting the compliment because I knew she'd say something like, *I don't think so.*

"Forget the napkin," the queen called over her shoulder. "I've already cleaned it."

The queen's gaze dropped to the glistening scars on Maxine's chest. Maxine stiffened and pulled her hand out of the queen's grasp, gently laying her fingers over her chest and hiding herself from Her Majesty.

"I envy you," the queen said. "For your courage."

Maxine stepped back into me and glanced up, brow furrowed, as if she didn't know what to say. "I'm not courageous," Maxine whispered. "Xorgor made me wear this. I'm sorry if this offends—"

"Offends me?" the queen asked, another laugh escaping her lips. "It pleases me that the next possible queen of demons has the courage that I never had to wear her scars on her body and not cover them with magic."

I placed my hands on Maxine's shoulders and pulled her behind me. "What did you say?"

The queen offered me a smile, then walked toward the entrance. "Usually, my lipstick stains the skin of prey, of men and women, of humans and demons who can only offer this world their bodies, who can only be hunted by hungry succubi. Not men and women who are born predators. Not men and women who are born to be leaders, rulers, kings and queens of kingdoms."

56
the dinner

maxine

I SAT NEXT TO XORGOR, staying quiet until spoken to by the queen. After what she had said to us outside before dinner, I wasn't sure what to say to her. Xorgor would be an amazing king, but his family had put him down for so long that he believed he wouldn't be.

My leg bounced underneath the table. I glanced nervously from demon to demon, from guard to guard around the room, my heart pounding inside my chest. I wasn't sure how I should feel about this. I didn't know why she had invited *me*.

And what was that comment about earlier?

"Xorgor," I whispered, trying to get his attention.

He glanced over at me, but didn't say anything.

My stomach twisted into knots, my legs bouncing even more underneath the table. I placed my hands on my knees to get them to stop, but they didn't. I wanted to go. The talking had been fun, but that was over. Now, everyone was silent.

"Are you okay over there?" the queen asked.

I forced a smile and nodded. "Yes, I'm fine."

"Xorgor, why don't you calm her down?" she suggested.

Xorgor looked at her for a moment, then at me. I stared over at him, my heart racing inside my chest. Neither of us knew what she was trying to get at.

Did she want us to fuck? For him to touch me? All so they could watch?

"She's fine," Xorgor said, but he placed his hand on my knee underneath the table. "As you were saying about the vampires ..."

I stiffened and swallowed hard. My gaze fell between my legs, and I pressed my thighs together. He snaked his hand around my thigh and slowly traveled it up my leg until he reached the hem of my lacy little dress, which he had made me wear today.

My throat dried. I balled my hands into fists underneath the table and tried to keep myself together. But all this lust ... all the eyes on me ... it felt so different. And in some weird, fucked up way I sorta, kinda liked it.

I curled my feet around the legs of the chair to give him better access. The queen sipped her wine and watched us, those red eyes so piercing that I wouldn't doubt I'd see them in my dreams later.

"Yes," she started, "I want one last glorious battle before I step down from the throne."

"So, that's why you didn't rat me out to the vampires."

She chuckled. "Oh, no, there are far more important reasons than that."

"Like what?" Xorgor said, slipping his fingers higher up my thigh until they reached my underwear. He brushed them back and forth across the lacy material, his claws against my clit making me clench.

"I don't think that is much of a discussion for tonight. We are here to talk about war."

"Then, speak."

I didn't know where the hell this sudden confidence from Xorgor had come from because as he talked back to the queen, he slammed two fingers into me. I grasped the edges of the chair and stared through wide eyes down at my empty dinner plate.

This really wasn't happening right now!

Sure, we had done stuff in public before, but in front of the queen?! Never.

He fingered my cunt until I could hear how wet I was. My cheeks warmed, and I hoped to God that nobody else could hear me. Even if they couldn't, I was sure that they could smell how aroused I was. How good he was making me feel.

I swallowed hard, the pressure rising in my core.

Xorgor must've sensed it because he shoved his fingers deep into my pussy and curled them against my G-spot. I jerked forward, my breasts slamming into the table as an orgasm ripped through me. I slapped a hand over my mouth, bit back my moans, and pressed my thighs together.

Everyone at the table stayed quiet, watching me ride out my orgasm.

And when I finally gathered the courage to pull my hand away from my mouth and sit back, I looked down at the table in front of me and opened my mouth. "S-s-sorry, I was having some t-t-trouble. It h-happens sometimes."

Xorgor slid his fingers out of me and stuffed them right into his mouth without any shame. After licking his lips, he returned to his conversation with the queen, who looked … *proud*?!

God, what the hell was happening?!

Maybe I was drunk off this wine, or—*gah*, I didn't know.

This was the weirdest freaking dinner that I had ever attended.

"Now that you've watched me finger-fuck the woman I love, will you tell us why we are really here?" Xorgor said. "Because it is not to talk about battles or war plans, having one last *glorious* time on the field before you step down. What do you want?"

She paused for a moment, as if she had been caught, then smiled softly. "Us demons don't find true love often. When we do, it's a wonderful thing. I just wanted to meet the woman my son has been infatuated with."

57

the mother

xorgor

WHAT DID SHE JUST SAY?

I froze and grabbed Maxine's hand, squeezing it hard. I wasn't sure how to react. She wasn't my mother. She couldn't be. My mother was a whore who slept with half the city and constantly put me down.

"Xorgor," Maxine whispered, nudging me to somehow respond.

"You're lying," I whispered to the queen.

Like it had yesterday, her magic faded from her body, the beauty disappearing and revealing the scars, the horror, the ugliness underneath her disguise. Jagged teeth, a half demon face, red eye. She looked like me.

"You're lying," I repeated, standing up and stepping back. "You're fucking lying to me."

"Why would I lie about this?"

"Because if it is true, you've been lying to me since I was a child. For years. Decades."

She swallowed, gaze falling to her dish, and then stood too. "And I apologize for it, but I did it to protect you." She walked around the large table toward us. "I shouldn't have waited for so long, but I wasn't planning on telling you so soon."

Pain rushed through me. I snatched Maxine's hand, yanked her out of her chair, and pushed her behind my back. I didn't trust the queen in the slightest. If she really was my mother, why hadn't she wanted me around? Why hadn't she wanted to tell me?

"Please, Xorgor, let me explain," she murmured, not advancing any further.

"What is there to explain?" I growled.

"Why I did it."

"No," I snapped, pushing Maxine back further. "If this is true, then you let me get bullied my entire life by that fucking family! You watched your own son get mistreated, stepped on, spit on, laughed at. And all because … what? You didn't want to deal with me?"

Maxine grabbed my bicep. "Xorgor," she whispered, "calm down."

But no matter how hard I tried, I couldn't. The queen had invited us over for dinner, dropped this fucking bomb on me, and expected that I wouldn't freak out. Had she really thought that I would let her do anything she wanted just because we looked the same?

If she really was my mother, how could she have sat back while the world bullied me?

She had to have seen it. She had the magic to make herself look beautiful. She had power. Why hadn't she made me look as she did? Why had she forced me to endure the constant bashing, the constant belittling? A mother didn't do that to her child.

"You're a fucking liar," I snarled.

"Yes, I am," she said. "I've lied to you your entire life."

I stared at the monster who had once been beautiful in front of me, hot, burning tears heavy in my eyes. When I was positive that I wouldn't shed a fucking tear in front of her, I ran my forked tongue across my jagged teeth and seethed.

"What the fuck do you want from me?" I growled. "The only time anyone is nice to me is when they fucking want something. So, what is it? Don't lie to me again either. I don't give a fuck if you're my moth—"

"I want you to rule after me."

"No."

She held out her hand. "Please."

"No."

"Xorgor," Maxine whispered again, moving in front of me. No matter how much I tried to push her back behind me, she wrapped her arms around my torso and gripped me hard. "Just listen to her for five minutes, and then we can leave this town forever if you want."

I glanced down at Maxine. The only reason I had stayed in Durnbone for so long was because of her. She had spent her entire life here, had a family home, had just gotten her friend Sina back in her life. Hell, she had a fucking job here!

But she'd give that all up for me so I could finally be happy, content.

She drew her fingers across my face, the soft touch making me warm all over. I slowly closed my eyes and nodded in agreement.

"Fine. Five minutes." I glanced up at the woman before me. "You have five minutes to convince your so-called son to stay."

"That's all I need," she said, sitting back at the table and gesturing for us to sit as well.

Reluctantly, I pulled Maxine's chair out again and sat down beside her. "Talk."

"I don't know if you'll want to stay after what I tell you, but I promise that I did what I did so you'd understand what it means to rule." She folded her hands on the table. "If Erthrol or Jaroth or anyone else ascends to the throne, they will not be for the people."

"Who says that I would be any different?"

"Because you know what it feels like to be a demon who isn't glamorized, who isn't lusted after. When you become king or queen of this species, you're not just the leader of incubi and succubi. You're the leader of all demons, of all subspecies. You're friends with demons who have been banished, who live on the corners and beg for money, who barely get by."

"How the hell does that matter?"

"Because you have a better understanding of how to help those people than Jaroth or Erthrol does."

"So, that's why you fucking gave me to those fuckers? So they *could* bully me, so I would fucking understand what it felt like to be dirt?" I growled, wanting to reach across the table and wrap my hands around her throat.

She was a sick bitch.

"Yes," she said. "Because I couldn't give you those experiences. I have never been a queen for the people. I've lived in fear of what people would say about my skin, about my ugliness for centuries. You have survived more experiences than I ever could."

I gritted my teeth. "I fucking hate you."

"I'm sorry, son."

"Don't call me that," I growled, slamming my hands on the table and standing. "Time's up." I grabbed Maxine's hand. "Come on. We're leaving."

58

the surprise

maxine

"XORGOR," I whispered, squeezing his hand as he whisked me down the hallway. I glanced over my shoulder and spotted the queen frowning from the double dining room doors. I swallowed and glanced up at him. "Are you sure you don't want to stay?"

"Yes."

Pressing my lips together, I followed him down the large hallway until we disappeared from her sight. Guards pulled open the exit doors and allowed us to pass. He continued to march with me all the way down the steps and into the forest.

"We're never returning," he said finally, halfway back to Carve's home.

"She's your mother," I whispered.

My mind was reeling with thoughts about what had just happened. Dinner had been quite literally insane. And the queen being Xorgor's birth mother?! I couldn't believe it in the slightest, but—at least from my perspective—I guessed it kinda made sense why she had done it.

I didn't agree with it. I didn't like how she had put her son through so much pain just so he could learn. He was the man I would do anything for, the guy I would protect with everything I had. But still, I wanted him to have a somewhat-decent relationship with someone in his life that wasn't just me.

He had been put down so many times by his fake family, bullied to no end. He didn't have to accept any of this, but she was offering him the chance to rule the entire kingdom—something he had thought he would never be able to do.

"I don't care who she is to me," he growled.

I snapped my mouth closed and stopped, jerking him back. I hadn't meant to be so harsh with him, but he had been pulling me the entire way. He turned around to face me, his face contorted into one of pain and so much pent-up anger.

We stared at each other for a few moments until I finally stood on my tiptoes and threw my arms around his shoulders. He stiffened for a moment, then slowly wrapped his arms around my waist and pulled me closer, burying his face into the crook of my neck.

"You're hurting," I whispered into his ear. "I can feel it."

Instead of responding, he pulled me tighter and squeezed his eyes closed. While I wasn't quite as tall as him, I held him as hard as I could and rocked us back and forth. We stayed in silence in the middle of the forest for a long time.

"Do you think I overreacted?" he finally whispered.

I paused because I did think he had overreacted. He had finally been given a chance at a real family who loved him and who wanted the best for him. Hell, he still had one of his real parents alive. But at the same time, I had no place to say anything. I hadn't been bullied by my family for all my life, and I didn't suddenly have the burden of seizing the throne that nobody wanted me on.

"No," I said. "How you feel is how you feel. I don't have a say in how angry and upset you should be about your mother finally coming forward and explaining why she made you endure such pain for all your life." I pulled back and saw the tears in his eyes, so I pushed them away with my thumbs.

"I never thought I had a chance on the throne," he whispered. "And part of me doesn't trust her. I mean, how could I? She fucking lied to me my entire life and stuck me with two bastards who hated me so fucking much. What if this is all some sort of twisted lie too?"

I pressed my lips together because, honestly, I didn't have an answer for him.

The first thing Xorgor had taught me was that demons never had true intentions. Most of the time, they spoke with the goal of gaining. What would they get out of their conversations? How could they benefit?

How could she benefit from Xorgor being king?

My stomach twisted, my head pounding at the thought. I didn't know the first thing about royalty. Hell, I worked at a bar where demons, wolves, vampires, and any other creature in Durnbone did the exact opposite of what any royals would do.

Plus, I was so much younger than Xorgor. Compared to him, I was so innocent, so impressionable. Humans lived much shorter lives compared to demons, and I didn't know the first thing about demon history, about demon royalty.

"You know I meant everything I said back there," I whispered, brushing some shaggy, dark hair out of his face and smiling up at him. "If you want to leave Durnbone, I will leave with you without questioning your reasons. You've lived your life before me, and you will live life after me, but I want to support you any way that I can, no—"

"Don't say that," he growled.

"It's true," I said, as hard as it was. "I want you to be happy whenever I—"

He wrapped his hand around my throat and lifted me into the air so we were face-to-face, my legs dangling off the ground. "You're mine, Maxine," he hummed. "You're not going to ever leave me. We're fated to be together in this world forever."

"I'm just a human," I whispered. "I can't live forever, like you can."

"You're not a human anymore," he murmured, bringing me closer. "I've told you before that I marked you the moment I came in your tight little hole. Incubi don't mark the same way that wolves or vampires do. You're more than a human now, Maxine, and one day —if I choose to be the king that my mother wants me to be—you'll be my demon queen."

59
the thoughts

xorgor

OVER A WEEK HAD PASSED since I had last seen my *mother*.

I had done everything and anything I could to keep my mind off her and the events of my life, the bullying, the harsh words … all of it. We had gone to see Maxine's friend, Sina, and her mates a couple of times, had traveled down to Durnbone once.

Yet, still, I couldn't stop thinking about the queen. And, today, I planned to get answers to my dire questions that I had about my life, my childhood, and my damn birth.

Why wait this long to tell me about our relationship? Why give me to a family who hated me?

After breakfast, I stayed in the dining area with Maxine and wiped up. Maxine hummed to herself, sneaking another piece of bacon from Carve's plate into her mouth before tossing the rest of his uneaten food in the trash.

The more I thought about the queen, the harsher I rubbed the wet rag onto the table. It didn't fucking make sense. She was the queen, who could give her son any experience that she wanted by herself. If she wanted me to learn how to be *for the people*, why hadn't she given me to a nobody family? Instead, she had chosen another family with royal blood.

If she wanted me to learn what it felt like to be bullied so I would *understand*, I was sure she could've done that all by herself while raising me. She wasn't as holy as she had pretended to be for Maxine the other day. She was evil by nature.

So, what the fuck was all this for? To keep me close, but not raise me.

Maybe she hadn't wanted to raise a son who looked as ugly as she did underneath all her magic. Maybe her magic didn't work on me. Maybe she was just a selfish bitch who hadn't wanted to care for her own son until the succession became clear.

Either way, I fucking hated her.

Nothing and nobody could change my mind.

"You okay?" Maxine asked, staring at me through wide eyes from the trash. She hurried over to me and grasped the rag from my hand. "If you squeeze this any harder, you'll give yourself a heart attack. What's wrong?"

I sighed and blew out a breath. "I'm going to visit her today," I said to Maxine, drawing her toward me and placing my lips on hers. "I have some things I need to talk to her about. The air needs to be cleared, and I think … I think I'm ready to ask the hard questions."

Like, why the fuck had she really left me?

Maxine curled her lips into a smile and pulled me closer to her, wrapping her arms around my waist and staring up at me in amazement. "You're not doing this for me, are you? I know I said you should give her a try, but I want you to be happy. If you don't want to see her, don't go."

"I do," I said honestly. "I want to see her."

After standing on her toes, she pecked me on the lips again. "Okay, have fu—"

"Oh my gods, I can't wait until you both leave my home," Carve said, walking into the dining room again with a gold-encrusted coffee mug that looked to be thousands of years old. He shook his head at our embrace and walked right out. "You make me want to gag."

"Don't listen to him," I said to Maxine. "This is the liveliest I've seen him in centuries."

A small giggle escaped her lips as she curled her fingers around my face. "He keeps asking me to head back to work so I can talk to that girl for him." She raised her voice just enough so it'd travel through the castle. "I think he has a little bit of a crush on her."

A knife whizzed through the air, nearly grazing against her ear, and slammed into the wall behind us.

"Don't you fucking say that again, Maxine," Carve growled from the other room. "I haven't asked you shit about her since you moved in."

He totally did, she mouthed to me, giggling.

"He has more than just a crush on her," I said, antagonizing him.

Because he had lived a thousand lives alone, just so she could survive. The curse that had been placed on them had been broken years ago, but Carve never pursued the woman he loved the most, mainly because she hated him now.

But … it'd be good for him to get out of this castle for once.

"I will literally kill both of you if you don't shut the fuck up," Carve snapped, banged his fists against what sounded like a table. He marched somewhere in the castle, then slammed the door closed, the echo traveling through the house.

After a couple of moments, I pulled Maxine closer by the waist. "I'll see you tonight."

"Be safe," she said. "Come back home to me."

"I always will," I said, then let go of her and walked to the door. "I always fucking will, Maxi."

60
the slaughter

maxine

AFTER XORGOR LEFT to see his mother for the first time in over
a week, I hurried outside to the quad so we could train. Usually, I
didn't want to do anything with Carve, but after seeing how broken
Xorgor had looked all week, I needed to protect him.

I might've been a human—or whatever kind of creature I was
now—and still weaker than a demon, but Xorgor was broken on the
inside. I had to do anything in my power to protect him. I didn't
care what it took. I would train hard so nobody could hurt him.

At least verbally and emotionally.

Halfway through training, Carve hurled a sharp knife straight at
my head, and I ducked. The knife split through the bark on a tree
behind me, cutting right through it until some of the damn handle
was stuck in the wood.

Another knife whizzed through the air, and I thrust my hip to
the left, swiftly jumping out of the way and dodging it. I regained
my balance quicker than I ever had and leaped up into the air to
miss another one he had lodged at my feet.

While I barely had a chance to get ahead, I grabbed the knives I
had stuffed in my waistband this morning before training and

hurled one in his direction. Another one of his blades grazed my upper arm, but I barely felt the pain. Blood dribbled down my arm.

Carve swiftly avoided my attack and continued hurling blades at me. I tossed another one in his direction, then turned on my heel and ran through the woods to use the trees as a shield. If he couldn't see me completely, he might get distracted.

"Maxine!" he roared. "Don't run away."

"I'm not running away," I hummed through the forest. "I'm utilizing my surroundings."

Another knife whizzed through the air and nicked my right ear. I winced but pushed my legs harder and faster. I analyzed the forest in front of me so I would know how I had to move and turned around, running backward while hurling a blade from my hand.

It didn't hit Carve, but it did slide into the tree trunk beside him. A smile curled onto my lips, and I faced the front and continued running. And I ran and ran and ran until my legs felt like Jell-O and I had wasted all my blades on the trees, not hitting Carve once.

A river came into view, and I slowed my pace to a stop. "Okay! I surrender."

After a couple of moments, he stopped a few feet behind me, sweating, like I was. "Improving."

"Thanks."

"That wasn't a compliment."

"Well, I took it as one," I said, leaning over my knees to catch my breath.

"Most demons aren't as fast as Xorgor and me," he said. "Especially not incubi and succubi. So, if you're worried about them hurting you, don't be." He glanced over his shoulder at the forest surrounding us. "Grab your knives and head—"

"I'm not afraid they'll hurt me," I interjected. "I'm afraid they'll hurt Xorgor."

A low chuckle escaped his throat. "Xorgor can handle himself."

Carve might've known Xorgor for much longer than I had, but he didn't understand Xorgor like I did. Xorgor didn't like many people knowing how much everyone's harsh words affected him, how all the bullying crushed his soul.

"I'm heading back," Carve said. "Don't stay out too late. Monsters lurk around these woods."

I nodded and walked back, collecting my knives from the trees.

If anyone hurt him—especially his brother—once more, then I would … have to take care of them. If he was really meant to be the king and would one day ascend to that position, then I would protect him. A king protected his kingdom, but the queen protected her king.

It sounded so cliché, so childish almost to think that a peasant girl like me would ever become a queen. And my insecurities wanted me to believe that Xorgor wouldn't choose me to become his queen, that he'd choose someone stronger and more beautiful, but deep down, I didn't believe that.

I loved Xorgor, and he loved me.

We would be together forever, whether he decided that he wanted the throne or not. And still, I would do whatever it took to become the best wife and mate to him that I could. I would try to stop being insecure and do whatever I had to do to protect—

"How'd I know he'd be stupid enough to bring you here?" someone said from behind me.

I gripped the three knives I had in my hand and twirled around, eyes widening when I spotted Erthrol hobbling closer to me. Dark circles underneath his eyes, his demon teeth showing, and all skin and bones, he took another step closer.

"Wh-what are you doing here?" I whispered, moving back.

"I'm here for payback, you little bitch."

My heart pounded. "H-how'd you get out?" I whispered, shaking my head.

It was nearly impossible. He had been locked in those chains, in that fucking cellar. Xorgor had visited him every day, bleeding him dry, not giving him any food or water so he'd die a slow and miserable death.

Wh-what is he doing here? Now?

"You can thank the queen for that," he said.

My eyes widened. "The-the queen?"

"The queen granted me freedom," he said, stepping forward. "Freedom to eliminate you."

"You're lying," I whispered.

He had to be lying. We had been at her palace last week, and she hadn't seemed like—I shook my head, still in disbelief. Hell, I didn't know why I was defending her—maybe it was one of her abilities—because I didn't know anything about her other than she had hurt Xorgor.

And now, she was hurting him again.

"Get out of here," I said, pushing my shoulders back because he wasn't going to kill me.

No, I'd promised myself that I would protect Xorgor in any way that I could.

"Put the knives down," he said, almost chuckling. "They'll do nothing to me."

"My bat did something to you," I growled, grasping my knives tighter.

He lunged at me. "You stupid little bitch."

Like Carve had promised, Erthrol's movement speed was much slower than his and Xorgor's. To me, he almost moved in slow motion. So, I swiped the knife through the air at an upward forty-five-degree motion and sliced right through the artery in his neck.

He doubled over and howled in pain, clutching his throat. "I'll kill you for—"

Adrenaline rushed through me. I dropped to my knees, shoved him over, and stabbed him in the neck over and over and over, like Carve had shown me when I asked him for advice about killing Erthrol. No way would I take any chances and let him explain himself.

Blood splashed up and splattered all over my face, but I kept stabbing him until Erthrol was dead underneath me.

61
the empty cellar

xorgor

"I NEED TO RETURN TO MAXINE," I told my … *mother* in the late afternoon.

While I didn't particularly love the word—I'd much rather call her the queen—she had been hounding me all day to call her mother. She had answered all my questions and concerns that I had, yet I couldn't shake this feeling that she was hiding something.

"Only a little bit longer here," she said, pinning her lips into a smile.

"No," I said, gathering my belongings. "I must leave now."

I'd been gone for far too long already today. This entire week, I hadn't set foot outside Carve's property without Maxine for more than a couple of hours. But I had been talking war with her and other high lords all day. And I just wanted to fucking go home, curl up in Maxine's arms, and forget about it all.

"We have much more to discuss," she said.

"Like what?"

She grabbed my elbow. "Like your place with all of us."

"My place?" I asked, ripping my arm away from her. "I already told you that I don't care what happens. You have never been there for me. Fucking ever. I'm not going to join another family who's going to hurt me just because *you* feel bad about yourself now."

She might've answered all these questions and thoughts that I had about her ditching me earlier, but I wasn't fucking over it. I didn't accept her. She was a bitch through and through for what she had done.

"That's not what it is," she said. "You have to understand me. I had no other choice."

"You always have a fucking choice."

"Xorgor, please stop with the swearing," she said, straightening herself out. With her shoulders pushed back, she intertwined her fingers in front of her torso. "I'm your mother, and I'm the queen. You will respect me."

"Like you respected me?" I scoffed. "After giving me away because I was ugly on the outside, like you're ugly on the inside? After watching me be bullied year after year after fucking year? You want my respect now?"

She didn't deserve any damn respect. None at all.

"I know you're angry," she whispered. "But you have to listen to me. There's danger lu—"

"A danger I don't give a fuck about."

"A danger you should give a fuck about," she said, arguing with me over nonsense.

We had spent all day together. What more could she possibly want?

"You will have to kill your brother if you want to live. If he becomes king, then he will take Maxine, or he'll kill her and you."

"You don't understand." I chuckled, shaking my head. "I'm taking Maxine far from here."

After today, she had made me want to stay in Durnbone less and less.

A guard walked into the room and up to her, whispering something in an ancient tongue that I couldn't quite understand. The queen tensed, her tongue gliding against her fangs.

"Is Maxine blinding you from what's important, Xorgor?" she

suddenly asked harshly, like she hadn't been sucking up to me for the past eight hours of pure hell. She balled her small hands into fists and glared. "Your family and your duties?"

"Maxine is what's important to me. She's my only family—"

The queen smacked me right across the face.

My cheek stung from the slap, but I blew out a low breath to control my temper and turned right around without saying another word. *Fucking bitch. Stupid fucking bitch.* I should've never trusted her, and I especially should've never come back here.

"I am your family!" she cried. "Your blood."

"Blood means nothing in this world," I growled.

I stormed out of her palace and headed through the woods toward the not-so-abandoned house, where I kept my brother. I should just kill him now. Get it over with. Skip town and never turn back. I'd be forced to take Maxine from her best friend, Sina, but it'd be for her own good.

The new owner watered some flowers outside the house. I cursed to myself and closed my eyes. I needed to get down to the cellar, but she was right by the door. So, I cloaked myself, like I usually did, and walked by her, slipping into her house and heading for the cellar.

Halfway down the steps, I froze and stared at the open door. *What the fuck?*

Once I finally regained my senses, I sprinted the rest of the way down the stairs and slammed the door open, storming into the cellar. The chains. The locks. The cage. They were all ripped to pieces.

And my brother was gone.

Fucking gone.

After uncloaking, I rushed out of the house. "What did you do with him?"

The woman spun around and widened her eyes. "What do you mean? Who are you?" She grabbed her watering can and tugged it to her chest, stepping back in fear. "Are you one of those ghosts? What do you want with me?"

"What did you do with the man in the cellar?" I growled.

"What man? I … I haven't been able to get into the cellar."

My heart was racing, my throat dry. Somehow, someway, my brother had gotten out of the cage. Out of the locks and out of those chains. And I needed to get to him before he got to Maxine. Because if he killed Maxine, then I would kill him … and then kill myself.

62
the fury

maxine

ERTHROL'S CORPSE lay on the table between me and Carve. I stared in horror at the stab wounds that decorated his body. One of my blades was still plunged into his abdomen, his abs covered in dried blood.

"What are you thinking?" I whispered, nerves bubbling inside me.

Why would the queen have sent him to kill me? What would she say now that I had slaughtered him? Would the demons exile me? Throw me in a dungeon and … *rape* me every day and every night? They were incubi and succubi, for fuck's sake! And I hadn't missed the way some of those guards watched me the other night during dinner.

Carve yanked the knife out of the corpse, examining it. "I'm thinking that your training is paying off." He chuckled and dropped his gaze to Erthrol's abdomen. "You did a hell of a job, killing this bastard."

"How are you not freaking out?!" I exclaimed, waving my arms in the air. "He's dead!"

"As he should have been years ago."

I rolled my eyes and walked around the body to stand next to Carve, not wanting anyone to overhear—as if anyone would when Carve lived alone. I glared up at him, mostly because I was scared shitless. The adrenaline hadn't left my body yet.

"What are we going to do?" I whisper-yelled.

He tossed the knife into the air and caught it. "I'm not going to do anything. I have plans."

"What do you mean, you have plans?!" I shouted. "You never have plans!"

Again, this stupid asshole chuckled, stuffed the bloody knife into his waistband, and walked toward the door. I ran in front of him and placed my hands on his chest in an attempt to stop him, but he continued to walk into me until I nearly fell over.

So, I stood by the door and placed my hands on each side of the doorframe to block him. "You can't leave me here alone with him! Who knows what the demons will do to me if they find me here without you and Xorgor?!"

"They're not going to find you," Carve said, his lighthearted face turning pissed. "Move."

"Erthrol did!" I exclaimed. "The queen will immediately know where the—"

"Maxine!" Xorgor shouted from somewhere in the house, his footsteps quick.

"In here," Carve called.

"Shut up!" I whisper-yelled at him. "Tell him we are not in here!"

While Erthrol had bullied Xorgor endlessly over the years, I wasn't sure if Xorgor actually wanted his brother dead. He hadn't done it himself yet. But Erthrol's body was literally lying on top of the dining room table, and my hands were covered in blood.

I listened to Xorgor's quick-paced footsteps echo down the hallway, my stomach twisting into knots. I rubbed my sweaty palms together and twirled around to face my lovely boyfriend, who was hurrying toward us.

When he reached the room, he threw his arms around me,

scooped me up, and spun me around, his face buried in the crook of my neck. "Thank the fucking gods you're okay," he whispered. "We have to get out of Durnbone. Erthrol somehow escaped the cellar. He'll try to find you and—"

Carve whistled lowly. "Little too late for that one."

Xorgor placed me down. "What do you mean?" he asked, gaze drifting behind us. A low growl escaped his lips. He pushed past Carve and hurried to his brother's side, staring down at the man's corpse. "He showed up here?"

"Yes," I whispered. "While we were training."

"You did this?" Xorgor asked, glancing back at Carve.

"Me?" Carve chuckled. "No. Her."

When they both glanced at me, I shrank down and grimaced, clasping my hands behind my back so Xorgor wouldn't see his own brother's blood all over them. I didn't want him to be angry with me because I had just … defended myself.

Maybe I had gone a bit overboard with the stabbing, but I wanted revenge on him for hurting Xorgor for all these years. I'd wanted to protect my boyfriend—my mate—from his evil, villainous brother.

"You did this?" he asked me.

I stared at him for a few moments, then nodded. "Yes."

He peered back down at his brother, gaze drifting from stab wound to stab wound. A couple of good ones would've done the trick, but so much adrenaline had rushed through my body, and my sanity had been thrown right out the window. I must've stabbed him over a hundred times in a blind rage.

While I expected Xorgor to be pissed, he turned around with a smile on his face. He walked over to me, grasped my chin, and forced me to stare up at him. "You're the strongest woman I have ever laid my eyes on. You're going to make an amazing queen."

Warmth exploded through me, yet I was still shaken to my core. "I-I don't know about that."

"Why?" he asked. "You don't think so?"

"I …" I opened my mouth, then closed it.

What should I even say to him? He had been so closed off about his mother. Maybe they'd had a great day together if he was thinking about becoming king. What would he say about it? Would he deny it? Accept it?

It didn't matter. I had to tell him, no matter what.

I took a deep breath. "Right before Erthrol died, he told me … your mother …"

"My mother what?"

I swallowed hard. "That your mother released him."

Xorgor's whole demeanor changed, his jagged teeth glistening with saliva, his eyes glowing. A ferocious growl escaped his mouth, and then he was out the door. "I'll kill that bitch!"

63
the king

xorgor

"I'M GOING TO KILL HER," I repeated in a growl, halfway to the queen's estate.

"Xorgor!" Maxine cried, attempting to keep up with me. "Please, slow down."

"Go back home with Carve," I growled to her. "You're not going to want to watch this."

Next to me, Carve whipped out his knives and counted them, like he used to decades ago during the Battle of the Species that had completely broken him. I stopped mid-stride, grabbed him by the collar, and slammed him up against a tree.

"Bring Maxine home," I said through gritted teeth.

"Fuck no," Carve said. "Not when you're about to go ballistic on the queen. Maxine can fight."

"She can fight, but I need to protect her," I growled, spotting Maxine from the corner of my eye, leaning over to catch her breath. "If she comes with us, the queen will attempt to kill her. There are far too many guards there."

"Which is why you're not going alone," Carve snarled. "A king protects his queen, but the queen does the same." He tossed Maxine his sturdiest knife, one that wasn't used for throwing, but for stabbing right through *bone.*

Although Maxine was doubled over, she lifted her hand and caught it in the air without even having to look at it. She finally stood up taller, cheeks flushed from running, and nodded. "You're not going alone."

I stared between her and Carve for a few moments, then released him and continued storming through the woods toward the queen's estate. "Don't get in my way, Carve. Stay outside of the building. Protect Maxine if she needs it."

"Don't have to ask me twice," Carve said, flipping one of his blades.

Once we made it to the queen's estate, I cut the throat of the first demon that I saw. Unapologetically. Because the only way to truly wipe out a monarch was to slaughter every one of her loyal subjects, her guards.

The news that we had arrived spread like wildfire, warriors running in from all directions. I stormed through them to the palace, leaving a trail of corpses in my wake. My hands were shaking in anger, my mind focused on one thing—kill the queen.

Carve and Maxine stayed outside, fighting off guards and men, while I walked right through the double doors and headed to the dining area. She should be having dinner right about now, her treacherous teeth digging into some poor girl as if she were steak.

I thrust open the doors and spotted her across the hall, sitting at the long table alone but with her men around her.

She smirked at me and cut her steak with a sharp knife. "Xorgor, my men mentioned that you had arrived."

"You attempted to kill my mate," I roared, literally seeing only red.

Her palace. Her guards. Her.

All drenched in a red film through my demon eyes.

I lunged forward and slashed my way through the guards who stood to protect her, tearing them all down one by one, two by two, ten by ten. Adrenaline pumped through my system. Anger. Fury. Pure rage.

How could she do this? How could she fucking do this?!

"She trusted you!" I growled. "She wanted me to trust you too."

Maxine had urged me to talk to her, to finally get along with her because I had never had a parental figure in my life who cared about me. But this had all been an act. All a fucking act so she could hurt me more.

Everyone had fucking hurt me.

"It was the only way," the queen said, sitting at the head of the table and sipping her wine.

Like she didn't give a shit that I was cutting my way through her guards to kill her.

I slammed my claws right into a guard's neck and pulled out his throat, his blood spraying all over my body, my face, my mouth. After dragging my forked tongue across my bottom lip to lick up the blood, I hurled his corpse in her direction. He smacked against the wall, inches from her head.

"I can't wait to kill you too. You fucking used me!" I shouted, slashing my claws through the air and moving closer to her with every demon I killed. "You stalled me all day today so you could have my brother attempt to kill my mate!"

"Yes," she said with a smile.

A guttural roar escaped my lips. My stomach twisted. "Why?!"

Everyone had given up on me. Everyone had hated me, hurt me. What was the fucking point of telling me that she was my real mother, inviting me to dinner with her, talking about war plans, my ascension, fucking all of it if she was just going to betray me in the end?

"I already told you," she said, patting her lips with a napkin. "It was the only way."

Once I finally reached her, I grabbed her by the neck, yanked her out of the chair, and slammed her up against the wall. I sank my claws into her throat and growled, my teeth dripping with blood, with saliva, with a need to murder this madwoman right here and right now.

"Stop playing stupid," I growled. "The only way for what?"

To fucking hurt me? Nice fucking try.

I was already twisted. Destroyed. Gutted.

"For you to take up your duties," she said, not even fighting me back as I squeezed her throat.

I crushed it in my hand, the bones ripping through her flesh and digging into my palm, her blood soaking my skin.

And in her very last breath, she smiled. "Now, my son, you are our king."

64

the true queen

maxine

CORPSES LAY in a trail of blood up the palace steps and to the double doors. I marched to the entrance with Carve behind me, who was licking the blood off his knives like some psychopath, and pulled the door open.

The vile stench of blood drifted through my nostrils and stopped me in my tracks. While the palace was eerily quiet, I almost didn't want to go farther. Xorgor had stormed in here in a blind rage, wanting nothing more than to kill the queen.

But what if she had killed him?

"Move," Carve said, walking down the hallway. "He's still alive."

I hurried after him and searched in each and every room we passed for any sign of Xorgor. Mangled bodies lay in pieces in the rooms, their guts splattered against the walls and their blood soaking into the bottoms of my sneakers.

"Xorgor!" I called, voice trembling.

Had he done all this?

"In here!" he said, voice traveling from the end of the hallway.

I sprinted past Carve and to the double dining room doors.

Xorgor stood at the opposite side, holding his mother's lifeless body against the wall and staring at her silently. He didn't put her down when we walked in, nor when we approached.

"She tricked me," he growled. "And I fucking fell for it. Again."

"What do you mean, she tricked you?" I whispered, glancing over his shoulder.

When he dropped her body, she smacked against the ground, her lips still pressed into a smile, a tear frozen on her cheek. I wrapped my arms around one of his to comfort him and rested my head on his shoulder.

"She did this so I'd be king," he whispered. "All this so I'd do my duties."

My eyes widened. "Is … is that what she said?"

He growled, his jagged teeth dripping with blood. "Forced me to kill her so I'd take the throne."

"What a bitch," Carve hummed from behind us. "I hated the throne."

"If you don't want it," I whispered, rubbing his bicep, "you don't have to accept it."

"I just murdered everyone, Maxine."

"Don't let her memory bully you into accepting a kingdom you don't want."

As much as I thought that him being king would finally get people to respect him, they didn't matter. All that mattered was us, family, friends. I didn't care what others thought about him, and he shouldn't either.

This was his choice to make. And a big one at that.

"I have to, Maxi. And I'm going to make this demon kingdom one where all are accepted." He stared at her for a couple of moments, snarling at her dead body. Then, he took the crown off the queen's head and placed it on my head. "Your crown, my queen."

65
the aftermath

"DAMN," Carve said, whistling and walking around the queen's dead body. He traced her open wound with the tip of his knife, then flashed me a smirk. "Brings back memories of the good old days ..."

Maxine arched her brow at him. "Memories? A dead queen brings back memories?"

"You wouldn't understand," he hummed.

But neither did I.

As far as I knew, Carve had lived a thousand lives in a thousand timelines. His memories of this life were clouded with those of before, with the lives he had spent with his now ex-lover, leading wars, killing gods. Carve had powers that far surpassed mine.

Who knew what memory he was lost in now?

I ran a hand through my shaggy hair. "Demons will rebel now."

"Not anyone important," Carve said, sliding onto the dining table.

"The high lords and those in line for the throne will rebel. The very people holding this kingdom together from unraveling will attempt to kill us, Carve," I growled, my gaze traveling to Maxine, who fiddled with the crown. I sat down. "To kill you."

She placed the crown on the table and walked over to me. "Then, we'll fight them."

While I didn't enjoy the thought of Maxine fighting anyone for me, she had proven she had the ability to defend herself during today's battle and with my brother merely hours ago. I didn't want her fighting, but I'd rather have her by my side through anything.

"Together," I murmured, gently grasping her hand and brushing my thumb across her knuckles. "Promise me that we'll do it together, that you'll stay with me to rule, because you're the only good part of me."

"Always," she whispered, smiling.

"Ugh," Carve hummed, strutting to the door. "Don't mind me leaving."

"Where are you going?" Maxine asked, sitting in my lap. "We need you too."

"I have a hot date."

"A hot date?" Maxine giggled. "With who?"

"Someone I'm going to carve my name into." He threw a wink back at us, disappeared out the double doors, then shouted down the hallway, "I'll be spreading the word that there's a new king in town."

"Carve!" I warned.

He responded with a chuckle, and then a door closed, signaling that he was gone.

I didn't want to know where he was going, but I suspected he was going to his ex-lover's home to pay her a visit. I had … mentioned that I had seen her out at the Dead Candle Tavern with another guy last week, and Carve had nearly lost it.

"I should head off too," Maxine said. "I have skipped far too many days of work—"

"You're not going back to that dirty job," I growled, tugging her closer to me. "You're the queen now. *My queen.* You're not working another day in your fucking life in that scummy bar, where you'll be in danger."

"But—"

"No buts," I said, my word final. "Choose any other job you'd like. If you want it."

She didn't have to work at all, if she didn't want to. I was willing to do whatever it took to keep her happy, healthy, and alive. I would sacrifice everything for this woman. No matter what she asked.

She sat in my lap, stroking the harsh edges of my face. "Xorgor ..."

"I fear that the demon high lords will attempt to hurt you," I murmured.

Which was one of the many reasons that I hadn't wanted the throne and this title. All I desired was a normal life with the woman I loved more than life itself. Not the money, the power, the responsibility that came with being king.

"As shitty as your mother was ..." Maxine said, dragging her fingers through my shaggy hair. She straddled my waist and gently took my face in her small hand. "She was right. You're the only one who'll lead the demons and be for the people. You have to do this."

I rested my forehead against hers. "I know."

"It doesn't matter what happens," Maxine said.

But if I had learned anything from Carve's thousands of lives and the hundreds of thousands of stories he had told back in the day, it was that it *did* matter. If anything happened to Maxine, I didn't want to be a lonely man in an abandoned palace, like Carve. Being king was more responsibility than even I understood. But love mattered even more.

66
the rebellion

maxine

"OH MY GOD," I whispered, heart racing as I stared at the mob of demons.

Carve had woken us this morning with a bang on our bedroom door in *our* new home and told us to get our asses to the demon sector of Durnbone as soon as possible. Xorgor had feared a rebellion, but not anything like this.

I stood next to Xorgor on a balcony that overlooked the demon sector and gripped his hand tightly. It had been exactly eight hours since Xorgor had killed the queen, and Carve really had told everyone.

"Release my hand, Maxine," Xorgor said. "I'll fight for my people."

Not his place in the royal family. Not to hold power. For his people.

I stared down at the furious lords below us as Xorgor descended the steps, and then I followed after him. Nerves zipped through my system, my stomach twisting and turning. What would happen to him? I'd expected to at least be able to prepare.

"Kill the king and his bride!" a high lord shouted in the crowd, storming up the steps.

Cursing under his breath, Xorgor stopped, his eyes growing dark the way he did before he lost all control and his demon seized his body.

He placed a hand on my front and gently held me back. "Go hide."

"No," I said, standing by his side. "I'm fighting with yo—"

A demon who looked similar to Xorgor with large, jagged teeth sprinted up the steps. I grasped Xorgor's hand in fear, gripping it as tightly as I could. But instead of running straight at us, the demon grabbed the high lord by the neck and threw him down the steps.

And suddenly, fighting erupted in the city streets.

Demons who had nothing were fighting against lords and nobles, those with royal blood. Killing and slaughtering, ripping out their throats and drenching themselves in the guts of the rich and the beautiful.

Everyone who hadn't had a voice in the kingdom before now did.

"You were right that people would rebel," I whispered. "But this is the kind of rebellion that I can support."

The fighting continued for a short time until corpses littered the ground and blood soaked the streets of the demon sector. Xorgor hadn't had to descend another step before demons rallied behind him and protected him from the royals.

All the time that Xorgor had drifted along with the nobodies in this town because his family didn't accept him was now paying off. Xorgor was king. He would reign as king, as leader, as friend to these demons for the rest of his life.

And when the fighting ceased, the crowd cheered in excitement.

"Long live the king!" Carve shouted from the crowd.

The demons broke out into a cheerful uproar, clapping their blood-covered hands together, whistling through their jagged teeth. I squeezed Xorgor's hand tighter and beamed up at him as he admired the crowd from the balcony.

For the first time in his life, I could tell that he was happy. He meant something to people—*to his people*. Wasn't that what we all wanted in life? To matter? To feel appreciated instead of rejected constantly?

"They really," he said, tears quivering in his eyes, "accept me."

"Of course they do," I whispered. "You're not corrupted by money or power. You're their friend, not their overlord. And you'll do everything in your power to ensure that they have the best lives they can have."

For a split second, his shoulders bucked forward, and a sob so quiet that only I could hear it escaped his mouth. He gripped the railing tightly as he stared down at the sea of demons who had finally accepted him.

"Long live the king," I whispered, wrapping my arms around his torso and placing a kiss on my man's tearstained cheek. I laid my head on his shoulder and admired his jagged teeth, glowing eyes, and the single horn that jutted out of his head.

Man of the people. Leader of the rebellion. King of my heart.

The end.

If you'd like to read the epilogue, sign up for my newsletter!

also by emilia rose

also by emilia rose

Scan the QR code with your phone to view all of Emilia's books!

about the author

Emilia Rose is a *USA Today* best-selling author of steamy romance.
Highly inspired by her study abroad trip to Greece in 2019, Emilia
loves to include Greek and Roman mythology in her writing.
She graduated from the University of Pittsburgh with a degree in
psychology and a minor in creative writing in 2020 and now writes
novels as her day job.
With over 18 million combined book views online and a growing
presence on reading apps, she hopes to inspire other young
novelists with her tales of growth and imagination, so they go on to
write the stories that need to be told.
Join Emilia's newsletter for exclusive giveaways, early chapter
releases, and more!